THE LAST FAMILY ROAD TRIP

VAMPIRE INNOCENT
BOOK FOUR

MATTHEW S. COX

DIVISION ZERO PRESS

THE LAST FAMILY

Road Trip

Vampire Innocent #4
© 2018 Matthew S. Cox
All Rights Reserved

Cover and interior art by: Alexandria Thompson

ISBN (ebook): 9781949174205

ISBN (paperback): 9781949174212

CONTENTS

1. Blood Gift   1
2. A Matter of Logistics   11
3. Are We There Yet   18
4. Fiends of the Night   29
5. Keeping Watch   39
6. Take Out   46
7. Cramped Quarters   53
8. Strange Energy   58
9. A Little Good, a Little Bad   63
10. Snooping Around   74
11. Family Time   80
12. Night Eyes   86
13. The Genuine Article   93
14. The Right Moment   102
15. An Unfortunate Escape   113
16. Next Moves   120
17. Lost Expedition   129
18. The Ruins of Nope   139
19. A Giant Problem   144
20. Portal Roulette   151
21. The Beast of Clark Caverns   156
22. Fey Amaranth   159
23. The Expedition   163
24. The Sanguine Grove   175
25. Wild Dreams   186
26. Catching Up   196
27. Love Bites   202

Acknowledgments   209
About the Author   211
Other books by Matthew S. Cox   212

BLOOD GIFT

Freedom is pretty damn complicated.

I mean, most of us spend the first eighteen years of our life demanding more of it... and as soon as we have it, it's like ugh... hang on. What's this responsibility crap that comes along with it? Some kids get their freedom in smaller doses, others have a whole lot dumped on them all at once even if they're not ready for it. Like this girl Mackenzie a grade ahead of me back in high school. Her parents both died during her junior year and she got stuck living with her useless aunt, so she wound up having to take care of her little sister as well as herself.

So, yeah... she got too much independence too fast—and not in the way anyone wants it.

In my case, I also got a boatload of freedom all at once and not entirely in a way I would've asked for. Not only did I hit the 'you just turned eighteen' plateau, I've also been given freedom from a lot of other small annoyances—like growing old or getting something awful like cancer for example.

And one of the best parts: I'm now free from the constant worry that some sick bastard is going to attack me if I'm out alone at night— or during the day, or anywhere really. They say most women who are murdered die at the hands of husbands or boyfriends. Yay. I'm a statistic. And Argh! I really need to stop thinking about Scott.

Okay, I admit I'm still a little concerned with being out during the daytime. If the stupid sun's up—and it's gloomy enough for me to set foot out of my room—I'm basically normal ol' me.

However, I'm feeling indestructible at the moment since it's about half-past midnight. Stupid sun. I'm still not quite used to being able to disregard certain behaviors ingrained in my head from a young age. Of all the things that have changed for me after waking up as a vampire, *not* having to be hypervigilant all the time when I'm out somewhere alone is the hardest to get used to. I keep catching myself falling back to my old fears.

It's stupid, reckless, and so totally unlike me, but I'm looking forward to the moment some creep tries to grab me or something... as if I want to punish some random guy for all the years my friends and I spent being afraid of our own shadows.

Speaking of grabbing, the echoes of two guys shouting at each other draws me into an alley somewhere in downtown Seattle. I think I'm on South King Street. The yelling comes from between the Phnom Penh noodle house and an I-don't-know-what-the-hell-it-is building with square green sections between bricks. Kinda looks like someone converted an old fire station garage into a strip mall.

Plastic banging echoes in the narrow space between buildings along with grunts and muttered curses. A ridiculous number of trash cans lines the wall on the left. Like wow... there's gotta be thirty of them, a row extending all the way down the alley. Two lay toppled by a pair of guys brawling. I have no idea who they are or why they're fighting, but they make as good a target as anyone.

It's pretty obvious the one getting his ass handed to him is *way* drunk. They both look about mid-twenties with a 'hipster dock worker' kind of air about them. I swoop in on the sober dude and toss him aside. He bounces off the wall to land atop the trash can row, stunned. In the time it takes him to recover his senses and scramble back to his feet, I grab the other guy by a fistful of his shirt, pull him nose to nose, and blank his memory of fighting or seeing me.

"What the f—" Sober man stares at me, fist cocked, clearly not expecting a girl on the smaller side of average to have been responsible for his flight lesson.

I drop the drunk guy, leaving him to crawl off home, and smile at the other dude. "Hey. You busy?"

The guy points at me. "Did you just—?"

"Of course not," I say, forcing my thoughts over his. Hmm. These two guys know each other and the drunk one randomly started fighting for fun. Geez. What is it with boys?

He stands there doing a spot on impression of a mannequin—or that guy who played teenage Anakin in the new movie—as I slip in close and sink my fangs into his neck. Ooh. His blood tastes like fried chicken. Wow. I can't even remember the last time I ate that. With Sophia being a vegetarian and Mom going all health conscious, it would've had to have been a 'home with Dad' day. Probably before I turned twelve.

Mmm. That's a dangerous flavor for my brain to loan to blood. Perhaps I drink a little *too* much. Finger lickin' good, right?

Still, I don't take enough to threaten the guy's life, though he's going to be fatigued for a day or two. In addition to making him forget me, I insert a craving for chocolate chip cookies and OJ before wandering off.

For no particular reason, I decide to take advantage of no longer being frightened to walk around alone at night and keep on going. My world is, for the moment, reasonably tame. Family's doing well. Friends are good. Boyfriend is good—well, mostly. Nothing's *wrong* with him or *us*. At least, nothing more than my continuous guilt over if I'm doing something mean to him by taking up his girlfriend slot instead of a living girl. All at once a storm of guilt and possessiveness grips me. I don't want to give him up. Does that mean I'm in love with him, too?

So yeah, I'm almost back to normal except for the whole, you know, being undead thing.

Best of all, I no longer have a homicidal psycho-bitch ex-actresses trying to kill me. Hopefully, she's more afraid of the Shadows than she's pissed off at me. My wounds from our last 'conversation' are all healed up, but sometimes I still feel a nip or twinge where her claws dug in. Whoever got the idea to call it a 'catfight' when a pair of women are trying to kill each other needs to burn in hell. Claws suck. If Dante hadn't given me that little boost... Then again, I wouldn't have dared confronting Petra without it.

I spot a liquor store across the street and get an idea.

The skinny old dude behind the counter gives me a 'yeah right' look when I walk in amid the peal of fake electronic bells. He proceeds to stare at me like he figures I'm going to steal something. I head to the back of the aisle, grab a six-pack of Busch from the cooler and walk up to the counter.

"Let me guess, you're buying it for your dad," says the guy, smirking.

"No, not my dad. It's for a friend of mine who's old enough to drink."

"Uh huh." He folds his arms. His mostly-bald head glows like a beige pool ball in the glare from the fluorescent lights. "And you and your friends aren't going to tip off into an alley somewhere with it."

"Nope." I grin. "I don't even like the taste of beer. It's for a friend of mine."

He opens his mouth, but the command to go put it back in the cooler never makes it off his tongue. "You're buying it for a friend of yours."

"Honest." I hand over a $10 bill. "I'm not going to have even one drop of it."

The man robotically rings up the beer and hands me change. "Not a drop."

"Thanks." I replace myself in his memory with Mrs. McMahan, my junior year English teacher. I have no idea if the woman drinks or not, but she's the first face that pops into my head trying to think of an adult woman who kinda-sorta looks like me. Memory changes stick better when they're subtle. She's also got brown hair and is a little young for a teacher, but clearly over twenty-one.

With my illicit haul in hand, I head out the door and slip into the alley. No, I'm not going back there to drink. I just don't need a cell phone camera recording me leaping into the air.

Did I mention I *adore* being able to fly?

FINGERS CROSSED, I ZIP ACROSS TOWN TO THE APARTMENT COMPLEX where I can usually catch Glim watching his ex-wife and sons. It's almost one in the morning, so he may not still be there as his family would be asleep now.

I glide in to land on the roof of the building he always perches on and emit a sigh at finding it empty.

"Sarah," says Glim from nowhere.

Gah! I scream in my head while clamping a hand over my mouth. "Umm, yeah."

He fades into view standing by the edge, his long black coat fluttering like Batman's cape around his legs. Okay, a really aesthetically challenged version of Batman with no money. Unusually strong moonlight makes his pale grey face glow, his yellow eyes sparkling like amber gems. "Your timing is impressive. I was seconds from departing."

"Whew." I fake-wipe sweat off my forehead and hurry over to him. "Glad I caught you."

"Is something wrong?" He asks, one eyebrow creeping up.

I still don't know how he can talk with such large un-retractable fangs and not sound like he's got cotton balls in his mouth. Mine aren't even half the size of his and I sound like an idiot if I try talking with them extended. "No. Nothing's wrong. I just wanted to hang out for a bit and… I got an idea."

"Oh?" He draws the word out, smiling.

"Yep." I hold up the beer, his favorite. "No memory reading this time."

"Sarah, you know I can't consume things like you."

I wag a finger at him. "Oh, but you can."

He smirks—I think.

"Look, remember when you found me at Petra's?"

"That's a sight I'll not soon forget." He eases himself down to sit, legs hanging over the side of the roof.

I flop beside him cross-legged. "I met these other vampires who also kind of had a problem with her. One of them, a Fury, gave me a little of his blood. With it, I somehow inherited his, umm... fury for a little while." I hold my arm out. "If he can let me share his rage for a little while, I can let you share my ability to drink not-blood."

Glim gives me the side eye.

"What? Is there something dangerous about it? I didn't like become a servant to that guy or something, did I?"

"No." He smiles around his fangs. "If the man had been an Academic, it might have been a concern, though not all of them can do such things."

"Ahh. No. Dante's definitely not an Academic."

He looks down and away. For a moment, he stops being the eerie character he plays who pops in and out of black smoky clouds. Next to me sits a man I suspect is still not quite ready to accept that someone *wants* to hang out with him. Maybe suggesting he bite me is too intimate.

"It's okay if you don't want to. I just got the idea since you like this stuff. I can't offer anyone super strength or mystical powers. I'm just a weaksauce little Innocent." I bat my eyes at him, then put a hand on his arm. "But, sometimes it's the little stuff that makes all the difference."

"Are you sure you're only eighteen?" he asks, not looking up.

"Last time I checked. Yeah, yeah. I know. My life ended before it started, but I don't think of it that way. More like flipped channels to a different station."

Glim takes my hand in his coarse, scratchy grip, and makes a silly smirk at my small army of cheap plastic and fabric bracelets. "You are sure about this?"

"Unless there's some bizarre side effect or hidden meaning I'm oblivious to, yeah."

Dante didn't explain it in *too* much detail, but as soon as Glim's painless bite sinks into my wrist, I concentrate on my ability to eat food, that aspect of me that's Innocent (the bloodline not the concept) and try to share it with him. He takes only a few sips, less than I did when borrowing fury, then closes the bite.

Glim's complexion goes from pale grey to a light brown like real-time colorization of a black-and-white film. He still has the odd features of a Shadow: the drawn cheeks, sunken eyes, and huge fangs, but his skin tone has become relatively lifelike.

"This is... unexpected." He studies his hands, turning them over.

"Better have one or two before it wears off." I offer him the six-pack.

He pops a can open and takes a hesitant sip—quite a task around his fangs. For a second or two, he braces for a fit of violent puking, but when it doesn't occur, he slugs down several gulps, and sits there with his eyes closed, savoring it. I figure his mind's going back to another time and place. He's got way more reason than I do to mourn a life lost.

Not that I intended this as any kind of experiment, but noticing how his body reacts erases any temptation I may have to suggest he borrow my 'lifelike' nature to visit his sons. He still looks pretty damn gruesome despite the color change.

"It's been a long time." He takes another sip, then lets out a gasp like he's been stuck in the desert and finally found water. "Thank you, Sarah."

"You're welcome. Is it weird that the first thing I think to do when I realize vampires can temporarily share stuff is bring you beer?"

Glim threads his arm around my back. "It's not weird. It's... human."

I lean against his side. "I feel like I should do a whole lot more for you than a six pack of cheap beer for helping me with that psycho."

He chuckles and starts on the second can. "It's not the expense of the beer that matters, but the thought behind it... and the memories it brings."

"Wonder if I could let another vampire deal with weak sunlight."

"Perhaps, but it wouldn't be worth it. The temporary exchange only lasts an hour or two at most. Though, if you ever wanted to trick a vampire to death, that would be one way to do it. Assuming you are even able to convey that aspect of your nature."

I shiver. "An hour or two... what's going to happen to you when this wears off?"

"I imagine the beer is going to come back out." He grins in an 'I don't care. Totally worth it' way.

We sit in silence, enjoying the starlight for a few minutes while he drinks his way into can three.

"Something's bothering you." He stifles a burp. "And, no, I didn't usually inhale it like this when I was alive. But... I'm on a timer and I can't become intoxicated no matter how much I have."

"Yeah."

He lowers the can. "Yeah, something's bothering you, or yeah you understand I cannot become intoxicated?"

"Umm. Both."

"Do you wish to talk about it?"

"My parents. Really, more my dad. He's insisting we go on the family road trip again. Every summer since I can remember, he's always dragged us somewhere kooky. I think he got the idea from those movies with Chevy Chase... only our trips don't usually end in disaster like that. They're just painfully lame."

He chuckles.

"Well, okay. When I was little, they were fun. Sometimes, he finds places to go that are kinda cool for kids. But past thirteen? Museums and stuff can't really compete with my friends. Like who really needs to see a six-thousand-pound ball of twine?"

"I'm sure he took you to Gettysburg."

"Yep. I was ten. We only got to see the place for three days since we had to drive. Most of that trip was in the car or motels. The only thing I really remember from actual Gettysburg was thinking 'It's so damn hot.'"

"Ugh."

"Yeah. Ugh is right. So, anyway, he's doing it again this year—or at least he wants to do it again this year. I don't know if I should go. Most of me doesn't want to."

"You're afraid you'll be a burden on the rest of your family."

I sigh and sulk for a moment until Glim's arm around my back squeezes encouragingly. "Yeah. They can't really go to any places that require being outdoors with me along. Not like it's going to be overcast the whole time. I'd be okay if they went without me. I mean, I'm eighteen now. I don't need to go explore Uncle Abner's Great American Goat Farm or the Great Midwestern Museum of Unusual Cheeses."

Big fangs plus aluminum can plus laughing equals geyser of beer foam.

He slings beer off his hand. "I am, for the first time in my un-life, glad I do not need to breathe. Fairly sure I've got suds in my lungs now."

"There's more. I'm worried about them, too. I'm trying to just be normal but it's only been two months and I've already nearly gotten them killed twice. Aurélie's influence to protect my family doesn't cover the entire country."

"Other vampires won't simply sense your presence and come out of the woodwork specifically to mess with your mortal family."

I shrug.

"You'd have to at least do something to become noticed. Petra didn't randomly target you out of spite."

"I helped a guy she was torturing! How was I supposed to know that would make some psycho bitch want to… to… you know." I grab two fistfuls of my hair and stifle the urge to scream in frustration.

"It is a vacation, correct? Perhaps you could try to enjoy it?"

"I dunno." I pick at my sneaker. "Nothing about my life is normal anymore. I just *know* something crazy is going to happen."

He sips the rest of can three while stargazing. "Oh, you're probably right. But if life were boring, what would be the point?"

"Some people *thrive* on boredom."

"I'm not so sure."

"Stamp collecting."

"Okay." He raises a hand. "I'll concede that point."

I lean back, letting my hair dance in the wind. "Bird watching. Fishing. Watching golf on TV."

Again, I get the glowing-yellow side eye. Wow. He's so good at that I practically hear the organ crash.

"Too much?" I ask with a wry grin. "Meatloaf."

"Perhaps. I believe the CIA once experimented with televised golf as a torture device. And what does meatloaf have to do with it? Not a fan of his music?"

"No, I mean the food. My grandmother makes this meatloaf that's so bland Sierra once called it a block of solidified boredom."

He manages to stop drinking before erupting in laughter. Humor lasts only a moment before somberness takes over his features. "The trip is more about your family than where you go."

"Yeah, I know." I bury my face in my hands. "That's why I think I should stay home. So I don't ruin it for them."

"If your father truly wants you to go, you'll ruin it by not going. He'll spend the whole time thinking about your not being there."

"Why do dads always wield guilt like a weapon?"

He salutes me with can number five. "It's what we do. And, thank you for this."

I smile through a curtain of hair at him. "You're welcome. Glad my random idea worked."

"Oh, you may have done something quite dangerous."

"Umm… what, like you might explode from the carbonation when the blood I gave you wears off?"

"No." He wags his eyebrows at me. "I may ask you to do this again sometime."

2

A MATTER OF LOGISTICS

Speaking of boredom, I wonder if the universe ever expected Thursdays to be like the 'middle child' among days.

No one ever looks forward to a Thursday for it being a Thursday, birthdays, holidays, and stuff notwithstanding—it's pretty uninspiring despite being named after the God of Thunder. Granted, no one hates it like Mondays. Nor does it ever cause the 'ugh, it's only Tuesday' feeling. I bet there's never been anyone coming down with a 'case of the Thursdays' either. But it's nowhere near as beloved as Friday.

Mostly, Thursday is a 'well it could be worse, it could be Wednesday' kind of day.

So here I am on the last Thursday in July, listening to Sierra's PlayStation shake the floor above my head. Her friend Nicole's over, along with a few other friends. The somewhat heavyset girl, Megan, from Sophia's dance class is here as well. Poor kid didn't have a lot of friends until Sophia cheered her up in dance class by sharing my mortifying story. Initially, she didn't trust an overture of friendship from noodle-thin, adorable Sophia, expecting it to be a setup for some cruel humiliation. However, Sophia is *so* damn sweet it didn't take long for Megan to realize she'd made a real friend. They both even adore unicorns.

Sierra still wants to write a video game when she gets older that somehow combines unicorns with machineguns and missiles. My sister is weird. Or maybe she's trying to get Sophia to play a video game they could both participate in. Sierra refuses to play the cute games and Sophia avoids anything violent, bloody, scary, or sad—which is pretty much everything Sierra likes.

A crashing rumble thunders overhead followed by a boy shouting, "I'm good!"

I send Mom a text: ‹What the heck was that?›

‹Daryl fell down the stairs. He's okay.›

This happens every year right before 'the road trip.' Not Daryl falling down the stairs... I mean friend overload. There are so many 'under eighteens' in the house, I think the place legally counts as a day care. Sadly, *my* friends are both at work. So is Hunter. So, I'm sitting in my basement bedroom avoiding a slightly-too-bright-for-comfort sun while studying a textbook I'll be using in a little more than a month when I start college.

Okay, I'm lying. I'm playing *Doom* on the computer.

I *did* want to read—not a textbook—but the explosions from the PlayStation plus six tween girls are so damn loud I can't concentrate on reading. An hour or so later, I sense a change in the air. The weather app on my phone shows clouds with a high chance of rain. Awesome. A door test confirms it's become gloomy, so I change out of my extra-long sleep T-shirt into a normal tee with sweat pants, then head upstairs.

The living room is basically a fifth-grade classroom... so I wave and go right to the kitchen. Out of sheer habit, I help myself to some cookies and plop down in a chair. Evidently, dad has sensed a disturbance in the force—my being among the living—and emerges from his office.

"Sam, c'mere a sec," he yells before saying, "Soph, Sierra, you too. Just for a few minutes."

He enters the kitchen right as I bite down on chocolate chip. Hey what's the point of having superpowers if I don't abuse them? Immunity to calories: check.

"Hey, hon." Dad takes the chair catty corner to me.

Sierra and Sophia walk in after him, lined up like they're expecting to be sent off to military school—except they're out of uniform. Soph's doing her usual pink dress thing while Sierra's sporting a black T-shirt with 'so what' on it as well as jeans. She does offer a small token on the altar of girlishness to the tune of teal polish on her toes. For the second time today, thunder comes down the stairs. For a second, I think Daryl's rolling down the steps again until I realize it's only Sam running. I still can't explain how a scrawny nine-year-old is so damn loud on those steps. My little brother skids to a halt, almost falling over when his sock-covered feet fail to stop on the smooth kitchen floor. Except for having socks on—and most likely *not* wearing toenail polish—he's dressed like Sierra.

The other girls in the living room keep playing the video game, and I can almost follow the conversation going on between Daryl and Jordan upstairs in Sam's room—but I don't.

"So," says Dad, clapping his hands together like a cartoon weasel with a plan. "I've decided where we're going for the road trip."

"Aren't we supposed to leave tomorrow? And you *just* decided?" asks Sierra.

"Well, technically, your mother and I decided a few days ago. But yes, we are leaving tomorrow." He waits, his face frozen in this expression like he's expecting us all to explode with excitement.

"Yay!" yells Sophia.

Sierra glances at her.

"What?" whispers Sophia. "Am I being too obvious? That was forced, wasn't it?"

Dad chuckles. "Okay, guys. We're going to the Lewis and Clark caves in Montana."

"Caves?" asks Sierra, a hint of a scoff in her voice. "Seriously?"

"They should be fun. It's also a campground. We're renting an RV, so we'll be camping there for four days. We decided on caves partially for Sarah's benefit."

I twirl the half-eaten cookie in an 'oh yay' gesture. "If it's not too roasty out for me to get *to* the caves."

Sam shrugs. "Okay."

"Do we have to go?" asks Sierra, a pained smile-grimace on her face.

"I guess it's cool." Sophia puffs at a strand of blonde over her eye. "I mean, I wouldn't mind staying home not to miss dance class, but a trip's okay, too."

"Oh, I'm sure one miss won't hurt." Dad smiles.

"Two." Sophia holds up two fingers. "We're going for a whole week, right?"

"It's okay guys." I stare at the last bite of cookie number one. "You guys should go and don't let me be a burden. There's no reason you need to visit caves for my sake. Do something fun."

Dad leans close and rests a hand on my shoulder. "Sarah, you're not a burden. I'd really like for you to come with us considering this is probably the last time the whole family goes on the traditional road trip."

My mother's sniffle comes from the archway to the living room. I'm surprised to hear it above the din of friends shouting over the PlayStation. I glance over at her. She hasn't even taken her coat off yet. Barely a minute in the door from work and she walks straight into Dad's super guilt bomb.

"Guys..." I hold my arms out to the sides. "I'm not dead."

Sierra raises an eyebrow.

"Well. Okay. Technically, I *am* dead, but... *argh!*" I sigh at the ceiling. "You know what I mean. No one has to be all gloomy about it. I'm not."

Dad pats my arm twice and sits back in his chair. "No, it's not *that*. I'm talking about time."

"You would've moved off to college and grown up," says Mom. "I mean, even if *it* didn't happen to you, I don't imagine you'd keep showing up year after year once you moved out. Especially if you started a fam—"

Sophia cringes, curling her toes. Sierra shoots Mom a 'nice one' glance. Sam looks back and forth between me and Mom without much of a discernible expression.

"It's okay, Mom." I smile at her. "I know what you meant. Really, I don't want to be a giant pain in the ass for you guys. My new existence presents certain issues that make road tripping a little annoying."

"Not a big deal this time." Dad smiles. "Like I said, we're renting an RV. I got some tint film to put on the windows of the back bedroom—that we can remove before returning it—so you'll have a comfortable hideaway if need be."

Both of my sisters look at me. It's too bright in here for me to be 'online' yet, but I don't really need mind reading powers to see what's all over their faces. At a guess, Sierra wants me to stay home so she can use that as an excuse to dodge the trip entirely. Sophia doesn't care as much about going or not going but will refuse to go if I don't. Sam, despite his neutral expression, wants to go... but not without me. Dad's desperate to have one last 'whole family' outing while I'm still not 'out of the nest.' And Mom... she's ready to start crying at any moment, probably thinking of me as 'all grown up and on my own.' I consider what Glim said about spending time with my family while I can.

Oh wow. Guess I'm really not quite dead yet. I'm kinda getting in touch with my old surly teen persona. My not wanting to go isn't *completely* because I feel bad about being pain in their asses. I don't want the interruption to my routine or separation from my 'friends time' which is already kinda limited by that stupid job thing. Right. I'm having a twinge of selfishness. Yay for normality. The last five or six months before Scott murdered me, I pretty much did everything I possibly could to avoid my siblings. Not that I was ever directly mean to them, but Sophia's clinginess *did* get on my nerves. I mean we had our moments, but I hadn't been the best big sis for a while. Seventeen going on spoiled brat. Nothing quite like a knife to the heart for an attitude adjustment.

"Okay." I hold my hands up in surrender at Dad. "I'll go. But don't drive too fast during the day or I can't make the cop go away. And if I have to hide in the RV due to sun issues, you guys are going to go out and do whatever without guilt."

"This *is* Dad you're talking to," mutters Sierra. "If he gets pulled over, it'll be for *delaying* traffic."

"Old ladies with walkers pull up beside him at traffic lights and challenge him to race," says Sophia, giggling.

"Very funny, you two. There won't be any speeding going on. Not in an RV. They can't go that fast."

Sam looks up at him. "So, we're going to get there in time to turn around and come home?"

Dad ruffles my brother's hair and laughs. "It's not quite *that* slow." He shoos the littles back to their friends, then stares at me with a bit of guilt in his eyes.

"It's fine, Dad. Really. I'm not going under protest."

"What's bothering you then?"

I pick up cookie two. "We'll be going away from Aurélie's territory. I'm worried."

"Well." Dad rubs his chin. "Have you angered any entities of great power recently? Stolen anything from a vampire elder? Taken any giant gems from the foreheads of ancient stone idols?"

"Hah. No." I grin.

Dad pats the table. "Then we should be fine. Keep an eye on the house, okay? Now that your mother is back, we're going to get the RV."

"That was fast." I bite cookie two in half.

"Put it on reserve last week." He winks at me.

"You knew I'd cave in and go?"

Mom kisses me on the head. "That. Was. Awful."

"Huh?" I look up at her.

"*Cave* in?" She sighs. "You and your father with the puns."

Dad wags his eyebrows. "That was deep."

"Argh." Mom tries to sound frustrated but winds up laughing.

"Like, totally, I didn't even say that on purpose." I toss the last portion of cookie in my mouth.

"Ahh." Dad clasps his hands together and bows at me like a Shaolin monk. "To pun without knowing is the final stage of transcendence. And give it a chance. I'm sure exploring caves is going to *rock*."

I stand and point at the archway. "Go... before Mom hits you over the head with a French bread or something. I'll get started on dinner."

Dad puts a hand to my forehead. "Are you sure you're feeling okay."

"You better go before the place closes." I poke him in the side.

"Yeah... good point." He eyes the living room. "You gonna be okay watching all these kids at once?"

Laughing, I head over to the fridge to check Mom's meal planning calendar. Ravioli tonight. "Yeah. Easy. None of them have claws."

3

ARE WE THERE YET

Temporary tint is a lot more effective than I thought it could be.

Granted, we put five layers on the window, so it's pretty much black. Dad's convinced it'll come off with some razor blade work before he returns this giant RV. Or maybe he'll leave it and see if they notice. So yeah... my parents rented this monstrosity easily the size of a city bus. The back bedroom is my temporary lair on wheels, with a queen-sized bed that extends a couple feet out the side to create space between the foot end and a slim entertainment center with a thirty-two inch TV. The window above the bed is (or was) the problem, but it should be fairly sun-proof after the modifications. If not, I can still hide in one of the three closets on the RV's rear-most wall.

Right outside the bedroom door, a set of bunk beds stands on the left opposite the bathroom with a tiny shower stall, toilet, and this cute little sink. Past that, it has a mini-kitchen and a booth table on the left with two bench seats. That whole section also extends out to the left like the bed for more interior space. On the right, there's a full-size fridge, the door out, and a sofa... then the driver and passenger seat with a pedestal table between them.

Roughing it, this isn't.

I decide not to be annoying and head out to the RV a little while before dawn. Regardless of how bright or gloomy the day is, I'm forced to sleep at sunrise. Assuming I haven't endured a supernatural ass-kicking, my wake up time is around two in the afternoon. Exertion or trauma can push it later... and every so often I randomly have a 'you're not waking up until it's dark' day, but that's only happened a few times so far.

Hey, I guess it's like being a normal person when it's raining really hard on a cold day. The body simply refuses to get out of bed.

So anyway, I crashed in the queen bed with the door closed and put my faith in Dad's first-ever attempt to tint a car window. Though he did have some practice on the basement windows, even if he didn't five-layer those.

I wake to the steady vibration of wheels on road. The time isn't readily apparent, but it has to be daylight out because we're driving. Dad's chosen destination of the Lewis and Clark Caverns is about an eleven-hour ride—closer to thirteen with Dad driving—and I know he said he wanted to be moving by seven in the morning. This more than likely involved them carrying my siblings out of their beds, still in their PJs and transplanting them to the bunk beds in the RV. Or maybe they bribed them with food.

Fortunately, this bedroom *is* dark enough for me to be fully online. That is a good sign. A little sun leaks in under the door like a strip of nuclear fusion. Ugh. I'm probably going to be stuck in this little bedroom all day. A Safeway bag on the entertainment center that wasn't there when I passed out catches my eye.

I fling the covers off and crawl to kneel at the foot end. With the bed retracted, there's barely an inch of space between it and the entertainment center. The bag contains a red cardboard box with saran wrap over the open top and the words 'break glass in case of annoying sun' on it in black marker. Hah. Dad made a 'fire alarm,' only it contains DVDs. Boredom buster for me.

The original *Robocop* is the top movie. Tempting, but I'm not quite bored enough to put on a movie yet. It's still strange not having to hit the bathroom or want to eat right after getting up. Wonder how long it will take me to get used to that? Or should I? I mean, I obviously can't force myself to pee, but I could still make myself eggs or whatever. Having human food purely for the sense of routine and all.

Except, there's no food in here and opening the door will probably hurt.

So, yeah. Dad and Mom went over 'the plan' last night after dinner when they gave us a tour of the monstrous camper. At night when I'm awake, the 'rents will use this bed while the sibs sleep in the bunks, Sierra and Sophia sharing one, Sam in the other. Contrary to every vacationer ever, I hope for crummy weather. The more overcast it is, the more time I can spend with the family instead of sitting in the bedroom all day before milling around the RV at night watching everyone sleep.

After stretching, I flop back on the bed and grab one of the books I brought along. Yeah, I know paper is not environmentally friendly, nor trendy. It's bulky and heavy—but these don't care about battery power or Wi-Fi. And, I'm quite capable of reading print in total darkness. Oh, very funny, Dad. He added *Bram Stoker's Dracula* to the top of the pile. Might as well… I've never read it.

Outside the room, the beeps of a PS Portable accompany the girls chatting with Mom. They're playing some kind of Pictionary type game on their phone. I push aside the mild feeling of being an outsider eavesdropping on someone else's family, and keep reading.

A few hours later, Sophia asks Dad to stop somewhere so she can go to the bathroom.

"There's a toilet right over there, doofus," says Sierra.

"Oh, this is so weird. I've never, umm, used a toilet in a moving car before."

"Some buses have them," calls Dad. "It's okay."

"Don't hit any potholes," adds Sierra, laughing. "Or she'll get all wet."

"Eww!" shouts Sophia.

It's quiet for about a minute, then Sophia lets out a shrill scream. I know that scream. It can mean only one thing. Three… two… one…

"Samuel!" yells Mom. "Why are there frogs in the bathroom sink!"

"Eww!" shrieks Sophia.

"Flush 'em," says Sierra.

"No!" yells Sophia and Sam at the same time.

"Alan and Edgar won't hurt anyone," says Sam. "They need water."

"Sam," says Dad with a hint of exasperation. "Why did you bring your frogs?"

"Because!" replies the boy, not quite shouting, "We're going to be gone all week and they're lonely. Besides. You said you wanted the *whole* family to go on the trip."

"Come on, do something," wails Sophia. "I gotta go."

"They won't hurt you," says Sam.

"I am *not* peeing with frogs staring at me!"

Mom's grumbling approaches. I picture her hovering at the bathroom door, surveying the situation, then backing out to ask Dad to move the frogs. She kinda shares Sophia's opinion about all things green and slimy. Don't hurt them because they're animals, but she doesn't want to touch them.

"Okay, okay," says Sam. The noise from his PS Portable stops.

Footsteps and clonking follows, then the *ka-chunk* of the small bathroom door closing. Yanno, that is kinda cool. Not having to stop anywhere for a rest break. I sigh at the thought of how expensive it must be to rent this thing, which makes me think of Hunter's family being poor. He can tell me it doesn't bother him all he wants, but I still feel kinda guilty—and miss him. Even though we spent two hours on the phone last night, it's already like we haven't seen each other for months.

Since frogmageddon is handled, I resume reading.

An hour later, the bedroom door opens and Sophia sticks her head in. "Hey. It's getting dark out."

"Oh, cool." I stuff a napkin in the book to hold my place, set it on the little nightstand, and scramble off the bed to change out of my oversized T-shirt into a normal one with jeans.

The most noticeable clue to me that it's becoming dark out is the stream of headlights going by on the other side of the road. Well, there's also the whole not going up in flames thing. So, I guess the headlights are the *second* most noticeable indication of dark. Having night vision is bizarre.

"What time is it?" I ask, glancing at a terrarium on the mini-kitchen counter containing a pair of green frogs, each about the size of Sam's fist. They appear indifferent to their surroundings. One's sitting in the water bowl, the other on the chunk of wood beside it.

"Almost seven at night," says Dad. "Gonna stop at the next exit for food."

"We've been driving for twelve hours already?" I blink.

"Eleven. We changed time zones, so we lost an hour," says Sam without looking up from his PS Portable.

The girls try to rope me into playing a board game, but we decide against it when the RV tilts slightly to the left on a turn. Dad's already taking the off ramp from the freeway, so we don't have time to get into anything.

Sam unpacks one of his canisters of food for the frogs and drops in some... mealworms or some such thing. Sophia shudders and looks away, then starts complaining to Mom about the frogs being in the RV. Sam does have a reasonable point that he couldn't abandon them for a week. Poor things. It's sucks being trapped in a small space like that. Trust me, I know. Hopefully, they're like Bree Swanson... not quite smart enough to be bored.

We eventually stop at a place called The Montana Club Restaurant in Missoula.

Everyone rushes to get shoes on, and we file out the side door. Dad parked all the way at the back end of the parking lot. It's actually kind of impressive he managed to get the RV in here at all.

"Are you hungry?" Mom smiles at me.

"Snackish. I've actually managed to go a couple days without a severe beating, so I think I'm okay." I glance at the building. "But I might nibble anyway. Not sure what I'll be able to get at the campground, but there's always nearby cities."

There's no wait, and we soon wind up at a larger table in the middle of the dining area. The waitress, who's probably a year or two younger than me, is overly chipper, pale, and based on her half-dark-blue-half-black hair, a goth forced to dressed 'normal' for work.

"Hi everyone. I'm Kari with an I. Can I get you anything to drink?"

Most of my family responds like normal people.

Not Sierra.

"Hi Kari with an I," says middle child. "Can I have an iced tea?"

The girl nods, either unaware my sister is teasing her for making a big deal over spelling the name of a person we'll likely never see again, or ignoring it.

As soon as the waitress leaves to get our drinks, Sierra leans over the table toward me. "You should bite her."

Mom gasps. Dad chuckles. Sophia shifts her eyes to Sierra with a 'did you really?' expression. Sam bounces in his chair while staring at the menu.

"Don't wanna make you guys waste money, but I can order normal food so I don't look strange."

Dad shakes his head. "If you enjoy eating it, it's not wasted."

A few minutes pass. Sophia's head lolls back and her eyes close. Sam keeps bouncing. Sierra sinks into this arms-folded glowering posture. Eventually, Kari with an I returns with our drinks and takes our orders.

"And for you?" asks Kari, smiling at Sophia.

"I dunno." She makes a face at the menu.

Mom leans over to her. They go back and forth whispering. Every dish Mom suggests, Sophia comes up with strange arbitrary reasons why she doesn't want it.

"It's not organically sourced vegan approved," mutters Sierra.

"I'm not a vegan. I'm a vegetarian." Sophia huffs.

Sierra rolls her eyes. "They probably shoot the cows right out back. This *is* Montana."

Kari with an I stifles a snicker.

"That's so cruel!" Sophia starts yelling at Sierra about the differences between vegans and vegetarians.

"Soph!" says Mom in a whisper shout.

She freezes, then puts on a sheepish look. "Sorry. Umm, I guess the garden salad."

"With bacon," mutters Sierra.

"No bacon!" wails Sophia.

The waitress nods at her and smiles at my brother.

"Fried chicken!" shouts Sam.

Half the people in the room stop and look at him.

Sierra blinks at him.

"Well okay!" Kari smiles. "It *is* good here."

I order a burger because… calories are meaningless to me. Dad does the steak thing, Mom a chicken Caesar salad. The waitress saves Sierra for last. Predictably, she gets chicken fingers with fries.

As soon as the waitress walks off, I stand. "Be right back. Umm, bathroom."

After spending all day on the road, I'm in a strange mood. I *do* go to the bathroom—at least in terms of physically traveling to a room full of toilets—but find it empty. Being that I'm in a weird mood, I float up to put my back to the ceiling and lurk there. Boredom wins out after a few minutes of being alone… so I start humming to myself. Then I wind up standing on the ceiling with my back to the wall.

"Eep!" shouts a small voice.

I look up (well, down really) and lock stares with a girl of around six. Before I can decide how to react to being caught on the ceiling, her mother bumps her forward, unsure why the girl stopped short in the doorway.

The woman spots me. Her scream doesn't quite make it from brain to mouth before I'm in her thoughts. Yeah, that's it. Stand there in a fog. I spin over and alight on my feet in front of them, taking a moment to enthrall the kid into a mental fog so I can feed from the woman. But before I can even break skin, I hesitate, my gaze shifted sideways, staring at the platter-eyed little girl. Supposedly, it's difficult to have sex when a dog is watching. Not that I've ever had that particular issue, but I understand it now.

I can't bite this woman on the neck while a catatonic six-year-old stares at me. Grr. I pick the girl up like a big doll and rotate her so her back's turned. Again, I go to bite the woman, and pause at the realization someone else could walk in on us. So, I relocate the kid to a stall, standing her on the toilet tank, before commanding the mother in after us. It's a little cramped, but I'm not in dire need of feeding so this shouldn't take too long. Finally free of distraction or worry, I lean in and bite down. A burst of cinnamon roll flavor floods my mouth. Like one of the hot, gooey ones that're about six bucks and nine billion calories.

Ooh! It's even warm. This is kind of amazing.

Once I drink my fill, I set the kid standing in front of the toilet like she's just about to take a seat, erase myself from both of their heads, then move Mom outside the stall. There. That was... awkward.

By the time I return to our table, the food's arrived.

"Wow. Did you fall in?" asks Sam, drumstick in hand.

"Had a little complication. Nothing to worry about." I smile, plop down, and pick up my cheeseburger.

"Darn. I should've done that. It's been forever since I had a mushroom-Swiss-cheese burger," says Dad.

"You *always* order steak when we go out." Mom smiles.

Sophia scrunches up her face at the word 'steak.'

"Well, I've agreed to limit the amount of red meat in the house for Sophia's sake."

The girl gives me a dirty look.

"This place doesn't exactly have tofu burgers," I mutter.

Our meal continues in uncharacteristic silence. Dad's bleary-eyed from the road. Mom's perhaps in the best mood of everyone. Compared to her usual day at the office, wrangling three tweens on a road trip *is* a vacation. Sophia's grumpy-tired. It's almost funny watching her try to eat and not fall asleep. Gawd. Sierra found this one video of a half-awake guinea pig or rabbit munching on something green. She *totally* looks like that critter now. Eyes half closed, a hunk of lettuce hanging out of the side of her mouth.

I glance away before I laugh at her.

Sierra's fist-to-the cheek glower worries me though... at least until I peek into her head. She's keeping quieter than usual to avoid saying something too surly. The girl wanted to stay home, and misses hanging out with her friends as well as her video games. Ahh. Normal Sierra. She'll be okay in a day or two.

Sam can't sit still. I haven't seen him this wound up in a while. Guess being cooped up in the RV all day left him with an abundance of energy. He ravages the fried chicken like a half-starved Tasmanian devil, inhales the French fries, and continues sucking on bones for a little while.

Yeah, so this is pretty normal for us on a road trip. And the burger's not half bad.

Sam balances the drumstick bone half off the side of the table. Right as I open my mouth to question what he's doing, he swats the dangling end, launching the bone into the air. Spinning end-over-end, it flies most of the way across the room before landing on a plate in front of a dude dressed like a cowboy, sticking in his mashed potatoes like King Arthur's sword.

Of course, a splat of potatoes-and-butter goes everywhere.

Neither Mom nor Dad noticed the launch, subtle as it was. Sierra caught it, and her glum mood improves a tick.

"What in the hell?" shouts the cowboy, who's older than dad... maybe middle fifties.

The woman seated across from him, also with a cowboy hat plus a denim dress, looks around the room. Sam clamps both hands over his mouth to stop from laughing.

People glance toward the guy.

"Is something wrong?" asks a waiter.

"There's a bone in my mashed potatoes," yells the cowboy.

A few people chuckle.

"Either this is a setup for a lame joke, or there's been some foul play," mutters Dad while eyeing Sam.

"I got it," I whisper, then stand and hurry over to 'ground zero.' "Oh, wow. You should've ordered the boneless potatoes."

The waiter and the cowboy both stare at me with the same look Bree Swanson gets from teachers whenever she tries to answer questions. Like, seriously, the girl once said she thought the country of Turkey got its name because that's where all the turkeys come from.

I swipe the drumstick bone from the mashed potatoes so fast none of them notice my arm move, and stash it behind my back. "You must be confused. There's no bone."

The woman blinks and stares at the crater in the potato pile. "I saw it too. It splashed on the table."

"Must've been a steam bubble trapped in the potatoes that exploded," I say.

"Steam bubble," says the cowboy in a not-quite-awake tone.

"Yeah, those steam bubbles are pretty volatile. You should bring this man some clean potatoes." I stare at the waiter, giving his cerebellum a prod.

"Of course. That's a good idea. I'm sorry the chef forgot to de-steam the potatoes first." He takes the plate and hurries off.

Once the couple firmly believes they suffered from a case of spontaneous-spud-detonation, I head back to our table and toss the bone back on Sam's plate. Sierra is still giggling about Operation Flying Drumstick. Mom can't believe Sam did something like that. Dad appears to find it hilarious, but he's trying hard not to laugh since Mom's pissed. Sophia's half awake, and I think completely oblivious to all of it.

"Sorry," mutters Sam, still bouncing in his chair.

"Don't you ever do anything like that again," whisper-shouts Mom. "You should be grateful to your sister for altering their memory or you could've caused big trouble. Really, Sam. You're nine. Not five. Five year olds throw food."

"He didn't technically *throw* it," says Sierra. "He was doing an experiment in applied leverage."

"I don't care what you call it. You should go over there and apol—" Mom blinks and glances at me. "They don't know what happened, do they?"

"Nope. They believe a steam bubble in the potatoes exploded."

Dad chuckles. "Have to be careful with those steam bubbles. Highly dangerous."

Everyone except Mom laughs.

Kari with an I returns and asks if anyone wants dessert.

Sophia wakes up.

"You want to give the boy *more* sugar?" asks Dad.

"Good point." Mom shakes her head. "I think he's had enough."

"Aww," says Sam while doing a spot on impression of Puss In Boots' pleading stare.

Mom's a sucker for it.

At least it's not too late. We still have a few hours' time where they can burn off energy.

"Anything for you?" asks Kari, looking at me.

I smack my lips. "You have cinnamon rolls? Got an odd craving."

"I'm sorry. We don't."

"Darn. Oh well. Thanks, I'm okay."

Sierra wags her head side to side making her long brown hair swish. "Yeah. Better for you. Anything you eat goes straight to your ass."

Kari gasps. Sophia blushes at the bad word. Sam ignores it entirely. Dad cracks up laughing since he understands what Sierra really meant. Mom gawks at her.

I laugh, which makes Kari feel better.

"What, Mom. Ass isn't that bad. It's not like I said—"

My hand's over her mouth before she can spit it out. "Don't. You're only going to dig yourself deeper."

Sierra grabs my hand in both of hers and pulls it down off her face. "I was going to say 'homework.' Now *that's* a bad word."

4

FIENDS OF THE NIGHT

The 'rents discuss Sam's uncharacteristic bone toss move over the next hour or so on the road. Dad thinks he's burning off pent up energy while Mom's worried they should take him to 'see someone.' They ultimately decide not to do anything yet, since we *have* been cooped up in the RV all damn day.

I mean, sure, sometimes I've wondered if the boy could be mildly autistic, but he doesn't really display many of the 'usual traits' that I found online. Really, the kid's just stoic. I'm not sure if muted emotions mean anything. He doesn't have a ton of friends but he didn't have trouble finding the ones he has.

The last mile or so is fairly hilly terrain, the road meandering between them. All three sibs press themselves against the windows to look around. Dad pulls off to the left soon after we pass a sign for the Lewis and Clark Caverns Campground. We make a brief stop in a small parking area by an office on the right before driving back out to the entrance road and hooking a left a little farther down. Dad takes the third left after that into the RV park. The area's arranged into a bunch of circles with RV-sized spurs sticking out from the ring. Dad drives around the circle twice, having difficulty figuring out which spot he's supposed to pull into.

Mom grabs the paper he got at the office and points him at one of the spurs. He drives past it, then backs up onto a gravel strip with a handful of boulders arranged around it.

"And... we're here," says Dad, grinning.

We all pile out the door and look around at the scenery. It's way different from home, mostly open grass with sparse trees. A row of hills facing the side of the RV with the door kinda resembles model terrain someone would build for an elaborate toy railroad set, only they did a shoddy job of spray painting on the 'grass' texture. It occurs to me after a moment of staring at it that what I think is 'green fuzz' are actually trees growing in patches. A few tiny cabins stand a good distance away, directly in front of the RV. The rolling hills continue to the rear and driver's side (the one without the door) of the RV.

"Wow," whispers Sierra, standing beside me. "There's a whole lot of nothing here. Grass, a couple trees... the land technology forgot."

"It's definitely different," says Mom.

Sierra leans around me to stare at Dad. "Remind me again why you drove us to 1865?"

"The caverns." Dad smiles. "The main attraction here is a giant limestone cavern underground."

"It's a two mile hike," says Mom. "That doesn't sound *too* bad."

"Uphill," mutters Sierra.

Sophia clamps on to me. "I don't wanna go into a cave unless Sarah's with us."

A few noises come out of Sierra that my brain translates into 'this is going to suck,' 'this is lame,' and 'I want to go home.' I suppose exploring caves and such can be cool for some kids, but Sierra's not one of those kids. Unless it involves computers, rides, or interesting science (and sure, cave exploration is somewhat sciency, but it's not exactly flashy) she's going to spend the whole time in 'can't wait to leave' mode. Then again, she is still cranky over being pulled away from her friends and PlayStation. She did the same thing last year but got over it in a day or two.

Dad whips out a Frisbee, and we burn off some energy for a little while. I cheat a little with a few diving (okay, flying) catches, but no one notices. At least, no one outside the family. Eventually, the family calls it a night. Or at least, 'family minus me' calls it a night. It's a little awkward having everyone trying to get ready for bed at the same time. Sophia changes in the tiny bathroom, Sierra goes for the 'master bedroom.' Sam simply waits for a moment where Mom and I aren't looking at him and changes while standing right beside the bunk beds.

Sierra and Sophia squeeze themselves into the top bunk. Soph's out in seconds. The 'rents retreat to the bedroom, probably to watch TV for a while. Again, yeah… we're totally roughing it. With the rest of the family otherwise occupied, and my being quite a few hours away from sleep, I decide to explore a little.

I head out and around the nose end, walking toward the cabins and the cluster of trees in the middle of the RV park. A sidewalk leads around the trees and cabins, past a little post with a water fountain and a large building with modern bathrooms. It's kinda surprising how many people are here. The spots hold an assortment of RVs, giant camper trailers, and ordinary cars. A few parking spaces without trailers or RVs have collapsible tents set up on the grass. I never imagined people still, like, did the 'camping' thing anymore. Sure, back when Dad was a kid, it happened, but now?

Ugh. The summer's halfway over already, more than halfway actually. Why does that bug me like I'm still in grade school? Is it that I don't want to go back to school (college) in the fall, or am I just not wanting time to pass? Is there still even any point to me going to school? How many vampires work 'real jobs?' Aurélie has a ridiculous amount of money, though how she got it, I have no idea. *All* vampires aren't from rich families, though. Glim sure seems the opposite of rich. But, what does he really need? Technically, it's not required to have a house or anything. We can't die of frostbite. It's also not like we need money for a grocery bill. Thinking of him sleeping in some dank, underground place puts me in a sad-guilty mood. It passes in a moment when I consider Aurélie's lavish apartment is really overdoing it. My family's home is—okay nicer than a lot of people's—but still not over the top. At least, not compared to *some* vampires I won't name with a weird thing for old dolls.

I don't *need* to earn a degree, or to work. Anything I want, I can mentally coerce people to give me. Though, the wandering rogue living off wit and guile may suit Dalton's tastes, but it's not who I am. My parents really wanted me to go to college, though they hadn't been *too* thrilled with USC purely because of the distance. In some way, I think they're both much happier that I'm going to a local school. Had I made it into some place really prestigious, they wouldn't have minded distance so much... but some of those options would've had to have come with a scholarship to be possible. My parents are doing fine, but some of those colleges are ridiculously expensive.

Yeah, okay, I'm kinda smart but not 'free ride to Ivy League' smart. Sierra could probably pull that off if she bothered to try, but she's a slacker. Sophia's either going to wind up going to an academy to learn professional makeup, or she's going to follow my friend Ashley's footsteps and study veterinary medicine, or maybe vet tech.

Yeah, okay. I'll keep with the plan and still go to college. Even if I don't wind up using whatever education I get to find a job, going to college will make me feel reasonably normal. And it'll make the 'rents happy. Honestly, it's not like I'm wasting time or anything. Forty years from now I'll still be an eighteen-year-old. Aurélie once told me something about how she sometimes forgets herself and still thinks it's the 1700s. Of course, I joked at her that it's probably because she dresses like it. But, now I'm wondering... decades from now, am I still going to feel like I *just* graduated high school and don't know what to do with myself? At least I know I won't be like Mom and obsess over which of her friends might be six pounds lighter than her or a half-size smaller.

Ugh.

Well, I also feel like the future is forever away. And I'm reasonably thin. I won't ever open the closet and feel like a slob for not being able to fit into the clothes I wore in high school. Oh well. Except for the inevitable somewhere-far-distant-future loss of my family, vampiredom is a big win for me. Maybe I'll get lucky and the teenage headspace *will* be permanent so I'll remain in the 'eep, I don't want kids' mindset. Then again, considering Ashley, maybe that isn't so much a 'teen' mindset as *my* mindset. Or maybe Ashley's the weirdo for wanting kids at our age. I mean, she's in no way going to get herself preggers until she has her life in order, but she's already made up her mind that she wants to spawn.

And whatever. If she does wind up with a kid before she's ready, I got her. Manipulating other people with my powers doesn't bother me at all if I'm doing it to help someone else. Like, forcing someone to hire me, or making a car dealership guy think I paid for a car I didn't? yeah... *no bueno*. But using my abilities to help support a pregnant-way-too-early Ashley? No regrets.

Anyway. I should stop thinking about that in case I jinx her.

I pass a small playground and a few more trees before reaching the other side of the campground, as indicated by the loop road going around it. It's pretty damn dark out, so I take the opportunity to catch an aerial view, flying straight up about a hundred feet. The campground consists of a D-shaped road surrounding five rings with bus-sized parking spaces jutting out from them at angles, making them resemble pinwheels. Big ass hills span along to the north of the campground, speckled with trees. Looks like a few trails lead into actual forests here and there on the far side. Wobbly flashlights here and there suggest people hiking. Cool. If people are dumb enough to go on forest hikes at night, I'll have no shortage of food.

And yeah. This place has *lots* of open nothingness.

Bored and with nothing better to do, I land again and proceed to wander around the road encircling the campsite. At the northeast, I cut the corner and stroll across the middle of the closest ring road to the street leading away from the parking area.

A pair of boys hanging out by another RV at the south end of the circle spot me and start walking over. I don't have Sophia's 'ugh, people' response to new faces, nor am I at all worried about what anyone may or may not do to me. I glance in their direction as they approach. The boys appear to be about fifteen or so, one a little shorter than the other. Both have light brown hair almost to their shoulders with zero effort put into combing it. Their faces are similar enough that I assume they're brothers. The tall one's wearing a khaki

T-shirt with an eagle on it and green camo pants, the other, a plain navy blue T-shirt and jeans.

"Hey," says the taller one. "Your parents drag you out into the boonies, too?"

His brother manages a weak smile.

"Yeah." I hook my thumbs in my jean pockets. "Something like that. Family time."

"Right on," says the taller one. "I'm Cody, this is my bro, Ben."

"I'm Sarah."

Ben pulls his right hand out of his pocket into a too-casual wave, a streak of glowing purple behind his fingers. "'Sup." He blinks. "Whoa..." He holds his hand up again, gazing in awe at a fat ring, the source of the light.

"Holy crap," says Cody. "Mom was right. They *are* here."

"Damn." Ben turns in place, holding his hand out, though the glow doesn't change.

"How long's it been glowing like that?" asks Cody.

Ben shrugs. "It lit up before when I tossed our plates in the trash. I dunno when it started again." He squints into the darkness. "That means... there's a fiend of the night around."

"Yeah." Cody nods.

I raise an eyebrow. "Umm. 'fiend of the night?'"

"Vampire," says Cody, still scanning the hills.

"Oh." I whistle. "You guys like seriously believe in that stuff?"

"Pff," says Ben. "Umm. Of course not."

"Dude." Cody swats him on the arm. "What are you talking about? Mom came here specifically because she felt a presence."

I lean back, pointing at them with a little twirl to my finger. "You two are here to hunt vampires?" It's all I can do not to laugh. What hits me funny is that I find it ironic to run into a pair of kid vampire hunters and I'm basically the vampire version of a kid, too. The two of them get into a rapid whispering argument. I don't need mind powers to realize Ben's developed an instant crush on me and his sudden denial of vampires is a direct response to me laughing at the idea.

"Look, dude, focus." Cody pats him on the shoulders with both hands. "Don't let your guard down. There's plenty of fangs around here."

"Most of them are attached to rattlesnakes," I mutter. "My father read that in the brochure."

"She knows." Cody points at me. "See? She said 'most.'"

"Well, there's also probably coyotes or mountain lions. They have fangs." I smile.

"Where are you from?" asks Ben.

"Seattle," I say, since I don't feel like explaining that Cottage Lake is both an actual body of water as well as the name of the nearby town.

"Oh, cool. We're from Oakdale."

At my blank expression, both brothers say, "California" at the same time.

"Wow. You guys had a ride. So… my Dad picked this place because he finds lame things fascinating. Like a six ton ball of twine. I didn't think this many people still actually went to campgrounds."

Ben shrugs. "Mom's got the sight. Last week, she—"

"Decided that we needed to come out here," says Cody.

"Do you guys do that a lot?" I ask. "Finish each other's sentences?"

"Sometimes." Ben chuckles. "Mostly, it happens."

I nod. "So… your mom has 'the sight.' You mean, she's psychic or something?"

"Yeah, basically." Cody nods. "I think we might have a little of it. You know."

"Psychics," says Ben. "Sometimes I get ideas or feelings without knowing why. Like, I think you're pretty cool."

I chuckle. "Thanks."

Cody elbows him. "Dude, she's like a sophomore. She's not going to be interested in a freshman."

"One," says Ben, holding up a finger. "A single year difference isn't a big deal."

I mentally roll my eyes at them mistaking me for fifteen, but somehow manage not to let my frustration show. Could be worse. Could be *way* worse. I could've turned into an Old Guard and become intoxicatingly hot. Or—I suppress a shudder—gone shadow.

Hey, I have nothing against Glim, but *I* look deeper than his appearance. Ninety-eight percent of people in the world are assholes. I'm not sure I could cope with it like he does. No wonder they hide. Though, I suppose it would be cool having so many friends. The Shadows are basically like the vampire version of an assassin's guild... or something. I mean, not that they run around killing people. Maybe I should think of them more as a guild of spies? Tight knit. Blah.

"Two," Ben holds up a second finger, "I'm getting a feeling about her."

"I'm sure you are," says Cody, before giving me a 'don't mind him' look.

Ben goes scarlet in the face.

"Well, okay. Maybe I don't really believe in vampires, but I've seen a ghost." I point at Ben. "And your ring is obviously doing something unexplainable. Mind if I look at it?"

"Uhh, sure." He keeps blushing but holds out his hand.

I clasp it—warm and sweaty, surprise there... *not*—and pull the ring closer to my eyes. It appears to be made of silver with a Celtic-type pattern on both sides around a black opal. The purple glow is definitely abnormal. It's not emanating from the metal or the gem as much as it's a thin sheath of energy shrouding the ring.

"Wow, that's pretty. What does the glow mean?"

"Well..." Ben doesn't seem to be in any hurry to pull his hand away from me. "Mom says it's used to detect sources of paranormal energy. Sometimes the light appears only on one side, sometimes the whole ring glows like it is now. I'm not sure what it means... or what the color means."

Cody again slaps him on the arm. "Dude. You know what purple means."

Ben fidgets.

"Vampire," says Cody, eyes narrowing. "Fiends and killers. Sometimes even ghouls, though maybe this weak glow means there's a ghoul nearby."

"It's not always purple?"

Cody shakes his head. "Nah. It glowed white when we were in Virginia City. I think that means ghost."

"Mom said if it ever turns red or black, we should find her right away." Ben tilts his hand back and forth, the constant, faint purple light painting his face in stark shadows. "Bet that's demons but she didn't say for sure."

"Wow. You guys are serious about this stuff, huh?" I smile.

Cody offers a sharp nod, like a soldier confirming his mission. Ben flashes a weak 'please don't think I'm a dork' smile.

"Well, I don't know about the whole vampire thing," I say, with a barely contained grin. "But that glow is kinda hard to explain."

"It's dark," says Cody.

"My brother likes to say random obvious things." Ben points at him. "Mom dropped him on his head as a baby."

"No, dumbass," says Cody. "It's dark and she's alone. We should walk with her."

"Oh, right." Ben fidgets. "Umm, what time do you have to be back to your tent or RV or whatever?"

Ugh. These two think I'm fifteen. For now, I figure it's probably not a bad idea to leave that alone. I'm kinda worried that ring might somehow be authentic and it's reacting to *moi*. The boys believe the faint glow means it's picking up a distant vampire, and if one had been closer, it would've been a lot brighter. More likely, it's sensing my Innocent nature. I'd like to believe it's because I generally consider myself, you know *not* evil, but honestly, it's more likely that my bloodline is pretty much the baby of the vampire world in more ways than physical appearance. Compared to mortals, I'm pretty über, but if a couple-decade-old Fury ever got pissed off at me, I'd be in big trouble.

"Umm." I pull out my phone and note the time at 11:18 p.m. "Oh, crap. It's after eleven. I should already be back."

"C'mon." Cody nods to the left. "We'll walk you to your camper if you want?"

"Ehh, sure. Why not?" I pretend to be nervous. "Probably not safe for a girl to be alone in the dark."

Ben ever so slightly puffs up his chest, and the boys fall in step on either side of me.

Great. This is my luck. I can't even go on vacation without running into a pair of vampire hunters... even if they *are* kids. I'm not too worried about them, but their parents might be trouble.

So much for a nice, relaxing road trip.

5

KEEPING WATCH

*I*t may or may not be smart to lead the brothers right back to our RV, but acting weird and evasive would probably make them suspicious.

I stop at the door and smile back at them. "Thanks for walking me, uhh, home."

"No problem," says Ben, a dazed grin on his lips.

"If you see anything strange, let us know." Cody nods. "You're pretty, which makes you a target. But you're still kinda young, so maybe the fiend or fiends will leave you alone."

I've never been called 'pretty' in such a matter-of-fact tone before. It's like he said 'that car is red, so the cops will give it more tickets.' This kid's going to grow up to be a mall security guard... way too serious about everything.

"Here's hoping. Though I'm more worried about rattlesnakes than legends." I open the door and whisper, "Gotta go. Little siblings are already asleep."

The boys nod, wave again, and trudge off.

I step inside, shut the door, and peer out the blinds at them as they leave, hoping that ring doesn't wink out when they get some distance away from me. Talk about dead giveaway. Fortunately, it keeps on glowing until they're more than halfway across the campground. I'm both relieved and perplexed. Maybe the ring didn't react to me after all. That also means that whatever it *is* reacting to is either close to them, or saturating the whole area.

Hmm. I wonder.

Eyes closed, I concentrate on trying to feel anything weird in the air. After a moment, I do get a faint feeling of unease, though that could simply be coming from sitting out in the middle of a wide open field far away from home.

Grr. I flop on the couch to the right of the door and pull out my phone. Attempting to text Ashley, Michelle, or Hunter gets me nowhere on account of a big fat 'no signal' message. Well, not a message really... more a lack of signal bars. Still, grr. I know the point of a vacation is to get away from the world for a while, but I still hate being cut off.

And now I'm stuck inside all night, too. Not that the vast open nothing out there held any offers of entertainment beyond messing around with other campers, which isn't really my scene anyway. Am I really paranoid that those two brothers might be observing us to see if I stay inside? Nah, neither one of them appeared to suspect me of being anything but fifteen and cute. Cody strikes me as the more pragmatic of the two. Even if I had Bree Swanson's looks, he probably would've still focused on how after the week is over, we'll never see each other again. Carrying on a relationship between Southern California and Seattle would be a pain in the ass for adults with careers. To fifteen-year-olds, it may as well be different planets. And I have absolutely no desire to start a relationship with a kid, even if I *do* happen to pass for one.

Ugh, this trip is like a giant dragon of lameness drawing in a big ass breath to spew its lameness fire all over me. I mean, it's cool to be spending time with the family but did we *really* have to go out into the boondocks to do it? Camping? Ugh. Lame. I mean there's nothing even here. It would be one thing if we could like go kayaking or swimming... or if they had rides. Nope. Open land and trees. Not very exciting.

I drape myself sideways over the couch, one leg up, one leg dangling. While staring at the ceiling, I let my mind wander over past family road trips. Snippets of a few from before Sierra was born come back to me. I would've been seven or younger. Mostly, it's a foggy recollection of sitting on top of a giant toy train some old man drove around. I think we went to Sesame Place the year I was ten. Sierra was three, Sophia two, Sam still not around. I remember it being cool, at least to my ten-year-old self. Anything with rides, I loved. But anything I'd consider cool, or that my sibs would consider really awesome, requires daytime. Yeah, this year's road trip is a cave because of me. Dad probably thought 'something away from sunlight' and cave happened. How excited did he really expect an eleven-, ten-, and nine-year-old to be about exploring a cave? Though, Sam actually *does* seem into it. Then again, he thought the giant ball of twine was awesome. And they do need a dose of outdoors.

But I don't want to drag down next year's trip. I probably won't go, citing 'being too old.' Or... no, I'm going to have too much guilt. I can't ditch my family. Once they're gone, I'll have all the me-time I can ask for. Hell, once my sisters turn eighteen, they probably won't want to do the road trip thing anymore. However, I will insist that Dad go somewhere the littles can have fun even if it's a sunbaked mess. I'll sit in the hotel or whatever I have to do until it's safe to go out.

I hope I'm not messing up my family by being around them. The more I stare at the ceiling, the more I start to fantasize about what things might've been like had Dalton not been delayed. If he'd found me at the morgue before I 'escaped,' and told me I was dead, a vampire, and taken advantage of that disorientation to convince me to go away with him... where would I be? Living like the Lost Ones from Portland? The two of us crashing wherever we happened to be when sunrise approached? Out of nowhere, my imagination puts us in punk outfits with bizarre hair. Fleeting daydreams of night clubs, wild parties, and synth music fill my head.

Ugh. I like to *watch* cheesy Eighties movies with Dad. I don't want to be *in* one.

Creak.

I sit up and stare at the source of the sound—the frogs.

The pair both stare at me from inside their terrarium on the counter of the mini-kitchen, side by side by the glass, beady little frog-eyes locked on me. I'm far from an amphibian expert, but something about them standing there doing the zombie stare doesn't feel right.

"What?" I whisper, shrugging. "You guys got a problem?"

They continue gazing at me. Go figure, neither one says anything.

Though, it feels oddly like something more than simple frogs is looking at me.

Creeeak, says one—don't ask me which.

"Okay," I whisper. "That's messed up."

It's impossible to win a staring contest with a frog. I swing my legs off the couch, stand, and crack the door, poking my head out. The campground has gone pretty quiet, except for a couple of guys around a campfire at the southwest end, whooping and firing beer-belches off into the sky. Slow and careful, I slip outside and pace around the RV, searching the area for any unusual sights or odd feelings. Nothing stands out as the least bit strange, so I go back inside and lock the door.

I turn away from the door and stop short—both frogs still staring at me. Their gaze pins me against the door with the weight of a physical presence.

"What?" I ask again.

Maybe two minutes later, the left frog hops into the water dish and the other one rotates a quarter turn, no longer interested in me.

"Well, that was messed up."

A rumble shakes my entire abdomen. Oops. Hamburger is unhappy.

Minutes later when I finish in the bathroom, I open the door to find Sophia staring at me from the top bunk. She doesn't appear to be freaking out, which is good. After the past two months, I half expect her to have constant nightmares. Seriously, this kid gets horrible dreams from the weirdest things. Like, two years ago, one of the maintenance guys at her school wore a dark green sweater or something and she had nightmares for two weeks that the guy wanted to drag her into the boiler room and cut her open.

Okay, maybe that wasn't so much the guy's sweater as Sierra tricking her into watching *Nightmare on Elm Street*. But seriously, the dude looked nothing like the character in the movie. Her brain makes strange associations.

"Hey," I whisper, approaching the bunk.

She manages a weak smile. "Hey."

Sierra's out cold between her and the wall, one arm draped across her face over her eyes. Another stark difference between my sisters: that girl can fall asleep anywhere. Sophia's like me. The first one or two nights in unfamiliar surroundings, I can't sleep. Well, at least that held true before I became a vampire. Now? As soon as that sun peeks up, I'm out.

"You okay?"

"I can't sleep," whispers Sophia.

I brush a hand over her head. "Anything wrong, or is it just the new place?"

"Mountain lions." She glances at the door.

"Umm. What?"

"I'm afraid of mountain lions getting us. Sierra showed me a video on YouTube with a cat opening the door of a cage in a shelter an' escaping. Mountain lion could open the door on the RV and have a snack box."

It's damn hard to resist laughing. "Soph, I don't think there's any mountain lions around here. And even if there are, they can't turn a doorknob. That cat in a cage reached between the bars and pulled a latch. Totally different."

"Okay. I'm worried about rattlesnakes."

"Heh. Well, they can't turn doorknobs either. But don't worry. I'll stay up all night and keep watch."

Sophia reaches out from under the blanket and pokes the tip of my nose with one finger. "Cheer up."

"I'm fine."

"You look sad." Sophia pulls her arm back under the blanket. "It's okay. None of us really wanna do the road trip. It's just to make Dad happy."

A brief chuckle slips out of me. "Aww. Well. It *does* make him happy. Sorry he picked camping for the road trip instead of something more exciting."

She shrugs. "It's okay. We don't mind. Sam actually thinks the cave will be cool. I'm glad you're here."

I pat her on the head. "Me too. Glad I came."

Her eyes well with tears. "No. I mean I'm glad you're *still here*."

"Aww." I hug her as much I can while standing next to her bunk bed. "Is that why you can't sleep?"

"No." She smirks. "I'm thinking of ideas for my story."

That pretty much means she's having trouble sleeping in new surroundings and her brain isn't helping, refusing to switch off. Mine used to do that to me, too. Before I sprouted fangs, going to bed almost always included an hour or so of staring at the ceiling thinking of random things.

"What story?"

"I'm gonna write a story about a princess who saves dragons from stupid knights."

I grin. "Sounds fun."

We talk for a while, mostly her whispering about the ideas she has for the story. Her whispery voice trails off to mumbling after a while, and she gradually drifts off to sleep. Once she's out, I help myself to Sam's PS Portable and relocate to the couch. I really don't know what the heck vampires did with themselves all night before the invention of video games.

Eventually, I sense the sun's on its way... sort of a 'ten minute warning' mechanism, give or take ten minutes. I drop the PSP back on Sam's bunk on my way into the main bedroom.

My parents are still asleep—in the bed that's supposed to become mine in five minutes. Yeah great plan to share the bedroom... because my parents always wake up at sunrise. I suppose I could crawl in between them. Yeah right. Well, this is awkward. I grab a long T-shirt from my bag and duck into the tiny bathroom to change. I'm amazed I don't wake up the entire campsite in my haste to beat the sunrise, banging my elbows and knees around this minuscule chamber with a toilet sized for a Barbie doll and a sink so small it looks like it came from a kitchen playset for six-year-olds.

I dart out of the bathroom, nearly gasping at the sight of blue in the windshield off to my right. Even though the weak sunlight of dawn won't torch me, I'm still going to pass out any second... and that actually winds up being a recipe for disaster—or at least boatloads of pain. Most vampires won't pass out if they're in danger of sunlight. Case in point: that time I had to bail Dalton out of a construction yard. But me? Weak sunlight isn't a big deal, so I'll pass out... and not wake up until I start cooking.

Like some bimbo in a horror movie barely escaping the monster, I leap into the bedroom, slam the door, and press my back against it. Only in my case, the 'monster' is that stupid ball of orange shittiness in the sky.

I didn't always hate the sun, but we kinda had a falling out over a boy.

Standing with my back against the door gives me about eight inches of clearance between my legs and the bed. Since I'm not five years old and I didn't wake up in the middle of the night, I decide against crawling in with my parents. Instead, I steal the comforter and burrito myself in it on the floor between the bed and the closets at the far-ass-end of the RV. That puts the bed between me and the door out, so I shouldn't ignite when the 'rents leave the room.

Now, I only have to wait another minute or so until the sun is up high enough and I pass—

6

TAKE OUT

I wake up in the bed. More like *on* the bed. Dad probably picked me up comforter and all, relocating me from the floor. Since I'm still a burrito, I figure he didn't want to see what I look like when I'm 'sleeping.'

According to Sophia, I'm rather corpselike while unconscious. Considering her response to finding me asleep was to start applying cosmetics instead of screaming and hiding under her bed, it can't be *that* bad. But, yeah, if ever there's a sight Mom or Dad *don't* want to see, it's one of their kids looking like a corpse when it's not Halloween.

Speaking of which, my mother did ask me to make her forget identifying my remains after Scott stabbed me. Now if only I could make myself forget seeing it, too. Not only did I have to see it in her head, I got to enjoy feeling Mom's heart shatter with grief. I mean, I pretty much figured it did, but sharing that memory with her. Ugh. At least it mostly feels like a bad dream to me now.

Heaviness in my limbs tells me it's an inferno outside before I even open my eyes. Sure enough, when I sit up, the room is *almost* in color. It's bright enough out there that five layers of tint film on the window above the bed isn't blocking all the light.

When I sit up, I spot a paper on the rug by the door. I reach for it, trying to do the Jedi mind trick thing. No luck. Bummer. Turns out paranormal crap is real and I have superpowers, but telekinesis is not one of them.

I flop back down.

Maybe twenty minutes of staring at the ceiling later, I summon the urge to move and drag myself over to the left side of the bed, reaching down to the floor to grab the note.

"Sarah," I say, reading aloud, "the sun's pretty brutal today, so your mother and I are taking the littles on a hike around the park. Signed, Dad."

Well, that's good. I'm not being a total drag on their vacation.

And, I'm stuck in the bedroom. Well, more room to move around than a steamer trunk at least.

It's sunny enough to make me lethargic, so I don't bother fighting it and flop back spread-eagle on this queen size bed. Despite being half awake, I succumb to boredom in minutes and wind up swishing my feet side to side while making faces at the ceiling.

Why did I let guilt convince me to go on this stupid trip? I'm so damn bored. I don't even have cellular coverage here, so I'm totally cut off from my friends and Hunter. That's like against the Geneva Convention or something, isn't it? Even when I'm stuck at home in my room, I still have a computer, the Internet, video games, and a stupid 4G signal. Okay, sure I have physical books with me but the idea that they're my *only* source of entertainment makes me not want to look at them out of spite.

I let out a groan of boredom. Going on this trip was a completely horrible idea. Not only am I forcing my family to do something lame, I'm still getting in the way. No offense to the caverns here, I'm sure people who are into that sort of thing find it *fascinating*... but, not me. Or maybe I would had I been alive and didn't feel like a boat anchor dragging everyone down. I totally could've done without this trip.

Whoa, hang on. I blink, stare at nothing for a moment, then break into laughing.

For a minute there, I felt completely normal. Like, you know, a moody teenager. I wonder if that means I've adjusted—or what is it the term the therapists use? 'Come to terms with it?' Yeah, well... I sigh. I'll have plenty of stuff to 'not be bored' in the future. And no, I'm not being maudlin again about my family growing old and dying. I'm sure the yearly road trips will stop at some point, probably once Sam's eighteen or nineteen. Wow that's so strange to think about. He's always been the small one.

Bored.

I spend a few minutes looking back and forth between the TV and the bag-o-books. Watching any of those movies would make me grumpier about being stuck here alone instead of out with my family, so I grab *Dracula* again and keep reading.

Twenty-six pages later, the RV door rattles. I instinctively close the book to get up and open it for my family, but... right. Damn sun. I expect to hear Dad grumbling while fishing out his keys, but there's silence instead. A moment later, delicate scratching, like someone scraping a tiny nail file over metal, tells me all is not as it should be.

Crap. Someone's breaking into the RV.

Normal people in my position would probably either reach for a weapon or a phone to call the police. Me? I reach for pants. Why, you might ask? Well, one... I *am* a weapon. And two, I just *know* if I get into a fight wearing only a T-shirt, my bare ass is going to make an appearance. Thanks, but I'll pass.

I hop to my feet on the closet side with the bed between me and the door. By the time I finish pulling my jeans up and buttoning them, the outer door squeaks open. Geez. Great locks on this thing, right?

Thumps shake the floor as someone tromps inside. He or she doesn't whisper or say a word, nor do I hear a second person moving around. Shit. This isn't a great situation for me. As long as this door stays closed, I'm 'online,' and not in any real danger. The instant the sun's on me, I go back to being Normal Girl.

Somewhere I heard that most thieves tend to run if confronted.

"Who's there?" I ask in a raised voice.

The strange person stops moving. I picture a guy staring at the bedroom door making 'oh shit' face. Come on. Run away. Get out of here.

Footsteps tromp *toward* the bedroom.

Double crap!

I leap over the bed and brace myself against the door. The knob twists, but I hold it shut.

"Get out here," says a man.

"Sorry. I can't leave the back room. Medical reasons. Highly contagious."

"Bullshit, bitch." He grunts trying to force the door. "Open it."

"Nope." I catch a whiff of something that stinks more like floor cleaner. "Did you get your cologne at a flea market or did you take a bath in Lysol?"

He growls. "Open this fuckin' door or I'm gonna shoot through it."

"Sorry, that's not the right password. And I don't think you've even got a gun. Besides, I'm too young. And my parents will be back soon."

"Look, kid. I ain't gonna hurt you. Just gonna tie you up so you don't go getting in my way."

"Umm, that's not happening," I say. "Besides. Wouldn't you rather I *don't* see your face? Can't describe you to the cops if I don't see you— and I don't think 'took a bath in a vat of shitty cologne' is going to be much for them to go on... unless they have scent dogs. But you'd knock them clear out."

The man growls again. For a second, I think he's giving up... but then I'm in the air.

Being amazingly strong is cool and all, but I still only weigh like 117 pounds. Grown man charging at a door is still going to knock me over. Or in this case, knock me back onto the bed. Time seems to freeze still. I'm nearly horizontal in the air, staring between my splayed legs at a guy in his middle twenties, flannel shirt, olive-drab wool cap, jeans, about three weeks late for his appointment with a razor. He's also holding a blade the size of a Bowie knife.

That's about all I take in before I realize I'm on fire.

The next thing I know, I'm on top of this idiot's who's half off the bed on the inner side of the room, my fangs two-inches deep in his neck. I have a vague memory of a tiger-like roar and a woman screaming. Wait, no… that wasn't a woman. That shriek came out of this guy. Since I'm no longer in a waking blackout, I trust the door wound up closed somehow. A brief glance over my shoulder confirms it.

His shirt has claw shreds at the shoulders from where I evidently grabbed him. While I don't remember a damn bit of it, the way he's slumped makes me think I dragged him into the room, threw him across the bed, and probably slammed the door before pouncing on him. I even slashed him across the face. Ouch. That looks painful as hell. Hopefully, whoever finds him thinks a bear did it. Or maybe a mountain lion.

I drink a few more mouthfuls of blood that tastes like cheap instant ramen. The bite wound is a lot bigger than I usually inflict, more a chomp and tear than a simple fang puncture. It does, however, still close when I want it to. To my amazement, I didn't sling too much blood around the room despite the obvious violence of the attack.

Oh well. Dude should've been more selective about which RV he burglarized.

It's still too bright out for me to risk checking the outer door to see if he left it open. With any luck, the guy didn't want anyone to spot him snooping around and closed it. Still, I can listen for trouble. What are the odds that *two* people will try to rob us in one day?

I grab his limp head and force him to make eye contact so I can dive into his thoughts. He's a simple thief looking for crap to grab and sell. And, the guy really did only want to tie me up so he could ransack the bedroom, expecting anything valuable to be in here. And dammit! Based on my voice, he thought I was only *fourteen*.

Argh!

Well, that's partially my fault. I *was* trying to sound harmless in hopes he would just panic at someone being here and run away. I take his knife and debate charging him an idiot tax of thirty bucks—all the bills in his wallet—but decide to leave his money alone.

"Okay, asshole." I grab two fistfuls of his shirt and pull him up so we're nose-to nose. "Time for a little creative remembering."

A FEW CHAPTERS FROM THE END OF *DRACULA*, A DOUBLE-KNOCK SOUNDS from the bedroom door.

Dad pokes his head in, smiling. "Hey, hon. We're back. About to start on dinner. It's almost dark."

"Oh, cool." Having had enough solitude for the day, I close the book.

"Umm." Dad peers down. "What happened? There's blood on the floor."

I shrug. "Oh. I ordered delivery."

Dad blinks at me. For a second, his expression makes me wonder if he thinks I'm serious and vampires really do have a take-out service.

"I'm kidding." I lower my voice so the littles don't overhear. "Some idiot tried to break into the RV."

"If he got in, he did more than *tried*," says Sierra, right behind Dad.

"Where is he?" asks Dad.

"Did you kill him?" Sierra pokes her head in past Dad's knee.

"What?" shrieks Sophia. "Someone broke in? Or was it a mountain lion."

I laugh. "Not unless this is such a bad area the lions have figured out how to pick locks. No, it was a guy. No I didn't kill him. And yes, he was an idiot."

"So, where is he?" Dad edges into the room, peering over the bed at the floor between it and the closets.

Bah. Hell with shoes. I scoot off the bed and stand next to him. "I sent him on his way with a bad memory."

Dad raises an eyebrow. "You made him think he went to a Barry Manilow concert?"

I blink. "What?"

"What did you make him see?" asks Sierra with a vindictive gleam in her eye.

"Oh, nothing too outlandish." I grin. "He now has the morbid fear that if he breaks into a place, there will be a mountain lion waiting for him."

Dad turns to keep facing me as I walk out into the RV. "Mountain lion? Where did that come from?"

Sophia emits a nervous laugh, then runs over to hug me.

I ruffle her hair. "She put the idea of mountain lions in my head, but I scratched him across the face pretty bad. As far as he knows, he opened the back bedroom here and a mountain lion attacked him."

"From what I remember of accidentally letting the sun hit you last time," says Mom, "a mountain lion is about accurate."

"Bad kitty," says Sam, before emitting an angry *rrreow!* and clawing at the air.

"Well, he obviously didn't steal anything." Dad pats me on the shoulder.

"Nope."

Sophia looks up at dad. "Are there mountain lions here?"

"According to the brochure, yes, but they're rare around this area."

Sophia leans at me, widening her eyes into a *see what I mean!* expression.

"Great, Dad. She's not going to sleep until we're driving home." I pat her on the head.

"Want to give me a hand with dinner?" asks Mom.

"Sure," I say, oddly chipper.

I grin and head over to the mini kitchen, thinking about how I used to love doing housework with her since it was about the only time we spent any time together. Whenever I'd complain about the ridiculous hours she worked, she'd always say something like the house won't pay for itself. Yeah... I'm glad I decided to go home. After all Mom (and Dad) have done to give us that house to grow up in, the least I can do is keep it.

Something tells me I'm going to live there for a long damn time.

7

CRAMPED QUARTERS

*M*om has declared that she is the only one who is allowed to open the fridge in this RV.

Mostly, because it looks like she invoked some HP Lovecraft levels of alien geometry in order to cram five days' worth of food in there. One wrong move, it'll all explode out onto the floor and take six hours to repack, not to mention the distinct possibility of tentacles from other dimensions.

Sam flops on his bunk with the PS Portable. Sierra and Sophia decide to play Frisbee outside, and Dad goes to watch them after checking Sierra's temperature because she preferred an outside activity to video games.

Tonight's dinner is true fine dining: grocery store chicken nuggets with canned string beans and box mashed potatoes. I reject the suggestion to nuke the nuggets since they'll turn to concrete in a few minutes, and set them up on the RV's tiny cookie sheet to bake.

"Are you okay about this trip?" asks Mom in a hushed tone.

"I'm here, aren't I?" I lean against her in a pseudo-hug since my hands are covered in nugget crumbs. "It's fine. I didn't come for the trip. I'm here to spend time with the family."

"You have to admit," mutters Mom, "a campground is kinda lame, even for your father."

I giggle and shrug. "I guess. But the whole point of this is to see the country, right? *Where* we go isn't as important as going somewhere we haven't been before."

Mom raises an eyebrow. "That's rather deep of you. Now I know you're too old for these trips."

"Do *you* hate it?" I ask.

"Nah. I'm only overthinking our new reality and hoping you're not miserable."

"Oh, today was boring as a hell, but I'm still glad I came. Look, if this happens again next year, please make sure Dad knows he can pick a place that the littles can enjoy. Don't need caves for the vampire. If I have to sit around a hotel room, I will. Let the guys have fun. They're still young."

She nods.

We set up around a folding table outside under a retractable awning. I don't bother eating any of this food. Having to cook for five instead of six helped with cramming everything in the fridge, and probably allowed Mom to get away with only invoking a *minor* demon to get it all to fit. Restaurants or emergencies (having to pretend to be normal) are different. Besides, it's Safeway nuggets. I'm not exactly missing out.

After we eat, I spend the last of the daylight with the sibs, tossing the Frisbee around. The sun settles into a glimmering sheen of dark orange along the top of the hills to the west. Clear sky, clean breeze free of the stink of any city, and grass at my bare feet *are* kinda nice. Maybe this place isn't so lame after all. The kids develop the habit of repeatedly reminding each other not to 'step in mountain lion poo' when chasing the Frisbee. Out of the corner of my eye, I notice the 'rents acting a bit romantic inside the RV.

Ugh. Guys. Seriously? Get a room. Wait, hold that thought. *Don't* get a room. I have to sleep on that bed, too.

The sun goes down, and after I toss the Frisbee straight into Sierra's forehead—she can't see in the dark—we decide to go inside.

Of course, her lack of night vision is my fault, so she punches me in the thigh.

"Butthead."

I grab her in a one armed hug.

Once inside, Sam goes back to his game. Sophia flops on the couch with her Kindle. Sierra also grabs her PSP and climbs into the upper bunk. I sit beside Sophia with Mom and Dad in the driver and passenger seats, which double as recliners. Sierra hops down and heads into the bathroom, a bundle under her arm. The parents tell me about the day they spent hiking around while showing off pictures they took of the sibs exploring the natural wonders they encountered. I try not to feel *too* bad about missing it.

Eventually, Sophia yawns.

"About that time," says Dad.

She emits a *mmm*, turns off the Kindle, and plods over to the bunks. After collecting her nightgown, she tries to go into the bathroom, but it's locked. She bangs on the door. "Hey. Time's up."

"Hang on," calls Sierra. A minute or two later, the door opens. She walks out wearing a towel. "I am taking over the back bedroom to change. No one's allowed in."

Sophia darts into the bathroom. The parents chuckle. Sierra tosses the previous day's clothes on the bunk, grabs a nightgown, and heads into the back room.

My ears pick up the squeak of the shower faucet, the patter of droplets, and even the faint squeak of her feet sliding around on the plastic floor. As soon as I cease *trying* to listen to Sophia, only the sound of running water remains in my awareness. Heh. Neat. I have like parabolic hearing. I focus on Sam and pick up the creaks from the plastic buttons on his game. Mom looks worn out and Dad's exhausted. While Mom is an office creature totally out of her element hiking in the woods, she at least leaves the house and walks around the building at Boeing. Dad spends almost all his time sitting in his little office at home. It's truly amazing how he's still thin.

Sophia lets out a scream like Norman Bates just ripped open the shower stall. A heavy *crash* interrupts for barely two seconds before she resumes shrieking. A few hollow *thuds*, heels on the shower stall floor follow.

"Soph?" I yell, springing up and running over there quite a bit faster than my parents are capable of. The door's locked. "Are you okay?"

Soft, echoey whimpering emanates from inside.

Using one claw as a screwdriver, I undo the lock and pull the door open enough to peek inside. Sophia's flat on her back on the floor in front of the toilet, curled up in ball, shivering. The shower's still blasting water.

"What happened?" I stoop, pulling a towel off the counter by the sink and holding it open for her.

She sits up into a terrycloth hug, still shaking. As soon as I squeeze her, I understand what happened. Her hair is frigid.

Mom skids to a stop at the doorway behind me. "Sophia?"

"C-cold," whimpers Sophia. "I w-was showering and the w-water just went ice cold in an instant."

I lean one arm into the stall, avoiding the spray like I'm trying to disarm some manner of Indiana Jones deathtrap, and turn the faucet off.

"Ahh," says Dad from a few steps back. "Guess Sierra used up all the hot water. Looks like we'll have to share showers out here, Allie."

Mom blushes a little.

I'm sure she doesn't at all mind the idea, but talking about it in front of the kids is about as awkward as me thinking about our parents being romantic. Ick. "No way, guys. The stall's tiny. I think it's even smaller than the fridge. You couldn't both fit in there, at least not and still move. It'd be like sharing a coffin. Soph and Sierra could barely share a shower."

"Uhh, that's not happening," yells Sierra from inside the bedroom.

"Well," says Dad. "Then everyone's going to need to wait between showers. This thing's only got a tiny water heater."

Sierra emerges from the bedroom in her nightgown—one of the few 'girly' things she likes.

"You showered too long," says Sophia, clinging to her towel.

"I didn't shower any longer than I usually do."

Sophia stomps. "But this isn't usual. We're in a camper."

"So, just wait a while and there will be more hot water." Sierra pulls herself up into the top bunk.

"That's not the point! You're being selfish." Sophia storms over to the bed, standing in front of Sam while screaming up at Sierra.

The girls fly into a full on bickering argument about 'showers of unusual length.' Sam peers around Sophia at me with a 'help' look, like a mouse trapped in a cubby.

I lean against the wall, arms folded, smiling. Ahh... everything's back to normal. "Wow. Feels like we never even left home."

Dad laughs.

8

STRANGE ENERGY

The next day is also relatively sunny, but we're blessed with moderate cloud cover. It's enough for me to tolerate going outside, though it's annoyingly roasty.

I wake up around two in the afternoon. Mom checks in on me a few minutes later, since they've learned my timing. In the absence of a severe ass-kicking and/or mega-sun, I almost always snap awake at two.

"We waited on lunch," says Mom. "Just getting back now."

"Back?" I ask.

"Your father got it in his head to try fishing. They have a trail down to the river. Spent the morning there. The weather looks like you might be able to handle heading up to the caves today if you are willing to try."

I shrug. "Might as well. The whole reason we're here, right? It doesn't feel worse than the day we gave Dalton a ride."

She smiles. "Keeping fingers crossed for clouds."

"Something almost no one ever says while on vacation."

Mom laughs and leaves me to my privacy. Ehh, screw it. I hop out of bed and change into my usual tee-and-jeans ensemble. For sun reasons, I put on socks and shoes, and snag a sweatshirt with a hood, but carry that for the time being.

I open the bedroom door and get a blast of ick in the face. The main space feels like it's over a hundred degrees. The area outside under the awning isn't much better, but it's also not worse. A lawn chair near the RV under the awning is about as safe from sun as I can get without going to the back bedroom, so I flop there while Mom and Dad set the sibs up with lunch. Everyone except for Sophia has chicken salad sandwiches plus whatever they want from a communal salad bowl. Sophia's munching on a crime against nature. It's a special mad-science project she invented. Similar to chicken salad, only made with tofu. I can't even… it has to be as squishy as eating a cottage cheese sandwich.

At least she's not like this girl Jennie I went to high school with. The girl's the kind of vegan that makes people hate them. She would refuse to eat the tofu sandwich because Mom used the same knife that touched chicken salad and didn't wash it between.

Dad mentions the cavern trip is on a schedule due to there being a tour. He opted for a late-afternoon one, so everyone has to be at the starting point at four. "The tour includes a hike from the campground to the caverns. It's about two hours."

The littles all shrug in a 'yeah, okay, whatever' manner. I nod. Not like I become tired anymore. The real question is if Dad can handle that much physicality. His being thin doesn't necessarily mean he's got endurance. But really, how bad could it be.

"They've got a warning sign for people with heart issues," says Dad. "Might be rough."

"They probably have to put that up because people sue," says Sierra.

"Thank you." Mom smiles.

Sierra gives her the side eye. "For?"

"Not blaming lawyers." She sighs. "It's so frustrating to constantly hear people going on and on about how lawyers ruin this or that."

"Well, *this* lawyer," says Dad, leaning close to her, "is presently ruining the mood with grumpiness."

Mom smirks, but eventually smiles at him.

"Hey," says Cody.

Crap. I force myself not to scowl, and look away from my family at Cody, Ben, and a pair of adults I assume to be their parents, crossing the grass toward us. The woman looks a little younger than Mom, with jet black hair and enough cheap jewelry to stock a Renaissance Faire booth. Denim jacket, tie-dye skirt, sandals, and giant moon earrings only add to the effect.

The dad's wearing an Army jacket, green camo pants, and a camo ball cap with a Remington Arms logo on it. He's fit in a 'suburban dad that goes to the gym sometimes' way, though I'm sure he sees himself as the last human left alive after the nukes come down. Dude's carrying three knives, a canteen, and a whole bunch of other little things on his belt I don't recognize. That certainly explains where Cody gets the whole 'soldier' vibe from.

The family approaches our campsite. Most of the jewelry on the boys' mother looks like new-agey Wicca stuff: pentacles, moon symbols, other rune-like things I have no clue about, and beads. *So* many beads. I'm momentarily glad the sun's on me, otherwise her aura of essential oils and incense would shred my nose.

"'Sup," I say, begrudgingly standing out of politeness.

The woman gives me an odd stare. Neither suspicious nor terribly warm. It's hard putting a meaning to her expression without reading her mind, but I'd say she looks like she walked into a room and can't remember why.

"Made friends already?" asks Dad, smiling. He stands and offers a hand toward the boys' father.

"Went for a walk the other night. Ran into Cody and Ben."

The parents introduce themselves as James and Melanie Peters. Mom and Dad shake hands. Mrs. Peters takes one look at Sophia in her pink dress with silver lettering 'SMOL' on the chest (the O is a kitten face) and melts. I'm sure if Soph was six instead of ten the woman would've started making baby noises at her.

Sierra shoots me a 'boys, really?' side stare.

Trying to be subtle, I wave at her from my hip like I'm refusing an offer of Brussels sprouts.

"So," says Cody, approaching me. "We haven't had any luck finding the vampire."

Ben holds up a crude stake they evidently made themselves from an almost-inch-thick branch.

Sophia sputters into choking. A piece of tofu hits Sam on the chest and falls to the table.

"You two seriously believe in vampires at your age?" scoffs Sierra. "You're like old."

Cody shows no sign of embarrassment at an eleven-year-old calling him childish. Ben blushes a little.

"Stakes don't work on vampires," says Sam in a matter-of-fact tone. "It's a trick so they can kill you."

Sierra picks up the piece of tofu and throws it at him, bouncing it off his head while trying to laser-burn 'dude, shut up!' into his shirt with her eyes.

"Vamp—" Sophia coughs and pats herself on the chest. "Vampires are only in games and movies."

"They're real," says Cody with an 'I'm gonna find and kill it' gleam in his eye.

"The ring's dormant," mutters Ben, examining his hand. The fat ring isn't glowing anymore.

Hmm. Does that mean I don't 'count' as a vampire when I'm offline? And ugh. 'count?' Really? I'm spending too much time around Dad. The bad puns are happening all the time now and I'm seriously not trying to do it. There's also my not knowing what the range is on that thing, since it kept glowing when they walked away. And I got a weird feeling at night. What the hell was up with those creepy ass frogs? Maybe it's picking up some other nocturnal creature that's quite a bit nastier than me?

The parents' conversation takes an abrupt 'needle-scraping-off-a-record' stop when Mrs. Peters waves her arm past her face and says, "I feel a strange energy here."

Mr. Peters doesn't react to the 'spooky-time' outburst, though it's unclear if he believes her or thinks she's weird. Any rational person looking at her outfit and mannerisms would probably assume she's overindulged in weed.

"What is it, Mom?" asks Ben, wide-eyed.

My sisters both look at me like they're afraid of getting in trouble.

"Something dangerous and unseen lurks nearby," says Mrs. Peters, gazing into space and waving her left arm sideways as if moving a curtain out of her way. "It is close… and quite powerful."

Sam swallows the last bite of his sandwich—and farts.

Wow. Nine full seconds. Impressive.

Sierra gags. Mom blushes. Dad's face turns red from how hard he has to fight to not die laughing. Mr. Peters grins.

"Aww, man." Cody pulls his shirt up over his face. "Little dude is noxious."

"Wow," gasps Sophia, staring at Mrs. Peters. "She *is* psychic."

9

A LITTLE GOOD, A LITTLE BAD

I didn't think this vacation could get any more awkward than sharing a bedroom with my parents.

Turns out, it can.

Dropping an ass bomb that bad within fifteen minutes of meeting a new person causes most normal people to forever remember you as 'that kid who farted,' usually followed by going the hell away. Alas, Cody, Ben, and their father find my brother's mastery of gastrointestinal warfare techniques hilarious. Somewhere between Sam inadvertently endearing himself to the Peters clan and the brothers insisting on talking to me like we've known each other for years, the dads get the bright idea to keep hanging out today… 'since the kids are friends.'

Neither of my parents mentions that I'm eighteen. I'm pretty sure the brothers and their parents believe me to be like fifteen. And it's far too damn bright out for me to give them all the idea to forget we exist.

So yeah. We're hiking up to the caverns and I'm basically being forced to hang out with a pair of teenage boys who both think I'm cute—and who'll probably try to kill me without a second thought if they ever figure me out. As to which one is more irritating, Ben's crush or Cody's weak Rambo impression, it's a toss-up.

Lucky for me I'm an Innocent. Going out in the day probably takes me off their suspect list for vampires. And wow, not a single joke about sparkling.

From Dad I mean.

Though, I *could* tell them my age, but that might get them thinking 'wow, she looks way young for eighteen—gotta be a vampire!' Sigh. It doesn't help that the sun's being a bitch today. I really want to pull my sweatshirt hood up and put on sunglasses, but it's weird enough that I'm wearing a sweatshirt in almost-August. Then again, we *are* kinda high up elevation wise. Not that I'd call this place cold, but it isn't exactly hot enough that everyone's staring at me like the crazy girl for having so much skin covered.

We pass a sign with a warning about heart problems or breathing difficulties. My heart's faking it and I don't need to breathe at all. Does that count as 'difficulties?' I smirk at the sign. Mom points out the 300-foot vertical climb warning as well as 600 steps inside the cave.

Dad, of course, thinks he'll be fine.

We head up a paved path flanked on both sides by shrubs and stacked stones. The width of the trail is enough for two people to walk abreast, and Ben falls in step at my right with Cody behind us.

While we walk, Mr. Peters tells my dad about his 'prepper' habit. The man sincerely thinks civilization is going to end within the next ten-to-fifteen years, so he's been training to survive... and also teaching his boys how to survive. Dad asks what he thinks will cause the apocalypse, and suggests zombies. I know his tone, and he's totally playing with the guy despite sounding serious to normal mortals. Mr. Peters takes the bait and starts discussing his opinions on why a literal zombie apocalypse might actually happen. Most of it sounds like he expects the CDC to make a zombie virus and lose control of it.

E-freaking-gads. No wonder those boys are wound so tight.

Of course, I *am* a vampire... so maybe I shouldn't be so quick to dismiss something like zombies as BS. If someone tried to tell me vampires are real before Scott killed me, I would've thought them nuts.

Ben and Cody chat about their attempts so far to find 'the fiend' in the area. The littles are a few paces behind us, small enough to walk side by side on the path. The four parents follow a short distance behind them. Dad insisted on all the kids being in front. He said he wanted to make sure none of us pass out from the climb or get lost, but I think he really wants to take pictures. Guess I can't blame him. I mean, I'll need something to look at and cry over when I'm centuries old. Trying to imagine my siblings as elderly people is bizarre enough, but thinking about looking at photos of them as they are right now when they're long dead is a whole new level of depressing.

It's almost tempting to ask Aurélie to show me how to make vampires so I can keep my family with me forever... but no. I can't trap the sibs as children for eternity. Talk about selfish. And *gawd*— the arguments. The way they can bicker at each other sometimes? Having to put up with that forever? No thanks. And I'm fairly sure Sophia would hate me. If the way she takes care of her stuffed animals is any indication, she's totally going to want kids someday.

Depressing thoughts plus the repetition of walking over hilly scrubland makes the rest of the world around me blurry and indistinct for a while.

"You okay?" asks Ben, pulling me back to reality.

A well-timed giggle from Sophia helps cheer me up.

"Yeah, fine," I say.

"Cool," says Cody, sounding a little out of breath. "You look kinda bummed."

I shrug without taking my hands out of the sweatshirt pockets. "Just thinking about summer almost being over."

"Yeah, that sucks." Ben tries to smile, but he's too out of breath.

"Ring glowed again last night." Cody plods along, looking around like he expects a vampire to come out of nowhere at any moment.

Chris, the tour guide, is mid-twenties with short sandy blond hair in a brush cut. Dad thinks he looks like Iceman from *Top Gun*, but I don't see it. Sierra called him a 'surfer dude lumberjack,' which is a little more on point. Sophia's on edge, but she's been somewhat fearful of hipsters since Eleanor St. Ives' two minions attacked us right outside dance class not long ago.

I should've asked them if the ass-kicking was gluten free.

"Wow," says Cody. "You do like yoga or something?"

"What?" I glance over at him, unable to help myself but squint at sun glare off the hill behind him.

"You're totally like not out of breath. Not even sweating."

Ben looks up at me, blinking as if he hadn't noticed.

"Nah, not yoga. Taekwondo," I say... a little too fast.

"She quit when she was thirteen." Sam looks over at us with an expressionless face. "Only did it for a year."

Sophia's so into dance class this hiking is easy for her, but her body language says she's totally *done* with walking. Sierra's handling the hike almost as well as I am. She doesn't appear tired in the least, though she is sweating somewhat. And Sam? He looks like he just bounced out of bed and ate an entire box of sugar bomb cereal.

All three of my siblings brushing off the exertion of the hike makes me not stand out so much compared to the Peters boys.

"Well, I did a bunch of hiking with the Girl Scouts, too."

"She quit that at twelve," adds Sam.

Dad, wheezing, emerges from the bend behind us, staggers a few yards, and sits on a boulder. Mom walks into view a few seconds later. She's not as destroyed as him, but the look she's giving him suggests he will be making reparations for this trip idea at some point soon. She flops down to sit beside him. Mr. Peters arrives next, unfazed by the uphill walk. He's not buff or anything, but I bet he could do this hike three more times.

Mrs. Peters strolls around the curve last, giving me a strange glance as she goes by.

I hope my expression doesn't make it too obvious I'm miserable. It only feels like I'm standing with my face inches from a raging pizza oven. This place has no damn cover.

"So, yeah, there's *definitely* a fiend of the night here at the LC Caverns," says Ben.

"Okay." I hold my hands up. "Let's assume for a second that you're not crazy and there are monsters. What exactly do you two plan to do to it? You're fourteen."

"I'm fifteen; he's fourteen," says Cody. "And we're prepared. We've hunted the fiends before."

"Oh?" I raise both eyebrows. "Please tell me you don't have a crossbow that chucks stakes."

Ben snickers. "No. That sounds lame as hell."

"What kind of loser would use something like that?" asks Cody.

I bite my lip. "Umm. Saw it in a movie once when I stayed up too late."

They laugh.

The brothers keep quiet for the remainder of the two-mile hike, focusing too much on walking uphill to talk. It's kinda cool not getting tired. Even though my vampire stuff isn't operational when the sun's on me, I don't really turn 'alive' or anything.

The cave entrance looks like a big crack in the side of a white stone hillside. It's low enough that adults (and me) have to duck to get in. However, it's like stepping out from the gates of Hell into central-air-conditioned paradise. Because my eyes have a habit of flaring red whenever I 'come online,' I fake a mild sneezing fit with both hands over my face.

A few people glance at me, though it's nothing more than reacting to an explosion of sneezes. It's a little claustrophobic in here, but I'm too busy being thrilled at not having sun baking me alive to care.

Chris the tour guide rambles on with a brief introductory spiel while giving us all a chance to catch our breath from the hike. After a few minutes, he leads us down a long, narrow stairwell cut into the rock with a black pipe railing on the left. Weird rock formations glow all around us, radiant in the glow from hidden electric lights. Some look like tall, thin cakes, others like spilled icing.

Eventually, the left side opens out into this enormous hole. Chris spends a while talking about 'the pit,' a hundred-foot vertical drop, before we move down the rest of the stairwell. At the bottom, we squeeze through a narrow passageway and around a bend into an enormous cavern.

We're left to explore the massive chamber on our own for a little while. Chris mentions the chamber dead ends on the other side, with only one way out... and reminds everyone that camera flashes are prohibited. No idea why, but... He also points out a formation of rocks near the ground that he calls 'cave popcorn.' I guess it kinda looks like someone spilled a giant bucket of popcorn on the floor. It's neat, and the place *is* pretty, but I'm not quite sure it's thirteen-hours-on-the-road cool.

"Okay, everyone," says Chris after about ten minutes. "To illustrate how dark it really is down here, we're going to cut the lights for a bit. Again, please remember that the use of camera flashes is prohibited."

"Why would anyone take a picture of dark?" asks a random man.

Ooh. Opportunity knocks. I lock eyes with Chris and give him a mental prod not to turn the lights back on until I un-prod him. A moment later, all the color leaves the world. People gasp in surprise. One guy mutters, "Whoa, it's dark." Sophia whimpers.

Since no one else in here other than me can see a damn thing, I zero in on the biggest dude in the tour group. He's probably in his forties, about six-foot-four in a John Deere cap and flannel. Good enough. A short flight puts me in front of him. While hovering, I stare into his eyes and knock him into a fog.

Careful not to brush against his wife, I clamp on and get a mouthful of... pancakes. Probably because Sierra made me think 'lumberjack' before. Having to endure the brutal sun on the way to the cave took a lot of energy. I would've had to feed later tonight anyway, so this is an awesome little convenience.

The wife goes to wrap herself around him, so I float up and away, hovering horizontally beside him like some kind of hybrid blimp-leech for the last few sips before I seal the bite and glide away.

"Dude," whispers Ben. "It's lit up again."

"Rad. Of course... the bloodsucker would be in the caves." Cody looks around, despite not being able to see much more than the violet glow radiating from Ben's hand.

"See that?" Ben waves his ring hand toward where I was standing before. "Sarah? Where'd you go?"

I zip over and land a couple feet away, then walk closer, pretending to wave my hands around so I don't walk into rocks. "Trying not to kill myself in the dark." The ring is throwing off quite a bit more light than it did the other night. "Whoa. That thing's really lit up. Does the brightness mean anything?" With the boys focused on the ring, I lean around Cody and lock eyes with Chris, releasing my command to keep the lights off.

"Yeah," says Cody. "We think that fiend is in here. The brighter it gets, the closer we are."

The ring didn't glow this strongly the other night when I stood right next to it. I rub my chin, looking back and forth between the brothers. "Are you sure?"

A few people yelp or gasp when color returns to everything—the lights turning back on. Cody cringes, squinting at the sudden brightness. The man I fed from stands there gazing into an alternate world. Oops. In my haste to get back over to the boys, I forgot to un-derp him. Hopefully, it'll wear off in a minute.

His wife pats his cheek, saying 'Hank' over and over.

"It could be like how powerful they are, too," says Ben. "Remember in Virginia City, it lit up weaker in some rooms than others. Maybe stronger ghosts." He glances around. "Mom would probably know."

People explore the Cathedral Chamber a bit more, taking pictures with their cell phones.

"Don't tell her yet." Cody shakes his head. "If she thinks it's too strong, she'll make us leave."

"Well, if monsters happen to be real, and that ring is suggesting there's a powerful one here, you probably shouldn't mess with it," I say.

"It's fine." Cody pulls the neck of his shirt down to reveal a metal pentacle amulet. "We're warded. Vampires can't do anything to us."

It takes every bit of my willpower not to laugh. Between his super-serious expression and total belief that he's wearing a magic amulet like something out of a video game, it's almost too much.

"Besides," whispers Ben. "It's daytime now. The fiend will be sleeping until the sun goes down."

"But isn't this a cave?" I ask, knowing full well he's pretty much right. At least, for other bloodlines.

Cody goes off on this whispery ramble about how vampires are beholden to some sort of cosmic law that forces them to turn back into corpses until the sun goes down.

Hank snaps out of it and acts like nothing happened. His denial that he'd been standing around like a mannequin for almost two minutes sets off an argument with the wife who accuses him of messing with her head.

"So what happens if one of them is on an airplane flying west fast enough to always stay where it's night time?" I ask.

They both stare at me with caveman faces.

"Okay, everyone. Time to move on," says Chris with a smile. "This way…"

He leads the group down another tunnel to a rock slide. Sam rushes for it while Sophia clings to Dad, terrified.

He kisses her atop the head and hands her to me, whispering, "Go with Sarah. She can make sure you don't go too fast."

"Oh, yeah." She sniffles and wipes her eyes.

I sit at the top of the slide with Soph in my lap. The girl's ten but she's so skinny I barely notice her weight. Granted, my being supernaturally strong makes a lot of things feel light. On the way down, I control our speed enough that she doesn't freak out at hurtling into a cave tunnel. Not that it would be *that* bad otherwise.

The tour lingers for a bit in the 'Grand Canyon' room before continuing past a spot Chris calls the 'brown waterfall.' *Naturally,* that name gives Sam the giggles. What is it with boys and poop jokes? It isn't water at all, but a rock formation that looks like a giant pot of chocolate pudding exploded and ran down the wall. The deeper we go, the more Mrs. Peters mutters to herself about something being 'not right' in here.

Chris calls the next chamber the 'Garden of the Gods,' and it's… pink.

And I don't mean trick lights. The rocks really *are* the color of raspberry sherbet. Dayum. This is kinda cool. Cue squee explosion in three... two... one...

"Ooh! Faerie castles," whispers Sophia, pointing at tall rock formations that do kinda resemble something a faerie might live in.

Sierra's eyes-half-closed sigh apologizes to the rest of the tour group for our sister being so twee.

At least my siblings are fascinated by the caverns. The awestruck look on Sophia's face at seeing a ginormous cavern of *pink* is totally worth this whole trip. I take about a dozen pictures of her, as well as Sierra and Sam who aren't quite as enthralled. Naturally, Sierra has decided to distance herself from acting impressed because she is the anti-pink. I spend a while following the three littles around making sure they don't break anything or fall down some treacherous shaft.

"Whoa," mutters Ben.

I glance over my shoulder. He's showing the ring to Cody while shrouding it with his other hand. The thing's practically a light bulb. Wow. That's not good. I don't think it reacts to 'power level' as much as proximity. And whatever it's picking up isn't me.

"Mom," whispers Cody.

Mrs. Peters spins in place like a woman trapped in a burning house with nowhere to go. She probably can't wait to get out of here at this point. I peek into her thoughts, and my eyes widen in surprise that she senses a dark presence pervading the area. She goes from scared to angry in a split second as the realization that someone or something is touching her mind reaches her awareness.

I back out and whirl away, breaking eye contact before she can look at me. Now *that's* trippy. The woman really *is* a psychic. Or something. She's definitely a mortal. That makes me wonder if Agent Han might have some real tricks up her sleeve. Of the two PIBs (People in Black) to check me out after my inglorious flight from the morgue, she was the most poised... almost like she didn't fear me at all.

Then again, I am the 'growling hamster' of vampires.

Wonder if she trusted my personality or if she had more faith in her secrets to protect her? If that woman is an actual psychic, what else is out there?

"This place is so cool!" chirps Sophia.

"Yeah," says Sierra in a begrudging tone. "Camping's kinda lame, but the cavern's pretty neat. These rocks all look like candle wax."

"There's definitely a vampire in this cave," whispers Cody... from thirty feet or so away.

I smile to myself. Well, he's not exactly wrong there. There *is* a vampire in the cave. But I resent being called a 'fiend of the night.'

"We should sneak back in here after the tour and find the entrance to its lair so we can stake it!" rasps Ben.

A little twinge picks at my chest where that idiot in the van shot me with the stupid crossbow. I'm briefly tempted to warn them that stakes don't do anything, but there's no possible way for me to say something like that without giving myself away. They'd probably think I'm messing with them anyway since I've been going the 'doesn't believe in vampires' route.

Honestly, I probably should give them a compulsion to forget they saw me... but ugh. Too much work. Fate should be happy I'm picking my clothes up off the floor now. That's me still being overjoyed to be home and alive, with my family. Well, not so much the 'alive' part, but I meant that in the sense of not gone. In twenty years, will I still feel that way or go back to my pre-death habit of sorting my clothing on the floor in a process of highly organized randomness.

Yes, I'm aware that makes no sense.

Ben and Cody keep whispering at each other, plotting their attack on the big, badass vampire who lives in this cave. Half of me wants to laugh at the absurdity of it, the other half worries there might actually be something here. At least they don't suspect me of anything, though I'm not sure why they would at this point. Going out in the sun is a pretty good technique to throw vampire hunters off my tail. Speaking of my tail, perhaps I *should* do something about Ben's fixation on me.

Nah. They're from California. I can't take away a boy's first futile crush.

But anyway, a little good news: they don't suspect me at all. Bad news: something *is* probably here. If it's tweaking Mrs. Peters out, it might not be too friendly.

"Hey," says Ben. "We should cool it with the vampire stuff in front of Sarah. She's gonna think we're nuts or immature."

"Dude." Cody grabs his brother by both shoulders and looks him in the eye. "You're never going to see her again. They're from Washington. It doesn't matter what she thinks of you. Besides, she's like thirteen. She might think it's cool."

My eyes narrow. Thirteen now? Grr.

"No way, dude. She's at least fifteen. She's too tall to be thirteen."

"Girls grow up different," says Cody.

"Her boobs are way too big for thirteen."

Okay, now I'm blushing. Without thinking about it, I tug my sweatshirt tighter.

Cody folds his arms. "Two words for you, man. Alisha Ralston."

Ben whistles. "Okay."

"Just don't get all worked up over her, okay? They live a thousand miles away. And, there's no time for girls. We have a fiend to destroy."

Ugh. I facepalm, shaking my head. These two are too much.

10

SNOOPING AROUND

oices murmuring inches from my head pull me out of sleep.

"Dude, look. It's totally blacked out."

"So? That doesn't mean anything. Lots of cars have tint."

The Brothers Dimm must be outside the RV, specifically standing *right* by my window. Once again, Dad evidently transplanted me from the floor to the bed after they woke up in the morning. My bones aren't made out of lead today, so I'm reasonably sure it's overcast, as the rest of yesterday was *not*.

Fortunately, I didn't need a lame excuse to get away from the boys after the cave tour as they hurried off to put 'Operation Fiend Kill' into motion. Seriously… that's what they called it. Anyway, I spent the remainder of the afternoon in the bedroom reading while the rest of the family went off for another hike. Sophia wanted to try one of the night tours of the cave since they go to different chambers, but Dad had no interest in another trudge up the trail so soon.

So, once the sun decided to stop messing with me yesterday, I took the littles… and I'm trying really damn hard not to think about what our parents might've done with two hours and the whole RV to themselves. With any luck, neither of them had enough energy left for much more than lounging.

The cave had a super-intense vibe, though nothing showed itself. Our tour guide, Joanne, called the end of the tunnel past the Garden of the Gods the 'Bacon Room.' I have no damn idea why they call the stuff on the walls 'bacon.' It didn't look anything like it to me—more like Banksy got high on tainted weed.

I did, however, notice a weird glowing spot on the wall, a circle a little bigger around than a quarter with a line dangling from the side and some weird little markings around it like something out of *Skyrim*. My sibs couldn't see it, so I asked the tour guide. She couldn't see it either. After she denied it existing despite us standing right in front of it, I erased my mention of it from her thoughts.

Anyway. I'm awake and I have stalkers. Great. Would they even know I'm in the RV?

"Dude, you've got vampires on the brain," says Ben. "You're seeing them everywhere now."

"That ring," snaps Cody, "didn't start glowing until that girl showed up. If you didn't *like* her, you would think the same thing I do."

"Don't be ridiculous, man. She was out in the sun."

Cody chuckles. "Yeah, wearing a hoodie. And she didn't sweat *at all* on the hike. Didn't even look tired."

"Her sisters and brother didn't look tired either," says Ben.

"Yeah, but they sweat. She walked the whole way up the trail and the whole cave, didn't ever breathe hard. And what about that guy who stood there like a zombie for a minute after the lights came on?"

"Maybe he's like epileptic or something and the lights messed with him?" asks Ben.

"Dude. Don't be a dumbass. She totally brain zapped him so she could bite him. One sec she's gone, then she appears out of nowhere? Probably thought we couldn't see. Your ring is pretty bright."

Ugh.

I roll out of bed and hurry into an Evanescence T-shirt, jeans, and my sneakers while the boys argue about breaking (or not breaking) into the RV and 'dealing with me.' Dammit. I should've made them forget me in the cave yesterday when I had my abilities. Or at least implanted the notion that I am not a vampire. Guess I have'ta do what I can now the old-fashioned way. Cringing for the expected blast of 'day heat,' I open the door to the outer area of the RV. The warmth isn't bad at all. Sam's frogs pivot to stare at me as I go by, but they're not giving off the super-creepy vibe they did the other day. Huh... wonder if anything happened there or I imagined it.

The day is dreary and overcast, threatening rain. A stiff but not overbearing wind rolls down from the hills. Were I alive, I might even find it chilly. I ease myself off the two metal steps attached to the RV and sneak to my right toward the back end, then creep around the corner to peer at the driver's side. Ben and Cody are still outside the window of the extended bedroom section, engaged in a whispered debate about my theoretical vampireness.

Without even trying to hide, I walk right up to them unnoticed. "Hey, what's up?"

The boys spin. Ben jumps back, looking about to faint.

Cody drops into a fighting stance. "How are you outside in the sunlight?"

I drop an epic eye roll. "What?"

"We're on to you, fiend." Cody points at me.

"You two *seriously* think I'm a vampire?" I laugh. "What are you planning to do, stake me?"

Cody narrows his eyes. "Well, my brother *does* want to stab you, but not with a piece of wood."

Ben gasps at him, then blushes hard.

I can't believe he actually said that. I'm too shocked to react for a good eight or nine seconds before I fall against the RV, in tears laughing. Ben shrinks in on himself, glaring at his brother with this look that makes me think Cody's the most likely person in this campground to have a stake jammed into his chest.

"Guys... seriously. I have a boyfriend already. *And* I'm older than I look."

"See!" yells Cody. "I told you."

Sigh. "I'm eighteen."

Ben blinks. "Whoa, really?"

"Yeah. And geez, guys. Come on. Vampires? Besides, *hello*"—I hold my arms out to the side, basking in the feeble gloom of a rainy day— "sunlight."

"Why's the window tinted black?" Cody points at it.

"How should I know?" I shrug. "It came that way. We're only renting this monster. It *is* a bedroom. Maybe it's for privacy."

They both take on this deflated 'oh, yeah, that makes sense' posture.

"Wait." Cody looks at me. "Your brother said you stopped taking karate at thirteen. If you're eighteen, how are you still in shape?"

I glance down at myself. "I'm not in that good of shape... unless scrawny is a shape. Guess I don't weigh that much or whatever. Besides, it's only walking. Running really kicks my ass. My high school was huge. Had to walk back and forth across the campus every damn day."

"Was?" asks Ben. "Did it get smaller?"

"No, dumbass. She graduated." Cody play-punches him on the shoulder. "*If* she's really eighteen."

"Sorry to disappoint, but I am." I step right up on Ben so he notices I'm... about the same height. "Okay, great. We're both five-three. So I'm a little short. Really, Ben. I'm eighteen, graduated from high school, going to college in a month or so."

He sighs.

"Hey, four years isn't that big a gap. Mom and Dad are six years apart," says Cody.

"One, it *is* a big deal when crossing the eighteen line, and two, I have a boyfriend already. No, I'm not just saying that to get rid of you. If I wanted to tell you to get lost, I'd tell you to get lost." I smile.

"So, umm, why are you still here alone?" asks Cody.

"Had some stomach issues. Didn't want to get too far away from a bathroom this morning."

"Oh." Cody shrugs in disappointment.

"What's wrong?" I ask.

"We thought you were a vampire. I wanted to finally get one."

I chuckle. "Why do you guys believe in that stuff anyway?"

Cody looks me up and down. "You're trying too hard to say they're not real. I call that suspicious."

"That's called being a rational person." I fold my arms. "Ask anyone in this campsite if they think vampires are real and you might find one kook who says yes. What makes you two so sure?"

"We saw one once," says Ben, staring at the ground. "I was six, Cody seven. We were at our grandma's place out on the back porch at night. This woman came by, walking her dog across the street, and a vampire grabbed her from between two houses and bit her. He didn't see us."

"As soon as he disappeared, we ran inside." Cody's expression hardens. "They found that woman dead a couple days later. Said coyotes got her... but we know what really happened."

"Wow. That's..." I shiver. "Are you really sure you saw what you saw? You were so little then. It could've been a mugger or something."

Ben shakes his head, still not looking up. "Muggers don't have red glowing eyes."

Grr. Guess I'm stuck hanging out with them for a while to prove I'm not a vampire. Ooh. I'll invite them into the back bedroom and do a little brain surgery. "You guys wanna watch a mo—"

"Cody? Ben?" shouts Mrs. Peters from the central area by the giant public bathroom.

"Crap. Gotta go." Ben finally manages to look up at me, heartbroken.

Despite him being only fourteen and living far away, I feel bad for the kid. Not that he had any chance whatsoever of becoming my boyfriend, but *argh*. It's like I went to the animal shelter to get a puppy, found one, and another one I can't possibly take home is staring at me from its kennel. Oh, who am I kidding? For puppies, I'd get both. But, that's an awful analogy. Boys aren't puppies (though I suppose they come close on comparative destructiveness). I can't have two boyfriends, and most definitely not with a kid.

They wave and run off toward their mother.

Great. I managed to throw them off my trail, but I broke—no. I didn't break anyone's heart. I refuse to feel guilty about pointing out the impossibility of a relationship that Ben convinced himself might happen. It's not like I flirted or anything. Okay, maybe it would've been better if I told them I was eighteen right away, but still.

If I learned anything from Scott, it's that I'm not responsible for what goes on in a boy's head with no input from me. Okay, these days, I *can* be responsible for what goes on in their heads, but only if I dive in. And ugh. If the two of them really did see a vampire attack some woman years ago, they might know enough to eventually catch me. Cody sure looks obsessive enough to have studied everything he can possibly find about vampires.

Between these two and wanting to get my family as far away as possible from whatever is lurking in that cave... maybe I should pressure the 'rents to cut this trip a little short.

FAMILY TIME

*W*hile it's overcast enough to be tolerable outside, no sense burning energy when I don't have to. I hide in the back bedroom and dig *Runaway* out of the box of DVDs. Wow… the special effects didn't age well at all. Their computer graphics look totally dated, and supposedly futuristic robots combined with cars that look old fashioned give it a real weird vibe. This movie is older than I am. Then again *all* my dad's favorite movies are older than I am.

My family returns around three to 'collect' me for a hike, so I stop the movie, put my shoes back on, and head outside. After everyone takes a turn at the bathroom, Dad puts on his giant green backpack and leads us off on a trail that goes north and east. The last time I saw him wear that thing, I was around eleven or so and we went camping (for real, no RV) somewhere in Colorado. All I remember from that trip is jumping into a lake so damn cold I crawled right back out— once the paralysis wore off—and refused to swim again the entire trip. That, and Mom going nuts trying to control a four-, three-, and two-year-old out in the wilderness.

Wrangling toddlers is why we didn't go camping again until now. And, neither of my parents are what you'd call 'outdoorsy types.' My dad could paddle a kayak in a kiddie pool and still wind up suffering a serious injury.

Anyway, it *is* kinda nice to walk in nature with the family. My condition has caused me to re-evaluate my relationship with rain. I used to hate getting wet when not in a bathing suit. Today's cloud cover is so thick I don't even feel like I'm in the desert. Risking a drenching in the rain is much better than baking alive. Not like I'll catch a cold if my clothes are soaked.

Since there's no one near enough to overhear us, I tell everyone about the brothers sniffing around the RV, suspecting I'm a vampire. And about the ring making them believe there's one in the area.

"So make them forget you exist," says Sierra. "Why are you stressing out over it?"

"I dunno. They seem mostly harmless. It almost feels like kicking a tiny dog for growling at me. All they're going to do is make noise. Not a real threat."

"They seem like reasonably nice people," says Dad. "Mr. Peters is a little intense though. And the wife is…"

"A space cadet," mutters Mom. "But not in a mean way. She kind of reminds me of your Aunt Jody."

Dad chuckles. "My mother's sister…. I still remember her going on about pyramid power and crystals."

The littles all laugh.

"Yeah," I say, "but there might actually be something else around here. That ring is picking up something in the cavern that isn't me. And I saw a… thing on the wall."

"I remember. But we couldn't see it," says Sierra. "Was it a lever?"

"No, more of a"—I scratch my head—"What do you call a funny glowing mark?"

"Glyph?" asks Dad. "Maybe sigil?"

"Yeah." I point at him. "One of those. Only I could see it, so I think it's something supernatural."

Sophia emits a faint whimper.

"It's okay, Soph. Don't panic," says Sam.

"But we're too far away for Aurélie to protect us." Sophia flails her arms. "If there's another vampire here, they might eat us."

Mom takes her hand. "There's nothing to worry about. Sarah will protect you."

"It might not even be a vampire." Sam looks around. "It could be some other kind of monster."

Sophia gasps.

"You're not helping," mutters Sierra.

"Maybe there's a bigfoot around here." Sam shrugs. "Hey, can bigfoots become vampires?"

"Only if Rich is running the game," mutters Dad.

"Huh?" asks all the littles (and me) at once.

Dad stops and checks his map. "Hmm. This should be Eastside Trail."

"Who's Rich?" I ask.

"Oh." He chuckles. "When I was your age, I played D&D, and—"

"You still do," says Sierra.

Dad pats her on the head. "Yes, but nowhere near as often. Anyway, this guy Rich sometimes ran, and things always got *weird*."

"I don't understand," says Sophia.

"It's really not worth explaining," mutters Sierra.

"It's actually funny." Dad grins.

"Yes, but as long as it would take you to explain it in a way for Soph to understand it, it wouldn't be funny anymore." Sierra taps a finger to her chin. "The guy making up the story did a lot of dumb things like vampire sasquatches or—"

"Blink wooly-mammoths," says Dad with an eye roll.

"Okay, now *I'm* confused." Sierra squints up at him.

Dad points, then continues walking down a branching path. "You know blink dogs?"

"Dogs that can teleport short distances," says Sam.

"Right. Well, same thing but a giant hairy elephant." Dad sighs.

"That's stupid." Sophia scrunches up her face.

"Exactly!" says Dad and Sierra at the same time.

Mom and I exchange the same sort of look we always exchange when the gamers start talking their own language.

Portions of the trek are nasty uphill slogs, but we eventually find ourselves among thick forest. It's not dark enough for me to 'go online,' but the gloom of an overcast sky plus tree cover gets to Sophia, putting her on edge. I'm sure Sam bringing up sasquatch has put that idea in her head. Or maybe she's wary of mountain lions.

We stop here and there, mostly so Dad can point out some plants that don't grow around home—not that he's into botany or anything. Guess he figures this is somewhat educational. Whenever she spots an interesting bit of scenery, Mom poses us for photos. It's a little annoying having her behave like I'm a kid again, but I tolerate it.

At one such moment, I'm in front of a giant rock with the sibs standing on it, a faint series of crunching footsteps approaches us from behind. Whoever it is keeps far enough back that I don't panic, but Sophia clamps onto my side and whimpers.

"Hey, relax," I say. "This is a public campground. It's probably more hikers."

She peers up at me with the same wide-eyed cute face as the kitten on her 'SMOL' dress. "Umm. Yeah. You're probably right. Not sure why I'm so scared."

"Because we were talking about scary monsters living in the cave," says Sierra before making an eerie 'OoOooowOoo' noise.

"Stop teasing your sister," deadpans Mom while taking the picture.

"Was that supposed to be a werewolf howling or Dad stubbing his toe?" asks Sam.

Sierra raspberries him. Dad raises an eyebrow, but laughs.

I watch the woods in the direction of the noises for a minute or so, but nothing catches my eye. Content that no imminent danger stalks us, we resume walking along the trail. Sam gazes around as if he'd never seen trees before. Sierra complains intermittently about how we'll be stuck out in the middle of nowhere when the downpour starts, and Sophia jumps at every *snap* or rustle in the woods. It *does* kinda sound like someone's following us, but I don't see anything.

"The monster's coming," whispers Sophia.

"It can't be," I mutter. "Sun's still out."

"It is?" mutters Sophia. "Could'a fooled me."

"Not online yet," I say. "So it can't be a vampire."

Sam jumps up on a fallen tree and walks it like a balance beam. "Doesn't have to be a vampire in the cave. It could be a bear. Or a werewolf bear."

"There's no such thing." Sierra rolls her eyes.

"It's probably just the stupid Frog brothers stalking their vampire," I mutter.

Dad laughs.

"Seriously." I huff. "They're even from California."

This is too much for my father, who needs to lean on a tree until he's no longer cackling like an idiot.

"Those two suspect something's weird, huh?" asks Sophia.

Sierra makes a fist. "They better not try anything. Sare would kick their asses."

"The heavy tint on the window made them suspicious, but I told them my dad runs with some inner-city Seattle gangs. They're so badass they don't even put cream in their espresso."

Mom's sudden laugh sounds like someone drop-kicked a chicken.

"Wow, I'm not sure I'm *that* tough. No creamer in espresso? Those are some *bad* dudes." Dad snickers, then continues walking.

Noises follow us for another few minutes, then stops. Sierra and Dad theorize everything from curious deer to mountain lion to bear scoping us out. I still think it's the brothers. Though, if it *is* them, they're a lot better at stealth than I gave them credit for. Granted, I'm no woodland survival expert, so maybe they sound much closer than they are. Again, assuming it's them and not some other group out hiking. We're hardly the only two families here.

A little after five, Dad homes in on a nice little clearing in sight of a creek. "This looks like a good spot."

"What for?" asks Sierra. "It looks like everywhere else."

"Figured we'd do the campfire dinner thing at least once since we're supposed to be camping," says Dad.

"Umm." I fidget. "Don't be offended if I sit back a bit from the fire."

"You're flammable?" asks Sophia, wide-eyed.

I giggle. "No more than any other person really, but it's a little scary since it can kill me."

"Right." Dad nods. "No bonfire then."

"Don't let him near the lighter fluid," fake-whispers Sierra while not-so-subtly pointing at Dad.

He sets his hands on his hips. "I am not *that* bad."

"He's not," says Sam. "My eyebrows *did* grow back."

"Hey!" Dad points at him. "I told you not to stand that close."

Everyone laughs, even Mom. It's such a pure moment with the family it's almost possible to stop feeling like there's something in the woods watching us.

Almost.

NIGHT EYES

*D*ad sets up a pit for a campfire while Mom rummages the backpack and pulls out a Tupperware container of shish kabobs. Sophia takes her sneakers and socks off and roams around for a little while before testing the creek with a toe.

She squeals at the cold, but it's evidently not *too* cold as she steps in. Sam's disappointed at the lack of swimming, but the creek's barely eight inches deep in the middle. Dad sends us out to find wood. Sophia continues playing in the creek instead of searching, though the 'rents don't say anything to her.

Five minutes into Operation Kindling, Sierra shouts, "Soph, help look for wood."

"I don't have shoes on and my feet are wet."

"Convenient," says Sierra to one in particular before looking up at me. "Bet she knew Dad was gonna do that. Ugh, there's—" She jumps back, with a "Gah!"

I don't need to ask, since the red glare from my eyes tinted her face.

She clamps a hand over her heart. "You just scared the crap out of me."

"What? You've seen that before."

Sierra blows out a forced sigh of relief. "Yeah, but not quite so close. You look kinda scary for a sec."

"Well, let's hope the cave monster thinks so." I grin.

"Is there really something down there or were you only trying to scare Soph?"

"There's… something. I don't know what it is, but that kid's ring legit glows like magic. Also got the weirdest feeling whatever's down there knows I'm here."

"Thanks for that. Now I'm not going to sleep again until we go home."

I ruffle her hair. "Haven't seen anything yet. If it *is* a vamp, it's not one that can go out during the day. I'm sure it didn't see me."

"Did you feel a vampire around?"

"No, just a weird energy in the air."

She picks up a two-inch thick branch. "Then it probably didn't sense you either."

"That makes sense." I spot a sizable rotten log and trot over to it. After making sure it isn't a hornets' nest, I sprout claws for a better grip, sink them into the wood, and haul the five-foot-long thing into the air.

"Show off," mutters Sierra, grinning. "Imagine the vamp you could stake with that sucker."

"Ouch."

I plod after her back to the campsite, which isn't *too* far off. Sam's presenting his find—a handful of twigs. Sierra holds up her branch, and Dad nearly faints when he sees me coming with half a tree.

Mom's face pales. She stares, wordless, as I carry it to a spot about ten paces from where Dad made the fire pit and drop it with a *thud* that startles birds out of trees.

"That's a little, umm, big," says Dad.

"I got it covered." Between clawing and ripping, I break off a couple of hunks good enough for a basic cooking fire.

Dad cuts Sierra's branch into a few sections and uses Sam's little twigs and such for kindling.

We sit around for a while watching Dad build a fire. Only, I'm not sure if campers are allowed to have fires out here. My father's not a rule breaker, but he's not above doing without asking then claiming ignorance. At least the stream's right there.

"Soph!" yells Mom. "Don't drink that."

My sister freezes, cupped hands a few inches away from her mouth. "Why?"

"It's not safe. Microbes or who knows what in it. We brought water." Mom waves her over.

She drops her handful of water and makes her way to the campsite, taking a seat in the grass by Mom. Eventually, my parents and siblings are all holding their shish kabobs over the fire. Sophia's got a custom one with tofu blocks instead of alternating beef and chicken. I break my own rule and sit maybe nine feet away, cross-legged on the ground.

"We're not gonna have to like sleep out here in tents, are we?" asks Sophia, her voice shaky.

"Nope." Dad smiles. "There's only so much room in that pack. We'll be going back to the RV after we eat."

"Whew." Sophia wipes 'sweat' off her forehead. "I don't wanna be eaten by a mountain lion."

Since we're sitting around a campfire in a dark forest at night, the urge to tell a ghost story comes out of nowhere.

"You know, I heard someone back at the RV area last night talking about there might be a haunt out here in the woods."

Sophia gasps. Sierra gives me a 'yeah right' smirk. Sam appears to ignore me, staring intently at his shish kabob cooking.

"This guy said like sixty years ago, a bunch of college kids came out here and tried to spend the night. No one really knows what happened to them. All they ever found were ripped up tents and blood. But every now and then people who come out here can sometimes hear people walking around when there isn't anyone there. He also said you can sometimes see a ghostly green campfire, but it's never there if you try to walk up to it."

Sophia shivers. Sierra's blasé attitude is gone, her expression 'non-panicking-concerned.' Sam keeps turning his food over in the flames.

"The guy I was listening to said he came out here when he was like twelve and someone told him about the story. So he and his friend walked up around this area at night looking for a ghost. It got real quiet all of a sudden. Like all the birds stopped chirping and all the insects shut up at the same time. Then, he felt like someone was behind him, walking closer... every step making a *crunch*." I lean forward, raising my hands like I'm creeping up to grab someone. "He knew the ghosts were right there, right about to grab him, but he was too scared to move—or even look behind him."

Silent tears roll out of Sophia's eyes. Sierra's gone pale, staring over the fire at me. Whoa. I haven't seen her that frightened since she was like five and had a nightmare. Sam's also looking at me with both eyebrows up. Mom's also shivering a little, and Dad stares at me, his mouth hanging open.

"Umm. Oops. Sorry guys... I think I might've been affecting your emotions by accident. Didn't mean it."

"No," whispers Sophia, trembling. "There's something behind you watching us with glowing red eyes."

I whirl around and stare at a large humanoid figure half hidden behind a tree about thirty feet away. Before I get much more than a half-second's look at him, he trucks off into the woods. The dude's like NFL linebacker sized and running way too fast for me to feel any urge to go after him. Any 'creature in the woods' intending to be dangerous wouldn't haul ass like that from little old me.

"What is it?" asks Sophia.

"Either a WWE wrestler is really lost, or this campground has a sasquatch."

"I don't see anything," says Mom.

"Duh." Sierra glances at her. "Sarah's got night vision."

I turn back to my family and check the thoughts of all three siblings. To them, the forest appears pitch black. They only spotted a pair of glowing eyes. Nothing in their heads suggests their thoughts had been tampered with or touched, though I don't think peering at surface thoughts is noticeable to the victim. He may or may not have tried knocking on my brain, but without eye contact, I don't think it's possible. According to Aurélie, it's a real pain in the ass to invade another vampire's head. *She* can do it, but she's older than hell and mental manipulation is like her specialty. Then again, I'm still not entirely sure what I'm dealing with. I know vampires exist, but that doesn't prove other stuff doesn't.

"Where'd he go?" asks Sierra.

"Gone. Ran like hell." I look around, but he's nowhere to be seen.

"I wanna go back to the RV," says Sophia. "I'm scared."

"Umm, the RV's walls aren't that tough. A sasquatch could break in pretty easy." Sam shrugs and nibble-tests his food. Satisfied, he takes a real bite.

Sophia bursts into tears.

"Hey Sare," asks Sierra. "Could you kick Bigfoot's ass?"

My turn to shrug. "No idea. Are sasquatch even real?"

"Sasquatches," says Sam.

"That's not a word," says Sophia, still a hint of whimper in her voice. "Sasquatch is an irregular plural like deer or fish."

"Book nerd," says Sierra.

Sophia sticks her tongue out. "Geek."

"Nerd." Sierra grins. "And Sare could totally kick its ass."

"I let the last one go, but I really wish you would clean up your language," says Mom.

"'Ass' isn't that bad a word." Sierra takes a bite of chicken from her kabob. "Be glad I'm limiting myself to that one."

"Be glad I'm not limiting you to no electronics for a week," says Mom, with a raised eyebrow.

Sierra hangs her head. "That's not fair."

Dad examines his food and wags the shish kabob at us. "Sophia's got a point. There's *something* out here, even if it's just an ordinary guy who might be up to no good. C'mon. Everyone eat quick and we'll head back."

No one objects. I stand and do my best impression of a sentry soldier from *Call of Duty* while my family eats. I've never seen Sophia wolf down her food so fast before—ever. As soon as her skewer's empty, she pulls her socks and shoes on, stands, and starts bouncing on her toes.

"Is that 'eager to go home' bouncing or 'gotta go' bouncing?" asks Dad.

"*Why* did you have to say that?" asks Sierra. "Now I gotta go."

"There's no bathrooms out here." Sam hands his empty skewer to Mom.

"I know that, dork!" snaps Sierra. "That's the problem."

"Well." Dad shrugs. "You can hold it until we're back at the campground, or water the bushes."

"It's like an hour walk!" Sierra fumes—and blushes... then looks terrified. "We can't split up. It'll get us one at a time."

"Eek!" yells Sophia.

"Will you two stop scaring your sister?" asks Mom.

Sam appears bewildered.

"He's not doing it on purpose." I wander over and pat him on the head. "He just says whatever pops into his mind."

"Your father does that too, but only after he's had a few glasses of wine." Mom smirks.

"So the boy will be a cheap date." Dad winks at him.

Sam glances up at me, bewildered.

"I'm not explaining that one to him." I wave at the girls. "Come on. I'll stand watch."

While my brother decides to water a tree close by, I walk my sisters into the woods until Sophia freaks out at the total darkness.

"Dude, I can't see anything," says Sierra.

"That's the point," I say. "Privacy."

"It's too dark," mutters Sophia. "Is the monster still there?"

I glance around. "Nope. C'mon, hurry up."

A few minutes later, I lead them back to camp. They cling to me since it's probably too dark for them to see anything. Dad's already doused the fire with water from the creek, so the girls both startle when I tug them to a halt, not realizing Dad, Mom, and Sam are right in front of us.

"How are we going to get back to the camp? It's too dark. We're trapped out here," whines Sophia.

Dad turns a flashlight on and points it at us. "Got lights for everyone." He smiles at me. "Well, almost everyone."

"Fly me back," whispers Sophia. "Pleeeease."

"It's okay," I say. "If I fly you back, then you'll be all alone in the RV while I go get everyone else. And if that… whatever he is comes back when I'm not here, he might hurt someone."

Sierra punches me on the shoulder.

"What was that for?" I ask.

She glares up at me, terrified of something attacking us at any second, and pissed off at me for scaring her into thinking about that.

"Oh. Sorry." I take her hand, too. "I think he was only curious."

It worries me that Sierra doesn't object to holding hands. Usually, she's 'too cool' for that. But then again, pitch-black forest plus ghost story plus actual monster would've scared the crap out of me at eleven, so I can't blame her.

Dad passes out flashlights, puts on his backpack, and takes one step. "Crap."

"What now?" asks Mom.

"I, umm… kinda got turned around."

"Geez, Dad… Hang on a sec, guys. Don't go anywhere." I fly straight up until I spot the telltale glow of cars on the road and a handful of lights around the RV park. We're way off, up in the hills on the far side of a peak. At least they're not *big* mountains. "Wow. We went pretty far." Even with enhanced vision, it's a little difficult to make out the trails from the air past the tree cover, but I think I spot one. "Okay. Got it. Everyone follow me."

I land, re-take my sisters' hands, and lead the way home.

Or at least, as 'home' as we can get right now.

13

THE GENUINE ARTICLE

Our trip back to the RV is uneventful, but nerve-wracking for Sophia.

She's still nervous even once we're inside behind a locked door, since Sam oh-so-helpfully pointed out a sasquatch could easily break the thin walls. I sit on the couch with her curled up in a ball on my left. As if her two-handed grip on my arm didn't clue me in on her fear, that she's not reading her Kindle or talking is a big red flag. Even Sierra's nervous. I can tell, because she sits beside me on the right with her PS Portable, one shoulder touching me. For her, that's about the equivalent of Sophia wrapping herself around my arm.

Sam flops on his bunk with his game system like nothing happened.

I spend a while trying to calm the girls down by saying the big guy probably saw the campfire and came to check it out. If he'd been dangerous, he wouldn't have run away. And, I didn't see anything at all on our walk back except for trees. When I finally admit the ghost story was all made up and I didn't really hear anyone talking about it, Sophia calms a little.

Eventually, Mom sends the sibs to bed due to the time. I hang with the parents for another hour, discussing random things from my upcoming first year of college to maybe we should go home a day or two early since there's *something* here.

"I don't think it's that big a deal." I catch myself before making the comment that no one would mind going home early. Fairly sure the girls are quite done with this place already. Sam's the king of 'whatever.' He'd be okay going home early or staying. "People camp here all the time and nothing noteworthy has happened. Whatever it is probably only wants to be left alone."

Dad nods.

"Perhaps we should skip the night hiking." Mom's tone makes it less of a suggestion.

"It's cool, guys. We have trees back home. If you want to roam around during the day, please, go. I hate being a boat anchor. You don't have to feel guilty about enjoying the daylight."

My parents stand from the recliners (driver and passenger seat) and hug me.

"All right," says Dad.

"I mean it. I'm *fine*." I grin, and again catch myself before saying 'if.' "Next year's road trip, please pick somewhere the kids can enjoy. I can either stay home or stay in a hotel room during the day if it's bright out. It will not bother me. Okay? Better they have fun."

Mom squeezes me tighter.

"I'll see what I can find." Dad pokes me in the side. "Thank you for coming this year. I get that you're eighteen now. If you wanna skip it next year, it won't bother me—much."

"Next year's a long way off," I say.

"Any plans tonight?" asks Mom.

"Well, I figured I'd fly back to Cottage Lake and hang with Ash and 'Chelle, then race back here to beat sunrise."

They both stare at me.

"Kidding, guys… It's like 700 miles home. It would take me three hours to fly one way. Totes not worth it." I gesture at the door. "Probably just going to wander around, grab a bite to eat, and maybe go do something I probably shouldn't do."

"What's that?" asks Dad. "Get too close to a bear cub? Start a land war in Asia? Put ketchup on a hot dog?"

Mom gives him the side-eye. She's originally from Chicago.

I giggle. "No. I was thinking of checking out that glyph on the wall… but you know what? I think I'm going to ignore it. This is supposed to be a vacation and I don't want to be the reason we nearly die. If there *is* a monster in that cave, poking it in the ass with a turkey baster is a stupid move."

Dad laughs.

Mom blinks at me.

"Wow, you're not really in a mood for jokes, huh?" I poke her in the side.

"Not really. I can never tell anymore when you're being serious. I thought that whole war between elder vampires thing was a sarcastic remark."

I cringe. "Nope. But you were right. Sophia's dance class *was* more important. At least to me."

"Okay then. We're off to bed," says Dad.

"Please tell me you guys aren't going to do anything unnatural in the same bed I've been sleeping on."

Mom blushes.

Dad rolls his eyes. "Hardly. Your mother hasn't let me touch her since the night we made Sam."

Mom gasps. "Jonathan!"

"Eww," says Sierra. "Guys… trying to sleep here."

I shudder.

"Allie…" Dad puts an arm around her. "You're supposed to laugh, since clearly that was not a true statement."

"Argh!" yells Sierra.

"I'm out." I plug my ears and walk to the door making "La-la-la-la-la" noises.

SUPERNATURALLY ENHANCED HEARING CAN BE A CURSE AS MUCH AS A benefit.

While roaming around the RV park, I catch all sorts of things I regret being aware of. At least four couples doing the deed, including one old couple. As long as I un-live, I'll never forget "oh, Julius, that's the spot, go a little faster" in a voice that sounds kinda like my grandmother.

When a man grumbles, "I'm gonna frickin' kill you, you stupid bitch," from another RV, I dash over out of concern… but he's talking to a video game. The 'bitch' in question appears to be some giant, vaguely-feminine, alien hive monster.

In addition to the awkward, the creepy, and the weird, I also catch snippets of bedtime stories, movies playing, and one guy strumming an acoustic guitar. For obvious reasons, I avoid going near the circle where the Peters Family is parked. The last thing I need would be to have the brothers spot me prowling around at night.

Eventually, I make my way across the middle of the RV park where the public bathroom building plus a few small cabins sit. A solitary man sitting with his back against a tree presents a perfect opportunity. He's evidently in the process of rolling a handmade cigarette. My nose tells me I want to bite him before he lights up. Not that I'd totally mind a little pot buzz on general principles, but I don't exactly feel comfortable out here. At least, not without understanding exactly what our unidentified cave monster really is.

I figured the girls wouldn't be asleep due to nerves, so I didn't tell the parents my real goal tonight: patrol. My plan is to make sure neither the unidentified cave monster nor the big guy creeping around the woods bother the fam while they sleep. Once I finish feeding to make up for my daylight exposure, I plan to sit on our RV roof all night and keep an eye out.

"Hey," I say, walking out in front of the guy by the tree.

"Shit!" He yells, fumbling his half-assembled joint. "What the hell is wrong with you?"

"A lot of things." I grin.

He stares up at me, caught off guard by my reaction. The guy's in his later twenties, wearing a sloppy T-shirt and camo pants so saturated with the smell of marijuana that I'm probably at risk of catching a high merely standing within three feet of him—despite being undead.

"C'mere." I curl my finger in a beckoning gesture.

"Okay." He stands and takes a step closer.

Hey, one good thing. This dude is so obviously a stoner, no one will think it weird that my charm leaves him staring into space for a minute or two. Also, given I'm five-three, it shouldn't surprise me that like *every* time I feed off a guy, he's seriously taller than me. This one isn't too bad though, I can reach on tiptoe. Don't have to hover.

His blood tastes like salt and vinegar flavored potato chips. Ugh. Isn't my brain supposed to pick flavors I *like*? I mean, I get that I associate a snack food with someone prone to the munchies, but yuck. A wave of revulsion makes me do something I've never tried before: consciously thinking about a different food. In two sips, I manage to change it to brownies.

Ooh. I'll take it.

Can't even taste the weed.

"Holy shit," rasps someone behind me. "You really are a…"

I whirl around, spinning Pothead with me.

Cody Peters… only he doesn't look ready to ram a stake into my heart. He's somewhere between worried and scared.

"Mmm," I mumble into Pothead's neck.

"Don't talk with your mouth full." Cody blinks. "Ben's missing." He pulls a two-inch diameter branch out of his jacket with a crudely sharpened point. "Did you hurt him?"

I hold up a finger in a 'give me a sec' gesture. Once I've taken my fill, I seal the bite wound and stare into Pothead's eyes, deleting myself from his memory and commanding him to sit back down and continue as he was doing before.

"Okay," I say, turn back to Cody—and walk into the point of his stake, which pokes me between my breasts. "Really?"

"What happened to Ben?" He tries to sound threatening, but he's too scared, so it comes out more like a desperate question.

I raise both hands. "Swear. No idea. I haven't even seen him."

Cody takes a step back.

I step toward him.

He backs up again, waving the stake at me. "Don't kill me."

Sigh. "I don't kill people. I'm not going to hurt you, only make you forget catching me feeding."

"Crap. You really are a vampire. I *knew* it. What are you doing to that family?" Cody backs up again.

I follow. "Nothing, jackass. They're really my family. Now sit still. This won't hurt at all."

He crosses his arms in front of his face. "Wait. Please."

Hands on my hips, I tap my foot. "Waiting. What?"

Cody peeks over his forearm. "Umm. Ben went looking for vampires because of that stupid ring. You know, I never really expected we'd find something real. I thought it was just like this weird phosphorescent thing. L-look. I swear I won't tell anyone."

"I'm sorry, kid. It's not personal. I can't risk it. There's more than me, and—"

He backs up another step. "Wait! You made the ring glow, but it wasn't that bright. Nowhere near as strong as it glowed down in the cave. Help me find him? Please?"

Okay. That's unexpected. I cock my head to the side. "How did you go from 'don't kill me' to asking for my help?"

"Umm." He shrugs. "Probably when you didn't actually try to kill me."

"Right…"

"What are you doing out here?"

"Feeding."

He shakes his head. "No I mean *here* at the park."

"Vacation."

"Seriously?" His eyes widen.

"Seriously."

"What does a vampire need a vacation from?"

I scratch my head. "Other vampires trying to kill me."

"Whoa, for real?"

"For real."

Cody replaces the stake in a harness he's rigged under his coat. "So, umm. You'll help?"

"Considering if there *is* some kind of creature in the cave, it's probably also a threat to my family... and I kinda feel bad about your brother, so yeah."

"Feel bad?" The 'you're a fiend and I'm going to kill you' suspicion returns to his eyes. "Why would you feel bad about Ben? What did you do?"

"Nothing. Just his crush."

Cody relaxes. "Oh. Hey, are you really eighteen? Or like only a total of eighteen counting vampire years?"

"I'm legit eighteen. Haven't been a vampire that long. I look young for... reasons."

"Oh. That's cool. So did you like make servants out of your parents?"

"Isn't that normal for every teenager?" I ask.

He blinks.-

"Wow, does *no one* here have a sense of humor? No. They are normal. I just live at home."

"Cool." He glances around, trying his damndest not to shiver.

I pat him on the shoulder. "Look, I'm not going to hurt you. I promise. It makes sense why you think what you do, but there's, umm, multiple kinds of vampires. We don't have to kill to feed. That one you maybe saw as a little kid was just an asshole."

"You ever kill anyone?"

"One guy, but it doesn't count for two reasons. One: he was already dead and two: he murdered me."

"Huh? Oh, I get it. You offed the one who made you."

"No. It's a long story. Maybe I'll tell you sometime if you wind up remembering vampires."

He looks around. "Umm. Why wouldn't I rem—oh. Never mind. So, Ben..."

"Haven't seen him at all tonight. Oh, by the way. Your mother is probably a genuine psychic."

"Yeah. And she thinks there's something bad in that cave. She got really freaked out when we went all the way to the bottom. Ben was kinda upset over, umm, you. So he went there alone."

"Really?"

Cody snugs his coat down over his shoulders. "He suspected you were really a vampire, but like *just* made so you hadn't turned all the way yet, which is why you could still be out in the daylight. Ben figured the one in the cave made you, so he went down there to kill him and, well, save you."

"Aww. That's sweet and tragic."

"Why tragic?" Cody's face pales.

"Because I'm too old for him and seeing someone already. As nice as he is, he's still only fourteen."

"Right."

I point toward the trail. "He's probably lost in the cave if he even made it inside."

"Why wouldn't he make it inside?"

"Oh, I dunno. Coyotes, rattlesnakes, mountain lions, that other vampire, a park employee, a sudden flash of rational thought making him realize he's being stupid. Take your pick."

Cody starts off toward the cave trail, edging sideways. "Come on, let's go."

Pothead's lighter emits a *chip, chip, chip* sound before a single flame lights his face orange for a few seconds. Might as well get out of here before my clothes stink.

"Yeah." I hurry after Cody. "You don't have to be afraid of turning your back on me."

"Umm."

I zip around in front of him too fast for him to react, and he walks straight into me, then jumps back with a startled shout.

"Really. If I wanted to hurt you, it wouldn't matter if you were looking at me or not."

He swallows hard. "Is that supposed to make me relax?"

"No. I'm only being honest. Let's go find your brother."

Cody stares at me for a few seconds. "Okay." He lets out a long breath and offers a hand. "Truce?"

I take his hand. "We technically can't have a truce since we weren't fighting. But I know what you mean."

After we shake hands, I grab his wrist and hurry toward the caves.

"Hey, what are you doing?"

"There's no lights up there. Follow my lead."

"I got a flashlight."

"Yeah, and if you use it out here, someone will see us going into the cave when it's supposed to be closed."

"Oh. Yeah. Crap. What if we get caught?"

I smile. "Don't worry."

"Maybe we should get a park ranger or something instead of going in ourselves?"

"I thought of that, too. But, they'd take forever to send in a search party, aren't capable of doing anything I can't do, and if whatever's down there is involved… they won't help at all."

"Crap."

We head out of the RV park, cross the loop road, and start up the hill to the trail that leads to the cave. Ugh. So much for vacation.

I just *knew* this was going to get weird.

14

THE RIGHT MOMENT

n eerie lack of darkness at ground level under a black sky makes the trek up the trail to the cave entrance feel as though I'm exploring an alien planet. The other day, this uphill walk winded Cody at a leisurely pace. Tonight, he struggles to keep up with me since I'm not trying to pretend I'm tired.

Not that I'm trying to lose him or anything, but my thoughts race with ideas of what might've happened to Ben. Everything from being merely lost in one of the chambers to having fallen to his death to encountering whatever is living at the bottom—or not living as the case might be.

A park ranger up ahead turns a flashlight toward us, no doubt at the scuff of Cody's sneakers coming up the trail. Seconds before the beam hits me, I leap straight up without a sound, flying in an arc to land a step behind him. The ranger stabs Cody in the eyes with the flashlight, making him cry out and cover his face.

"What are you doing up here at night, son?" asks the ranger, his tone a mix of worry and suspicion.

"Umm." Cody looks around, having no idea where I went.

I step up to within a few inches of the ranger. "Excuse me?"

The guy jumps and drops the flashlight. It takes him a few seconds to remember how to breathe. He turns and squints generally in my direction. What the clouds do for the sun, they also do for the moon. It's nearly as dark outside as it is in the cave.

"What are you kids doing out here at night? The cave's closed… and it's off limits except for guided tours."

"Kids?" I ask, staring into his eyes. "What kids? There's no one up here but you."

Cody, rasping for breath, stumbles over to the dropped flashlight and picks it up.

"You should just stand here and think nothing's out of the ordinary," I say.

"Whoa," whispers Cody. "Are you mind controlling him?"

I hold up a pinching gesture. "Just a little."

The ranger resumes his patrol, ignoring us entirely.

"That's pretty cool." Cody twists to watch the man go by. "Also pretty evil."

"It's not evil," I say, before grabbing his hand and pulling him over to the cave entrance.

Cody ducks under the giant rock, then points the flashlight around at the first chamber. Apparently, the park service discourages people from going into the caves after hours by turning the lights off. "Messing with people's heads is evil."

"It depends on what I do with it. Making someone forget they saw me or forget vampires exist isn't bad. It lets people keep their sanity. Forcing people to do things or using my abilities to steal is bad. And I don't do that."

"Uh huh. Sure you don't."

I creep forward, looking around. "I'm serious."

"Okay. I believe you," says Cody in a tone that says he really doesn't.

It's tempting to give him some line about how vampires change based on their nature, and as an Innocent I'm all cute and such… but that logic doesn't work. Take Glim. Visually, he's pretty damn harsh, but he's an awesome guy. So our outward appearance isn't at all reflective of who we are. Maybe I could get away with a half truth?

"You know how I look like I'm sixteen?"

"Fifteen, but yeah."

I sigh. "Really? Whatever. Anyway, it's because of my bloodline. I'm about as sweet and harmless as vampires can get."

"It's a trick, right? Like that kid in the movie. Act all innocent so people get close and you can drink their blood."

Okay, I can't help but chuckle. "While I doubt deceptive hunting is the reason for my looks, I *have* used that trick. But I don't kill anyone. Mortals kill each other all the time. Does that mean every mortal is a homicidal maniac?"

"No. But it's different."

I pause at the top of the stairs and look back at him. "So you expect *all* vampires to be killers because you might have witnessed one kill a woman, but not all mortals to be killers despite there being murders all over the place?"

"Yeah basically."

"Umm. Why?"

He shrugs. "Everything you read about vampires describes them as bloodthirsty monsters."

"You're being a species-ist."

"That's not even a word." He points the flashlight down the stairs. "Come on. Ben's in trouble."

With a sigh, I march into the cave, taking the lead. "You do realize that you're basing your opinions on movies and stuff people just made up. I bet one out of every thousand people responsible for any bit of vampire fiction has seen one for real and remembers it. Do you believe everything you see on the Internet?"

"Of course not."

"My mom works with a guy who used to be in the military. He was in the Middle East somewhere. The guy's super racist against anyone from that part of the world because he'd spent years being shot at. It's still wrong. Not *everyone* over there wants to kill him."

"My grandpa hates Germans still, 'cause of what happened to his father during the war."

I stop again and whirl to look at him. "A bad experience is hard to get over, but it doesn't make hating an entire group correct."

"Are you a vegan?"

"What?" I stare at him. "What does that have to do with you hating vampires?"

"You sound like my Aunt Wilma."

"Whatever."

We continue down the stairs. A minute or so later, he mutters, "Sorry."

"Forget it. You're upset over your brother. It's okay."

He's quiet until we reach the spot where the stairwell overlooks the 'pit.' "Ben?" His voice echoes over itself a few times and fades to silence. "Crap. What if he fell?"

"Wait here."

I leap the railing and fly down the vertical shaft.

"Hey!" shouts Cody.

"Relax," I call back.

If not for trying to find a missing boy, I'd snap some pictures on the way down. Dad would love this. I swoop to the bottom, which thankfully has no sign of any Ben-shaped splat marks, so I return to the stairs above. Cody's pale as a ghost and white-knuckling the railing. I float up to eye level with him, hanging in space over the hole.

"I said relax. You don't look relaxed."

"You jumped."

"Technically, I'm flying, not jumping."

Cody peers down at my sneakers. "You can fly?"

"Either that or you've done entirely too much pot." I tap a finger to my chin. "Is this where I'm supposed to launch into a five-minute song about how awesome it is to fly while you stare at me like I'm nuts?"

"What?"

I hop the fence and land next to him. "Never mind. Just making a Disney joke. And he's not down there."

He slouches with relief. "Where do you think he went?"

"I have no idea. I'm a vampire not a psychic. You should ask your mother."

Cody frowns. "She'll kill us both if Ben really did go into the cave on his own."

"Better being 'killed' by your mother than what's down here."

He grabs my shoulder. "Didn't you just try to tell me that most vampires won't kill people?"

"I did. But one, I don't know for sure that what's down here *is* a vampire at all. And while most of us are just like normal people with a few extra bells and whistles, there are still killers."

"Are you trying to scare the crap out of me or make me feel better?"

I jog down the stairs. "I'll let you know as soon as I figure that out."

At the bottom, I take a few deep breaths in my nose. Crap. I can smell Ben... and about a hundred other people, but his scent is strongest. "He was here."

After a moment of a flashlight beam dancing across the floor at my feet, Cody reaches the end of the stairs. "Are you psychic or not?"

"Well, not like your mother. I don't see visions or anything. Guess tweaking people's memory counts as psychic. But anyway, I can smell him."

"We don't have BO."

I glance sideways at him. "Keep telling yourself that."

He cringes.

"Seriously though, I don't exactly have a normal nose anymore."

"Oh, right."

We walk for a few minutes in silence.

"Do I really stink?" asks Cody.

"Probably not."

He jogs up to walk beside me, nearly tripping on uneven ground. "Probably?"

"I can pick up scents like a dog. It's kinda hard for me to tell anymore what's strong enough for normal people to smell."

"Oh."

There's no sign of Ben in the Cathedral Room, so I keep going downward. That sigil on the wall needles at me. While no one but me saw it, their mother had a strong reaction to the Garden of the Gods room... so I bet that's where Ben went. Careful not to go *too* fast that Cody hurts himself trying to keep up, I head straight there. This time, I go down the rock slide at full speed... and yeah, it probably would've scared Sophia.

Despite not needing air, having a few hundred feet of earth over my head is kinda scary. I've never considered myself claustrophobic, but I'm developing a strong urge to hurry back to open sky. Being caught in a cave-in is *more* frightening when the cave-in itself won't kill me. An instant crushing death sucks but it beats being trapped under tons of rock for-possible-ever, starving while going feral.

Cody skids out from the bottom of the slide and stands, shining the flashlight around at various dark places and holes. "I hope he didn't fall down there."

"I have a feeling I know where he went. If he's not where I'm thinking, I'll check down there." Pretty sure the tour guide called this hole the 'Green Well.'

We hurry past the Brown Waterfall—that totally sounds like a tragedy involving a septic tank—to the chamber full of pink. Sure enough, his scent is in the air. Of course it's so muddled with thousands of other people being in here I can't follow it. I decide to trust my hunch, ignore my better judgement, and approach the spot on the left side where a small glowing sigil marks the rock.

"Hey, let me outta here," cries Ben, so faint that human ears wouldn't notice. The far-off echo makes me picture another tunnel behind this wall. Metallic banging follows.

"He's alive, and... trapped," I whisper.

Cody grabs my arm. "What? How do you know? Trapped?"

"What else would 'hey, let me outta here' mean?"

"Dammit. The vampire got him."

I brush my hands around the stone, looking for a way to go in.

"Hey," says Cody from a few feet to my right. He crouches and picks up another crude stake. "This is Ben's. He was here."

"Well, obviously." I point at the wall. "I can hear him."

"How do we get in?"

"Working on it."

My frustration level rises until I find myself slapping and kicking at the rock. The stone isn't impressed. Having no other ideas, I try pushing the sigil like a button. That, too, doesn't work, but I do notice a faint tingle upon contact.

"Hmm. That's something."

"What?" asks Cody.

"There's a mark on the wall here that's glowing."

He leans closer, squinting. "I don't see anything."

"It's like paranormal or something. Maybe like ghosts. I can see it. It's two circles inside each other a little bigger than a quarter, with a swoosh around them that curves into a vertical line going down. Right... here." I jab my finger at the center of the circle part—and it sinks into the rock like peanut butter.

"Whoa." Cody blinks.

"Eww." I cringe at the sensation.

Before I can pull my finger out, a section of wall opens like candle wax melting on sped-up video, revealing another cave tunnel. Ben's repetitive shouting of 'let me out' becomes loud enough for Cody to hear.

"Ben!"

I grab him before he can run in. "Shh. Be careful. Let me go first."

He leans back. "Wait. How do I know you're not trying to trick me? Maybe you're with him. You went right to this spot. A little too fast."

"Cody..." I sigh. "I wouldn't need to trick you. If I wanted you to do something, I'd *make* you do something like I made that ranger forget he saw us. Second, if I was really luring you in here, wouldn't I want to be behind you so you can't run?"

"Oh. Duh. Right. Sorry."

"Hey!" shouts Ben. "Cody?"

Grr. He's going to give us away.

I dash down a thirty-ish foot tunnel with glass-smooth walls. At the end, it meets the narrow end of an oval chamber. Muted colors tell me there's a weak source of light somewhere. I gasp and hold my breath at the overwhelming stench of rotting meat. Cody skids to a stop behind me and gags, shielding his mouth and nose in the crook of his elbow.

"What the"—he coughs—"heck is that?"

"Dead stuff," I mutter.

Several rugs, three old sofas, a table, and a bunch of chairs stand at the center of the chamber next to a natural rock column that resembles the other 'drippy' formations in the rest of the cavern. Most of the ceiling and walls have a blue-green shade that reminds me of a hospital operating room—or an abandoned mental asylum. While I don't see any ghosts, I do have the distinct sense of being watched. A pair of glass jars hang from mounts, both containing a tennis-ball-sized sphere of glowing pale yellow... something.

"Hey," says Ben, from up ahead on the right.

He's in a big cage roughly the size of an Old West jail cell made from iron slats. The prison is elevated from the floor on a natural dais of dark teal rock, and stands against the wall midway across the long part of the oval. Okay. That's strange. I jog over and climb a series of three stone ridges like a natural stairway, and stop by the cell door.

"Sarah?" asks Ben. "What are you doing down here?"

"Your brother said you disappeared... something about trying to rescue me."

Ben goes scarlet in the face. "Umm."

I examine the door. The cage slats are about two inches wide and a quarter inch thick, arranged in a grid with a rivet securing every point they cross. A lock plate—again like something out of the Old West—secures a full-sized door on the front face. I grab it and pull, trying to rip the thing open, but it doesn't give.

"Umm." Ben chuckles. "What are you doing? Trust me, you're not gonna break it. I've been trying for a while."

"Shh," I rasp, then adjust my grip and pull again. My feet slide over the ground toward the cage, but it doesn't break. "Damn, this thing is tough."

Ben reaches out and puts his hand on mine. "Go for help. Get out of here before the fiends catch you." Fear's obvious in his eyes and shaky voice. "They could come back any minute."

I stop. "Huh? What do you mean *they*? Fiends... plural?"

The rapid scuffing of feet on rock emanates from the interior passage.

"Too late," whispers Cody, pressing his back against the cell.

I spin left, caught off guard by the sight of a group of five dudes and two women rushing toward us across the chamber, loping in not-quite-human strides. All have glowing red eyes and fangs with barely-sentient expressions. Ugh. Scraps. A huge figure steps into view at the mouth of the passage opposite the one we entered from. I'm sure it's the same guy I saw in the woods yesterday.

The scraps charge at us, but I don't get the sense they're planning on tearing us to pieces... yet.

"What now?" asks Cody, his voice way too high for a fifteen-year-old.

"Nothing. Don't fight."

I keep my head down, hoping that avoiding eye contact with the big guy will fake him out into thinking I'm mortal. The last thing I need now is some territorial BS and another Petra 'ripping the shit out of each other' situation. When the Scraps swarm us, I pretend to flail at them like an ordinary girl too weak to fight them off. One guy unlocks the cell door, and the mob tosses the two of us in the cell, then slams it. Ben grabs Cody and tries damn hard not to break down in tears with me watching.

"Umm," mutters Cody. "We're in deep shit."

"Shh," I whisper. "Wait."

Fortunately, the scraps are too dim-witted to recognize me as a vampire. A few mutter about 'stocking the fridge' as they disperse. Two head out the entry tunnel while the rest go down the passage that leads deeper into the cavern.

Their clothes don't look out of style, though they all have a shabby, homeless air about them, like they'd been living in the same outfit for months. No surprise there, since I doubt they have enough brain left to process the concept of dirty laundry. Whatever they had on when that big guy killed them is theirs for the rest of their short unlife. I don't like that this guy hasn't destroyed them. Both Dalton and Aurélie agreed on that one point: Scraps should be put down. That tells me this guy's pretty dark and probably likes having minions.

I grab the bars and keep my head bowed, pretending to be a terrified mortal. Through a curtain of my hair, I peer at the tunnel where a few of the scraps surround the big guy. Like some sort of bad cartoon henchmen, they brag about 'finding more food' as if their master hadn't watched the whole thing.

While he's distracted by his sycophants, I stare at him long enough to get a sense that he is, in fact, a vampire... and I don't recognize the 'feel' of his bloodline. I've met a couple Furies already, one of whom was a rather normal-looking woman. Dante wasn't terribly huge either in a muscular sense. Not like this guy. He's beyond ridiculous. His biceps are bigger than my thighs, and he's probably close to seven feet tall. All he needs is fur pants and a battleax and he'd make a perfect cover for a fantasy barbarian novel.

Yeah... I'm gonna let that guy continue believing I'm mortal. I don't want him thinking I'm a threat, nor do I want to wind up his concubine or something. Dude might see a female vampire who's *not* a Scrap and decide I'm his. Maybe expecting the worst of him like that is a tad unfair, but he looks so much like Gonad the Conqueror it's hard not to think along those lines. And he *did* have his minions put me in a cell.

Grr. Also, that's *twice*. The last time I ran into other vampires, I wound up in a cage, too.

What the hell is it with vampires and dungeons? At least this time I'm not stuck waiting hours for the sun to go down.

"Dude, you were right," whispers Cody. She *is* a—"

I clamp a hand over his mouth and pull his head around to make eye contact. *If that big bastard realizes I'm a vampire, he's going to tear me to pieces.*

Cody blinks in shock at my telepathic message, then thinks, *Aren't you like super strong and stuff?*

Compared to normal people? Yes. I twist his head so he looks at the enormous dude in the tunnel for a few seconds. *Compared to that monster? No.*

Ben glances at us. "What are you two doing?"

I take my hand away from Cody's mouth. "Just getting on the same page."

"What do we do now?" whispers Cody.

"We're gonna die," mutters Ben. "Sorry. This is my fault for being stupid."

"Chill out." I whisper. "We just need to wait."

"Waiting is exactly what we can't do." Ben flails. "We have to get out before they come back to tear us apart." He pauses. "Hey, how did you get in here?"

"We walked."

Ben points. "No, I mean the secret tunnel."

"How did *you* make it in here?" asks Cody.

"I didn't. I was out in the pink room and they jumped me."

"Secret button on the wall," I whisper. "Shh. Just wait."

The boys stare at me in disbelief, Ben clearly the more upset of the pair. I look around at the cell, the top about ten feet off the ground. No benches or anything else inside, not even a chamber pot. I'm not at all interested in learning what the stains on the floor are. Based on the bars overhead, I'm pretty sure this is a free-standing box, but the floor is smooth rock. Either this cage has been here so long that more sediment poured in to cover the bottom, or it somehow sank into the rock the way my finger did at the switch.

I've caught the occasional rumor that the Academics can do weird things that basically amount to magic, and temporarily liquefying stone pretty much counts as magic. Part of my brain wants to laugh and reject the idea outright, but I once felt the same way about vampires.

"He's leaving," whispers Ben.

I wait for the big dude and his Scraps to completely disappear down the interior tunnel.

"Okay," I whisper. "Now, we leave."

AN UNFORTUNATE ESCAPE

*B*oth brothers blink at me.

"Leave? Just like that?" asks Ben. "I've been trying to get out of here for over an hour."

I jump up and hang off the ceiling bars. After a few seconds' concentration on wanting to be stronger, I mule-kick the door with both feet and it flies open with a tremendous *clang* against the cage.

"Guess you're not doing subtle," mutters Cody.

"Much easier to break from inside," I whisper after dropping back to stand.

"Holy shit," mutters Ben, pulling a stake out of his coat. "She *is* a vampire!"

He goes to lunge at me, but I swipe the stick out of his hand so fast I'm basically taking it away from a statue.

"I swear, if you do that again…"

"Incoming!" says Cody.

The Scraps spill out from the inner corridor, heading for us. One guy with butt-long dreads dashes way ahead of the group. He springs at me, but I sidestep and hammer the crude stake into his chest. Thick, cold blood that stinks of rot sprays over my hand. He keeps flailing, but I swing him around and hold him up by one hand on his back, one hand on the stake like I'm showing off a science project to the boys. The scrap keeps trying to bite my face, but can't overpower me.

"And besides, stakes don't work."

Three more Scraps sprint up the dais toward the cage. I hurl the staked guy at them, knocking all four to the ground in a moaning heap.

"Run! Now!" I whisper-shout.

The other two Scraps, a skinny chick and a dude with lime green hair, charge out of the entry tunnel, heading at me.

Ugh.

I catch the woman with a right hook that leaves her seeing stars for a second. The guy tries to claw me, but I'm way faster. He swings so hard at empty air, the momentum pulls him over sideways and he lands on his face. Cody and Ben scramble to catch up, running from the group of four. Dreadlock hasn't even bothered pulling the stake out.

Lime-hair ignores me and pounces on Ben, growling, fangs out.

"Grr!" I spring at him with a flying tackle, sinking my claws into his shoulders.

Pain makes him release Ben, who bounces away in a logroll across the floor. I wind up kneeling on top of Lime-hair, and plunge my claw-tipped fingers into his throat once we stop sliding. Cody stands rigid, staring in shock.

With a grunt of exertion, I rip his head off and throw it across the chamber. It bounces with a hollow coconut-like *thok* and rolls out of sight. The skinny woman grabs me from behind and drags me off the headless body, which sits up and grabs at the air. At the sight of blood burbling up from the neck stump, Ben lets off a scream worthy of Sophia having a nightmare.

Damn, Scrap blood stinks... like carrion or liquid death or pure distilled evil. It's even worse than Dad's socks.

I spin and drive my left knee into the chick's side with enough force to catapult her across the chamber. She crashes into the wall like twenty feet away and flops to the ground.

The headless guy totters off in search of his head.

Despite us being closer to the way out, Ben shrieks and dashes away in a panic—heading *deeper* into the place. The other female scrap, a fortyish woman with a prematurely grey ponytail, grabs Cody from behind in a bear hug and lifts him off the ground.

For two seconds, I stare helplessly back and forth between the brothers, not sure which way to go. Since Cody's right here, I launch myself at the scrap and grab her by the ponytail. She abandons her grip on the boy, flailing as I wheel her around and around. Seconds after her feet go airborne, she careens off, leaving me holding a ponytail, most of her hair, and a patch of scalp.

Oh. Eww. I squeal like a little girl stepping barefoot in dog poo and fling it aside.

Damn. That's nasty.

Two male Scraps rush at me from opposite sides. I drop to the ground, letting them collide face first. After rolling back to my feet, I shred at them with my claws, throwing fetid blood everywhere. They shriek and howl in agony, shying away. Evidently, it *finally* clicked with their tapioca brains that I'm a vampire.

I grab Cody's wrist and drag him up to a sprint for the tunnel Ben disappeared into. It weaves around in a triple S-curve before straightening (somewhat) into a passage with multiple offshoots. Gagging in Ben's voice leads me to the second opening on the left side. I round the corner at a full run and nearly crash into him.

He's stopped short at the entrance of a smallish room containing the decaying remains of thirty or so corpses. Cody clamps a hand over his mouth and starts heaving. I grab his other hand, as well as Ben's, and run back out. Cody hurls on the run, barely managing to stay on his feet.

At snarling and growling from the right, I veer left, following the cave around in a gradual rightward arc. At every opening, I pause to look, hoping that this guy is smart enough to have chosen a lair with a back way out. Even a vampire has to dislike being trapped in a space with one way in, right?

"Where are you going?" rasps Cody.

"Umm... away from the big guy."

"This isn't the way out," says Ben.

"No kidding." I smirk. "If you two were in a boy band, it would be called *Wrong* Direction."

Cody chuckles despite looking terrified.

"We can't go that way." Ben points at the actual exit.

"I'm hoping he's got another way out. Even if it's straight up."

The constant scuffle and snarl of Scraps chasing us provides the brothers enough motivation that I don't need to keep dragging them along. A few turns later, an opening on the left catches my eye for being much larger than any of the other passages. I head in, finding a sharp corner to the left only a few feet later. The tunnel curves back to the right and becomes a near-vertical slope for about nine feet.

Easy enough to jump and climb, even without flying.

I pull myself up over the ledge, get to my feet, and… stop short at the *last* thing I expected to find in a cavern.

An ornate bedchamber.

A carved lion face dominates the headboard of a massive bed in the far right corner of a squarish room. Thick rugs of red and purple cover the floor. Bookshelves stand wherever they fit between the stalagmites jutting up from the floor. Papers litter the surface of a large writing desk straight ahead against the rear wall, along with multiple ink jars and actual quills.

The far left corner extends into a sub-chamber with a downward-sloping floor and a rounded end with a wooden door in the middle. Two shelves on either side of that door hold an assortment of boxes, a couple backpacks, and some bundles of fabric.

"Whoa," whispers Ben at my right.

Cody climbs up and stands to my left. "Holy crap. Hey, the uglies aren't following us in here."

"Good," says Ben.

"Not good," I mutter. "The only reason they wouldn't come in here is if they're either afraid or were commanded not to. This is big boy's room."

Ben leans around me, literally talking behind my back. "Is she gonna kill us."

"No, dumbass," says Cody.

I turn a one-eighty. "We shouldn't be in here."

"Uhh." Cody gestures at the tunnel. "Those other vampires are in the way. We're kinda trapped."

"Damn." I spin in place, considering for a few seconds, then dash across the room and down the hill into the second chamber. "This might be the back door I was hoping for… though I didn't expect a literal door."

"Maybe it's an old mine shaft?" asks Cody, hurrying along behind me.

Ben follows walking backward, staring at the way we came in.

I stop by the door, which looks more like it belongs inside some country manor house than deep in a cavern. "Oh, this is too weird. How old do vampires have to be before they go insane?"

"Eccentric," says Cody. "Rich people don't go insane, they become eccentric."

"What makes you think he's rich? He lives in a cave."

"Did you see that bedroom?"

"Okay, good point. Still, why would he be out here?"

Ben gulps. "Probably because he likes killing people too much to stay in civilization. Picking off tourists is like easier or something."

"But no one said anything about disappearances. It's not on the news," I whisper.

"Media control." Cody shakes his head. "It might not even be the vampire doing anything. If word got out they had a serial killer living in the caves, tourists would stop coming. It would cost the state too much money so they don't let anyone talk about it."

I give him the side eye. "Conspiracy much?"

"Did you hear about anything in the news?" asks Cody.

"No."

"Did you or did you not see a cave full of bodies back there?"

"Okay. Okay." I raise my hands in surrender. "Keep your fingers crossed this is a way out."

"It's probably a closet," says Ben.

Cody shakes his head. "No way. Door's too fancy."

I grab the knob. Admittedly, I haven't had good luck with closets. "Hopefully, I don't wind up in Kansas as a five-year-old again."

"Huh?" asks both boys simultaneously.

"Forget it. Long story." I pull the door open… and my jaw drops at the sight of a vast forest. It's as if I'd opened the front door of a cabin deep in the woods. Only, this forest is way more lush than what we hiked in around here.

"Dude. We found frickin' Narnia," says Cody.

"That's a big closet," whispers Ben.

I close the door. "Okay. That's too weird. Guess you guys get to see my boobs tonight."

They gawk at me.

Ben's the first to recover enough composure to ask, "What?"

"Only way out of here is to fight through the Scraps. Every time I get into a fight with other vampires, my clothes end up in shreds."

"Scraps?" asks Cody.

"Those other vampires? They're not full vamps. Closer to mindless creatures driven by pure animal instincts."

"Oh… Cowboys fans," mutters Cody.

"Huh?" I glance at him.

"Not into football?"

"No. Not really."

A low, rumbling growl comes from the outer chamber. Heavy, stomping footsteps approach.

"Uh oh. Dad's home," whispers Ben.

"Screw it. Run!" I rip the door open and jump in, taking a few quick steps before turning to look back.

A swirling… portal hangs in midair, a thousand varying shades of blue forming an oval ring around a hole in reality that looks in at the cave behind it.

The boys rush in not a second before the shadow of a huge man appears at the top of the hill, running toward us. Orange glowing eyes stare straight into my soul. In that brief glimmer of mental contact, it occurs to me why the dude is so huge. He's a Beast.

Ben snags the knob and pulls the door with him as he runs in, slamming it. The boys scramble over to stand on either side of me again and spin back to gawk at the portal.

"Should we keep running?" asks Cody. "He might come after us."

Light glimmers across the portal—and it disappears, leaving us staring at thick, verdant forest.

"Or not," says Ben.

"Shit." Cody stares at the sky. "Did we really think going through a door to the woods at the bottom of a cave would be a good idea?"

"Sorry," I mutter. "Maybe going through the door wasn't such an awesome idea. Kinda panicked."

NEXT MOVES

Forest surrounds us in every direction.

The trees appear more or less like normal oaks, but they're enormous, two or three times the size of trees I'm used to seeing. Dense carpets of green moss cover most of the trunks, along with long runners of draping ivy hanging between branches. Unseen birds whistle somewhere overhead, along with a constant undertone of insects clicking and chirping.

"Damn, that guy was huge," says Cody.

"He's a Beast." I bite my lip while looking around for any sign of a landmark.

"No kidding." Ben shakes his head. "Dude seriously needs to lay off the 'roids."

I laugh. "No. I mean a literal Beast. It's a bloodline."

"Is that good or bad?" asks Cody.

"Bad," says Ben. "He's a vampire."

"So's she." Cody pats me on the shoulder. "And she's kinda cool."

Ben gives me this heartbroken stare. "You're not really eighteen, are you? You died when you were like fourteen and you've been a vampire for four years."

"Do I really need to go through this again?" I ask, still kinda giggling. "I've been a vamp for like not even two months. I turned eighteen a couple weeks before."

"Oh, that sucks," says Cody. "How'd it happen?"

I give them a brief explanation of my ex-boyfriend Scott stabbing me to death when I dumped him for cheating, and Dalton saving my ass. "And I look younger than I am because of my bloodline. That's also why I can kinda go outside during the day if it's gloomy. Bright sunlight will still cook me. But, as vampires go, I'm kinda weak."

"Whoa. Sorry you got killed. What an asshole," says Cody.

"Thanks."

"And Beasts aren't?" asks Ben. "Weak I mean?"

"I've never seen one up close before that I've realized. No one's really explained too much about them other than that they're the closest to surrendering their minds to becoming monsters."

"Dude. His arms were bigger than her waist," says Cody. "Pretty sure he's not weak."

"So pretty much bad news." Ben cringes.

"Like a Kodiak bear with opposable thumbs." I sigh at the trees. "At least we got away from him."

"Yeah, but where the hell are we?" asks Cody. He pulls the stake out from his harness, and tosses it.

"Dude?" asks Ben.

"You weren't paying attention, were you?" Cody points at me. "She rammed your stick right through the one dude and he didn't even slow down."

"Oh, shit." Ben blinks at me. "Your little bro was telling the truth. Stakes are a lie made up to fool people. Like, does your family know you're a vampire?"

"Yeah. Hang on a sec."

I float straight up until I'm over the treetops. As far as I can see in every direction, forest continues all the way to the horizon. Miles away on the right, water cascades down the face of a rock ridge that has to be over a hundred stories tall. It's dark, so I can't tell which way is which. If the ridge is north, to the southeast, I spot a crumbling ruin that looks so much like a medieval castle I decide not to believe my eyes. Of course, there *are* ruined castles in Europe that don't look much different, so maybe things aren't as weird as my brain is trying to make them out to be.

My iPhone isn't any help. I pull it out to use the compass app, and it's stone dead. Black screen. Won't turn on at all. Grr. Guess I'm not calling for help either.

I land between the brothers, pretty sure Ben's mouth has been hanging open the whole time I hovered. With one finger under his chin, I lift his jaw shut.

"You… saved us. But you're a vampire." He blinks.

"Not all are monsters. Some really are, but I'm way on the other side."

"So, what do you want with us now?" asks Ben.

"Umm. Just trying to help Cody find you alive. What I want is to be as normal as possible."

Cody puts an arm around me. "Relax, man. She's cool. He's only upset because he had a thing for you."

"I know."

Ben turns white.

"It didn't take powers of mind reading." I poke him in the stomach. "You were way obvious. And no, I don't think you're being immature for believing in vampires."

"But you said they don't exist." Ben fidgets.

"I was trying to keep it a secret. It's not easy to attempt being normal when I have idiots with stake-chucking crossbows showing up every month."

"That really happened?" asks Cody.

"Yeah. Hurt like hell." I rub my chest.

Cody whistles. "Did you kill them?"

"No. Just a light ass kicking and sent them on their way after making them forget vampires exist. And you two should really stop worrying about hunting us. I'm basically still a baby, and the weakest bloodline… and even I can pound the snot out of four guys at once. You'd have more luck beating up an Army tank with a baseball bat than taking on an older vampire."

They exchange a glance.

"Okay," says Cody. "Back to the 'where are we' issue. How do we get home?"

"Shouldn't we wait for the portal to open?" asks Ben.

"Oh, sure, and have that monster be there waiting for us?" Cody flails, gesturing at the portal.

Ben takes a couple steps, turning as he walks. He pulls his hair off his face, listens to the wind for a moment, then points. "I think we should go that way."

"Based on?" I ask.

"Sometimes he gets feelings like Mom." Cody looks at me. "Did you see anything when you went into the air?"

"Nothing promising. A big waterfall and an old castle."

"C'mon." Ben walks in the direction he seems to like. "There could be another portal somewhere."

I shrug, but follow. "I love how you're talking about portals and stuff like it's real and normal."

"Either portals are real, or there's a giant forest beneath the caverns." Cody punts a brown lump that resembles a walnut the size of a baseball.

"Fair point."

"Crap, my phone's dead," says Ben.

"Mine too." I groan.

"Watch is toast," says Cody. "And the flashlight."

"Great, so anything electronic died." I squeeze my hands into fists. "Question is, did the portal do that or is it this place?"

"Does it matter?" asks Ben. "It's not like we're planning on moving here."

"But where is 'here?'" Cody picks a bit of moss from a tree on the way past it. "Are we still even on Earth?"

"Where else would we be?" I ask.

"Some other dimension," says Ben. "Maybe another time period. Maybe another planet."

I swallow a sense of rising panic. It's rather difficult to disregard that swirly blue thing I saw around the door. "Another planet? Don't get crazy. That's a little far-fetched."

"But alternate dimensions aren't?" asks Ben with a hint of a laugh.

"There has to be more than one vampire," I say. "There's no way a Beast knows how to make portals like this."

"Why, are they all dumb?" asks Cody. "Or are you just guessing because you think no dude that ripped could be smart?"

I roll my eyes. "No. It's not because he's huge. Everything I've heard about Beasts says they're real close to being feral creatures."

"Whatever that door was, it closed and trapped us here," says Ben. "And I don't feel like waiting around there for that monster to open it again and grab us."

"Good point." Cody nods.

We walk among the trees across flat ground that would be a welcome change from the hilly forests around the park, if not for us being trapped and lost who-knows-where. Our conversation drifts from where we wound up to what we're looking for, to how long we have before our parents collectively freak out at our absence. When it turns into the 'what's the wildest thing you've ever done' competition, the only thing I come up with is passing out drunk headfirst in Tiffany Hoffman's hamper.

"Wow, really? That's the craziest thing a vampire did?" asks Cody.

"Okay, how about literally ripping my ex-boyfriend's head off and burning him to final death in a staged car accident?"

The boys stop walking and stare at me.

"What?" I ask. "He *did* murder me first."

They blink.

"And he was already dead. A Scrap like those people back in the cavern."

"Oh." Cody nods like that makes it all okay, and resumes walking.

Ben shrugs and keeps going as well.

"What about you guys?" I ask. "What's the wildest thing you've ever done?"

"Two years ago, we suspected a guy who lived down the street from us was a vampire. We spent half the summer scoping his place out, trying to find proof," says Cody.

"His yard was way overgrown and stuff. We kept getting ticks." Ben shivers.

"So, late August, we figure the summer's almost over and we haven't found any proof." Cody gestures like he's grabbing an invisible box. "So we decide to step it up a notch."

"A couple notches," mutters Ben.

"Did you ever think you didn't catch him being a vampire because he wasn't a vampire?"

"I'm getting to that." Cody chuckles. "So, we break into his house and, figuring a vampire would lair underground, head for the basement. Only we didn't find coffins or anything."

"Lots of old paintings and stuff," says Ben. "The guy's like an art thief or something. Or he works at a museum."

"Holy crap. You really broke into a house?" I blink. "I guess you got away since you're here and not like, in jail."

"Yeah. We scared the shit out of the dude, but he didn't see us. Fell down in a giant pile of junk and crap. Dust everywhere." Cody grins. "Cops never showed up, so he didn't see us."

"Or he *is* an art thief and didn't want the cops involved," adds Ben.

"You two probably almost killed an innocent old man."

"He wasn't *that* old," says Cody. "Like fifty something. And, what exactly are we looking for?"

I gaze around at the trees again… noting everything is pretty much the same. "I dunno. Some kind of landmark or a sign of civilization so we can figure out where we are."

"What if we aren't anywhere?" asks Ben.

"We have to be *somewhere.*"

Ben sighs. "No, I mean we might not be in our world anymore."

"Could there be other portals?" asks Cody.

"Argh!" I grab two fistfuls of my hair. "There's no such thing as magic portals to alternate worlds. Dammit! I just *knew* going on a vacation was a bad idea. Ever since I woke up as a vampire, *nothing* is ever simple anymore."

Ben stops again, and whirls to face me. "You're saying the supernatural doesn't exist?"

I let my arms fall, my hair draped over my face. After a momentary stare of defeat, I huff at it, but clear only one eye. "Okay. Whatever."

"My brother has a good sense about stuff like that." Cody pats him on the shoulder. "Pretty sure he's got the gift like Mom."

"Yeah... yeah..." Ben looks around again, then resumes walking.

A few minutes later, a sudden twinge of alarm washes over me. I peer up at the sky, brightening to a clear blue directly ahead of us. "Oh, shit."

"What?" The boys ask at the same time.

"The sun's coming up." I point.

Cody glances at the sky. "Wow. That can't be right. It isn't late enough. It should only be like one in the morning."

"Maybe we're in a different time zone now," says Ben. "Or, you know, an *alternate dimension* that's on its own separate time."

I look around in a mild panic. "Shit. Shit. Shit. I'm gonna die. I gotta get out of the sun. It feels like it's gonna be too strong for me."

"We have a little time." Cody points. "Maybe fifteen minutes."

"Look!" I shout, flailing wildly at the trees. "It's the same shit in every direction. We're not going to make it anywhere before the stupid sun comes up."

"Hey... Hey..." Ben runs over and grabs me.

I sink to my knees, on the verge of sobbing. God dammit. Try to help someone out, and now I'm gonna die for real. "You should get away from me before I go nuts. The sun makes me crazy... Just tell my family what happened, okay?"

"Sarah, don't be a dumbass." Cody pulls off his jacket and throws it over my head. "We got you."

"Huh?" I peer up at him, too overcome by grief and panic to think straight.

"You said you can survive weak sunlight, right?" He grins, then pulls his jacket down over my face. "Just gotta cover up. Ben. Jacket. Come on."

I curl up on the ground as the boys cocoon me in their coats.

Something small and uncomfortable—probably a flask of holy water —presses into my cheek. Dread of imminent doom wells up deep inside my soul. It takes every ounce of willpower I have to sit still and not surrender to blind panic. Exploding into a hissing, growling, clawing wildcat wouldn't do anyone any good right now.

Cody's right. I'll be okay. I'll see my family again.

Did Dalton feel this scared when he wound up hiding in those sewer pipe sections? I do my best to shield my face and keep my skin covered. Snaps and splintering crunches come from nearby. The boys chatter back and forth but I'm too wound up in panic to comprehend what they say. It doesn't get any easier on me when the oven starts. I feel like the meat inside a dumpling after it's been dropped into a deep fryer. The jacket cocoon is at least preventing me from vaporizing, but holy shit is it hot.

"Gah!" I yell. "It's burning."

Arms scoop under me and drag me a short distance before setting me down on a hard branch. When it tilts back, I realize they must've made some kind of stretcher or drag sled. Amid the searing agony of bright daylight, I huddle in as tight a ball as I can manage. We're moving, I can tell that much by the constant jostling around.

I'm aware only of twigs breaking beneath me, the vague murmuring conversation of the brothers somewhere above and behind me, and the vibration of being dragged across the forest floor.

Oh yeah, and pain. Lots of that. There's smoke too. I really don't like how I smell cooking.

Bit by bit, my panic ebbs. 'Oh shit I'm gonna die' gives way to 'ow, ow, ow, ow.'

Heaviness spreads over my body, the grip of vampiric sleep fighting my reaction to sunlight. There's nothing I can do at this point but trust a pair of wannabe vampire hunters. If I'm going to *foom*, I don't want to be awake for it.

I try to think about feeling safe between my partial tolerance for sunlight, the jackets covering me, and my hope that these two won't actually try to destroy me. Of course they won't, right? If they wanted to, they wouldn't have wrapped me up in their jackets. They'd have run when I told them to and left me to burn to death.

Yeah. They're going to help me.

My eyes grow heavy...

...and I lose consciousness.

LOST EXPEDITION

*W*ith a gasp, I lurch upright and find myself sitting on a patch of damp mulch inside a small one-room hut. Flaps of ancient burlap hang over two small windows, the glow of sunlight under them obvious. Despite the covering, the room's got enough color that I imagine the boys can see fairly well.

Walls of dark brown wood mottled with white spots reek of wetness and mildew. The seat of my jeans has soaked damp; however, cold, wet butt beats burning so I'll deal. Pretty sure the lingering aroma of medium rare steak is coming from me. The smashed ruin of a table, two chairs, and a shelf lean against the wall to my right, the only furniture in here. Ben sits in a ball at the opposite corner from where I am, staring at me. His expression is a weird mixture of freaked out and sad. Cody's flopped on the floor by the wrecked table, half asleep.

"Whoa," I mutter, examining my intact hands. "I'm not charcoal. You okay, Ben?"

"Don't mind him," says Cody. "He's over his crush."

I glance at him. "Huh?"

"You, umm… look a bit different when you're sleeping."

"Oh." I cringe. "Sorry. Hope I wasn't too gruesome."

Cody sits up. "Nah, you don't look like a mummy or anything. Just obviously dead. Even paler than you are normally, with blue lips… and cold."

I narrow my eyes at him. "Cold?"

"He, umm, might've tried to kiss you."

"On the cheek," mutters Ben, turning scarlet. "You know, just like an 'I'm glad you're okay' kiss."

Considering how unnerved he looks, I drop it. An innocent peck on the cheek is hardly taking advantage of an unconscious girl. "Thanks for dragging me out of the sun. You saved my ass." I brush at my sweatshirt sleeves, making the smell of grilled hamburger stronger. "Ugh."

"No problem." Cody leans over and fist-bumps me. "You saved Ben. And I guess me, too."

"Any clue where we are?" I ask.

"Nope. We walked for a couple hours until we found this little cabin. Haven't seen another person or anything else bigger than a rabbit." Cody yawns. "I'm so messed up, I have no idea what time it really is."

I check my phone, but it's still dead. "No luck on calling for help."

"Everything electronic is useless."

"Maybe electrons work differently in this dimension, so our devices can't work?" asks Ben.

"Do you have to keep calling it another dimension?" I ask, head in my hands.

Ben shrugs. "If you have a better name for it, I'm all ears."

"Umm. Maybe it took us to Europe or wherever that guy is originally from, and whatever energy powered the gateway blew out our devices."

Cody scratches his head. "Maybe. That could also explain the sun coming up so fast."

"Well, that answers that question," I mumble.

"What question?" ask the brothers simultaneously.

I explain my earlier mental debate about a vampire's sleep cycle being tied to chronological time or the actual sun. Since I either jumped across the globe to a different time zone or wound up in another universe, and became sleepy when the sun came up—it's tied to the sun.

"So, theoretically, if a vampire hopped on a plane and kept flying west to stay in the dark, they might not need to sleep," I say.

"That's kinda dumb." Ben's eyes widen and he shakes his head. "Uhh, I didn't mean your theory. I mean why would they do that? Stay awake constantly but be trapped in a plane?"

Cody laughs. "Might be a way to actually finish Mr. Santos' homework in one night."

"Ugh. Don't remind me." Ben shivers in dread.

"Freshman biology teacher," says Cody. "I had him last year. Ben's got him this year coming up."

"I had bio freshman year, too. Teacher was such a basket case. He was so weird the school wouldn't let him in the lab, so we never did any lab work at all."

"Wow." Cody blinks. "Sounds hilarious."

"The guy hit a deer on the way to school one morning. He threw it in the back of his pickup and came in anyway. Said he was going to clean it and make steaks out of it when he went home."

They both cringe.

"I think we should probably go back and hope that portal opens again," mutters Ben.

"What about that giant Beast dude?" asks Cody.

"He could've come through the door after us, but didn't." Ben flicks at his shoulder-length hair. "Maybe he can't. We can go back to the spot we came in. If the portal's open, we peek through and see if he's there, then try to sneak out into the caverns."

"Why would a vampire have a portal in his bedroom that he can't go through? That doesn't make any sense." I rub both hands up and down my face, massaging my sinuses. Ugh. I'm going to be smelling smoke for days. "But… Beasts can't fly. At least, as far as I know. I could peek in and check things out. If he's dangerous, I should be able to get away."

"That's more of a plan than I can think of." Ben shrugs.

"Okay. So we wait for it to get dark and head out." Cody scratches his stomach when it growls.

Over the next few hours, we trade stories of high school, mostly about stupid stuff our friends and teachers did. It's kinda funny hearing a lot of the same sorts of things from them as what I experienced, despite us going to school so far from each other. I guess high school, in and of itself, comes hand in hand with a certain degree of derpitude regardless of location.

This gets us theorizing on what high school might be like in other countries… if teachers there are the same. Or if the usual cliques show up all over the world. Ben keeps rubbing his 'magic ring,' which has no sign of a glow at the moment.

"I don't think your ring was reacting to me at all," I say. "That first night we met, I watched you walk off, and it kept glowing long after you got far away."

"What about the big guy?" asks Ben.

"Maybe… but what if it sensed the portal?" I draw a circle in the air with my finger. "It glowed rather bright in the cave the closer we got to his lair. But, I suppose it could still have picked him up."

"Do you think it works like light?" asks Cody. "If that big guy's old and powerful, he might be giving off so much energy it can't even see you."

I stand with a grunt, brushing dirt and forest bits off my butt, then hobble over to Ben. He presses himself against the wall, though he doesn't appear frightened of me. More nervous. I grasp his hand and touch the ring, but it doesn't do anything.

"Maybe because I'm not a vampire right now." I shrug.

"Huh?" asks Ben. "How can you be not a vampire?"

"It's not dark enough in here. I can tolerate some degree of daylight, but when the sun's on me, I'm basically a normal person. No speed, strength, super hearing or anything like that. I can't even make my fangs come out."

"Still better than being a corpse," says Cody.

I point at him. "Damn straight."

We sit around staring at each other for a while. The boys venture outside and return half an hour or so later with strange fruits that look like apples only they're the size of grapefruit.

"Tastes like an apple," says Cody after a test bite. "But almost rotten."

"They were on the ground. The others are too high up in the trees."

So, yeah. Killing time until sundown gets boring. How boring? We start talking about what random movie or cartoon characters might be like as vampires. Ben goes outside to pee. Cody follows. When they return, they invariably ask me if I need to go to the bathroom anymore. I'm not going into gruesome detail about what happens if I eat normal food, so I simply say 'no.'

Ugh. Why are boys so obsessed with bathroom stuff? The most hilarious thing in the world to Sam is farting. The only thing funnier to him than that is a fart that makes someone gag. And fart jokes *still* make Dad laugh. Men always accuse us of being mysterious and beyond explanation, but they shouldn't throw that stone. Stuff *they* do makes no damn sense either.

Eventually, the sun sets.

The brothers jump back and gasp when a brief flare in my eyes paints half the cabin bright red.

"Relax," I say. "That's just me, umm, 'coming online.'"

"You have signal?" asks Cody.

I laugh. "No. That's just what I call it when my powers kick back in. I think I got the idea from some old movie my Dad showed us with a space battleship. They always said 'weapons online' right before they got into a fight."

"Cool." Cody stands. "Let's get the hell out of here."

"Any idea where to go?" I ask.

"Well, the sled we used to carry you left a drag trail we should be able to follow." Ben points at a pair of arm-thick branches tied together with twine with a sort of sling-like arrangement of vines at the bottom.

"Oh." It's a little embarrassing to think about how much I panicked, but neither of them make a big deal of it. "Thanks."

Ben once more takes the lead, following the trail they left bringing me to this cabin. I glance back over my shoulder a few times as we move away from it, mystified at how they could've found it. Barely a minute's travel away, it's pretty much invisible among the foliage. Huh. I guess the boy *is* psychic. Or, maybe they simply got lucky and stumbled across it.

We pass more of those fruits, most of which are little more than rotting brown lumps on the ground. One or two are as big as small pumpkins. Ugh. I don't like that. Apples should not be that big.

"We're either in an alternate world or outside of Chernobyl," I mutter.

They chuckle... and their stomachs growl.

I glance upward. Non-rotted apples hang from branches well over thirty feet off the ground. That certainly explains why most of the ones down here look exploded. I glide up into the trees, pick two that appear ripe enough to eat, and carry them back down.

"Oh, cool!" says Ben, all trepidation at being near me gone. He grabs one and attacks it like a starving dog as he walks.

Cody nods his thanks and eats as well.

Great. Everything about my life is weird now. Alternate worlds, apples the size of cantaloupes, undead minions, vampires trying to kill me. I can't even take a damn vacation in peace. I wonder... if I hadn't been a vampire, would I have even been aware that one lived in a secret chamber at the bottom of the caverns? Probably not. And my aversion to sunlight is the only reason Dad even picked this as our road trip destination. What better place for a vampire to go on vay-cay than a huge-ass cave. Mr. Beast certainly seems to share that opinion.

My parents have to be completely freaking out. Sophia's going to be a total mess.

Shit. What if that vampire somehow figures out they're my family and goes after them out of revenge for 'stealing his food.' Stress and worry build and build until I let out a scream of frustration.

The boys whirl.

"Sorry." I breathe into my hands for a few seconds. "I'm really stressing out over my family."

"Yeah. Dad's gonna kill me," mutters Ben.

"What are you going to tell him?" asks Cody.

Ben grimaces. "Umm. If I give him a BS story, I'll only get it ten times worse when he finds out."

"You're going to tell him you were hunting a vampire?" I ask, incredulous.

"Yeah. He's not going to believe they're real, but he'll believe I was trying to find one."

They fall into a glum silence. Maybe an hour later, I catch a whiff of death on the wind. And no, Sam didn't fart again. I mean actual death.

"Guys…"

Ben looks back at me over his shoulder, but before he can say anything, he wipes out and lands on his ass.

"Oof!" Ben rolls to his left, rubbing his rear end. "Stepped in something slippery."

Cody stops short. "Ugh. That's disgusting. What the hell is it?"

I creep closer and crouch to examine a dark red smear. It looks as if Ben stepped on some manner of internal organ that ruptured and took his foot out from under him.

"I think it's a spleen."

Cody gags. "Seriously?"

I stand, shrugging. "No, not really. That just sounded funny. I have no idea what a spleen looks like."

"It's a dead guy," says Ben.

"Awful small for a dead person," I say.

"It's a piece of a dead guy," mutters Ben, giving me the side eye.

Cody pokes at it with a stick. "Could be from an animal."

"No." Ben points. "It's people."

I look to the left. A person's head sticks up from the foliage, so pale he's clearly dead. Blood stains his face below the nose like he vomited gore. A hand juts out of the weeds not far away attached to a different body. Time to take advantage of my not needing to breathe. I advance toward the carnage, looking around.

Five men who look anywhere from mid-twenties to fortyish lay sprawled around a fairly small area. They're wearing normal clothing, but it looks like they got into a fight with a steamroller and lost. Three have crushed torsos. One guy looks like he flew into a tree so fast he burst open—he's probably the former owner of whatever Ben stepped on. Number four is missing both arms, and the last guy looks like an action figure that some kid ripped in half at the waist.

"God damn," whispers Cody, between gagging. "Okay. I'm officially 'concerned' now."

"That means he's scared shitless," says Ben, as he stoops to root around the bushes.

"What are you doing?" snaps Cody. "Don't touch dead people."

Ben stands back up, lifting a modern pulley crossbow out of the weeds. "Check this out."

"Awesome." Cody stares at it.

"Not that awesome." I gesture at the dead guys. "It didn't do them much good."

Ben struggles to cock it, his face reddening. "Damn. This thing is stiff."

I offer a hand. "Let me try."

He gives me a 'but you're a girl' stare for about three seconds before his brain engages and he passes it over. I grab the string, pull it back with two fingers, and toss the thing back to him.

"Don't fire it with nothing in it," I say. "You'll break it."

"Here." Cody squats and removes a nylon quiver from one of the corpses' belts. "There's nine bolts left."

Ben blinks. "That was on a dead man."

"Yeah, so? He doesn't need them anymore. And we might wind up dead right next to them if we're helpless." Cody looks around at the dead, still struggling not to throw up. "Is this a search party? Did they send people looking for us?"

"Maybe. But... that would also mean that the park rangers know about a vampire living in the caverns with a magical portal to another dimension." I fold my arms.

"Right, so this search party wasn't here for us." Ben loads a bolt.

Cody walks away from the gory scene, waving a hand back and forth in front of his face. "They don't stink *too* much. They haven't been dead all that long. But they stink enough that they were probably here before us."

"Which makes me wonder what brought them here." I say.

"Yeah. They had a crossbow, so they must have been expecting trouble." Ben turns in place, gazing around. "But we haven't seen anything."

"Something smashed them." Cody nods toward the dead. "Those rabbits we keep seeing didn't do that."

"Not unless we've wound up in Monty Python's world," I mutter.

"Huh?" asks Cody.

Ben blinks, perplexed.

"Not worth explaining. Old movie. But if only one of them had a bow, I think that means they weren't expecting *definite* trouble, just the off chance they might run into something. So whatever they came here to do, it didn't require combat... or hunting. Otherwise, they would've all been armed."

"Why don't they have a gun?" asks Cody. "A crossbow is kinda weird, right?"

"Dude." Ben pats his pocket. "None of our tech works. Maybe guns stop working, too?"

I raise a hand, shaking my head. "Now hold on a sec. Guns aren't dependent on electronics or computers. Are you suggesting that *gunpowder* might not work in here? A gun's basically a simple machine. Simpler even than the mechanism in that crossbow. And chemical reactions..."

"Umm." Ben scratches his head. "Good point."

"Maybe they wanted to be quiet?" asks Cody. "Hoping nothing noticed them."

"Nothing like what?" asks Ben.

"Like whatever smashed them to death," I say.

The boys look at me for a few seconds of tense silence.

"Hey." Cody points. "The ring!"

Ben shifts the crossbow to his right hand and holds the left one up.

A brilliant spot of teal glow clings to the side of the ring, covering only about a quarter of its top.

"Weird." Cody leans close. "I've never seen it do that before. Usually the whole thing lights up."

"Yeah that's messed up." Ben looks around at the forest, the luminous spot moving around as he turns.

I point. "The light's moving when you turn. Maybe it's like a video game. Just follow the waypoint?"

Ben holds his hand flat and spins around. Sure enough, the glowing spot slides around the top of the ring like the needle on a compass. "It's pointing us at something. Yeah. They don't make video games like they used to. All the new ones basically handhold you the whole time, leading you straight to every objective."

"Umm." I laugh. "Aren't you like fourteen? How are you talking about 'the good old days?'"

He grins. "I play my Dad's computer games. The graphics kinda suck but the stories are way better. Sometimes they get pretty hard. Used to be, they sold 'hint books' with all the answers for people who got frustrated trying to figure out where to go. Dad has all the hint books, but he says they're only for collection purposes and he's never read them until after he beat the game."

"Bull," mutters Cody.

Ben snickers. "So what does teal mean?"

"It *doesn't* mean vampire," I say, smiling. "And hey. I'm fully powered up and it's not reacting at all to me."

"Well, you are only a few months old," says Cody. "Maybe you're not powerful enough yet. You're like still level one."

I roll my eyes. "Okay. Whatever."

"Do we follow the ring or not?" asks Cody.

"Let's go for it," I say. "It's bad to look a random magical emanation in the mouth."

18

THE RUINS OF NOPE

*B*en hands the crossbow to Cody. "Here. I can't look at the ring while carrying it."

His brother takes the weapon. After attaching the quiver to his belt, he checks the safety (a sliding button on the trigger guard), and nods once, his expression grim.

The glow leads us onward. Ben holds his left hand flat in front of him, gazing down at the light every so often to make sure we're still on course. After what feels like two hours, we arrive in a small clearing of trees beside a steep, but passable hill studded with frayed roots and sprays of tiny white flowers. If not for being trapped somewhere unknown and worried sick about my family, I'd find the scenery beautiful.

Being unencumbered by trivial things like gravity or fatigue, I make it to the top of the hill first and let out a whistle of awe at a sprawl of ruins scattered around a much thinner growth of trees than we'd been walking in all night. Low-lying fog drifts over stacks of stones and a few grave markers. On the left, waist-high crumbling walls outline the corpse of a larger building. Rocks of various sizes lying upon the ground trace the path of a fence that disappeared a long time ago, the rusting remains of wrought iron bars partially sunken in the ground. A stone table that looks suspiciously like an altar stands about sixty yards away straight ahead near a thicker copse of trees that shroud the spot like the roof of a little chapel.

"Damn," whispers Cody. He stopped climbing as soon as he could see over the top of the hill. "Totally creepy."

"This seriously looks like that movie *Evil Dead*," I say. "If either of you guys see a demonic book, don't frickin' touch it."

"Klaatu, verrata, screw that." Cody chuckles. "Are you sure this is where we need to go?"

Ben holds up his hand. "Umm. The ring's pointing straight at the altar."

"Of course it is." I sigh. "We only assumed it's detecting helpful stuff. It might just sense power, good or bad."

He starts walking. "We're already here. Let's check it out."

Cody tries to grab him, but Ben ducks. "Hey. This is how you wound up in a vampire's cage."

"Come on. There's nothing here but fog." Ben walks faster.

I hurry after him. "This place feels creepy."

"Graves, fog, and ruined buildings always feel creepy," says Ben.

"Do you make a habit of visiting abandoned cemeteries?" I ask.

"No, but the one where Mom's parents are is almost like this… minus the sacrificial altar."

The fog thickens almost in response to our presence. By the time we're halfway to the stone table, it's difficult to see much more than ten feet in any direction. Of course, this sets the brothers into 'soldier overdrive' and they start swiveling around looking for danger.

"Every damn game," mutters Cody. "Graveyard plus fog equals skeletons."

"Except, we're not in a game." I listen at the surroundings, but hear only distant birds. "No idea why the fog is thickening. Nothing's moving but us."

"Hey." Ben points ahead. "I see a runic arch on the other side of the altar."

A tall stone structure in the shape of an upside down U stands on a round platform a short distance past the stone table. It's a little hard to see with the fog, but I'm sure the sides are covered with engraved symbols that don't belong to any language I've ever seen.

"Come on dude, this ain't *World of Warcraft.*" Cody sighs.

"It really does look like that." I pinch the bridge of my nose. "This keeps getting weirder and weirder."

"No, I'm serious." Ben hurries up to a jog, ignores the table, and jumps a knee-high stone wall behind it before running over to the arch.

Cody edges past me, and I catch myself staring at the side of his neck. Ben's hair is long enough to hide it, but his is short. Surviving that sunbaked trip took a lot out of me. Grr. I avert my gaze, clenching fists at my side. Biting either one of these guys wouldn't do much to keep us friends.

I follow at a safe distance. Fortunately, the table is empty—no cursed books.

Up close, the arch is bigger than I thought. The center of the U at the top is about twelve feet high and it's wide enough for a van.

Ben walks around it, holding his hand up. "The light's following this arch. This is what it led us to."

"Great. So what do we do with it?" asks Cody.

"Don't ask me." I shrug. "I still don't believe any of this is really happening. There's no such thing as portals or magic."

"Says the vampire," mutters Ben.

"Okay. I can't explain how when I bite someone, the wound goes away when I want it to."

"Magic," says Cody.

Ben pokes the arch, tracing his finger along one of the runic carvings. His touch leaves a trail of teal light. "Whoa."

"Dude. Stop. Something's happening," says Cody, reaching for him.

The instant Ben's finger reaches the end of that rune, all the carvings light up at once. I cringe back from a tangible blast, almost like someone switched on a ten-foot-wide fan in front of me for only a few seconds. Neither boy reacts.

"Ouch," I mutter.

They look at me.

"That thing just hit me with a wave of like, I dunno 'spirit force' or something. You didn't feel that?"

"No," says Ben.

With a noise like a raging waterfall, a swirl of teal-blue energy appears inside the U, expanding until it touches stone on all sides. The air crackles with electricity and the smell of ozone. Unlike the one we came in from, this portal is solid light, not an open circle peering into another place.

Cody aims the crossbow at the portal. "What's inside?"

"You know as much as I do," I say.

"Do we go in?" asks Ben.

Cody shrugs.

I pick up a nearby branch and poke it into the swirl. At the instant of contact, a tingle spreads over my entire body. When my hand comes within a foot of the field, I stop, wave the branch around a little, then back up. The branch comes out unscathed.

"Okay, so it is a doorway of some kind." I toss the branch aside. "Wonder why we can't see past it?"

A huge leg emerges from the portal, the knee as tall as my chest and even more muscular than the Beast. Hair like steel wool covers it down to a foot sporting cracked yellow toenails easily a quarter inch thick. A stink of male musk rolls over me strong enough to make my eyes water. I jump back, hand over my mouth and nose, as an enormous humanoid creature steps into view.

He's clearly a guy, bald in front, beard down to his rounded belly, shaggy, unkempt black hair going wherever it wants. Mercifully, he's wearing pants made of... animal hide or some such thing. The face is part caveman, part back woods hermit. Standing a little shy of being eye-to-eye with his groin hits me in the nose with a sour cheese odor. All manner of flying insects swarm around him, crawling in and out of his ears, navel, and even mouth. They seem to be feeding off stuff in his teeth.

"Umm," says Ben.

"Nope," I say, shaking my head. "No way."

"That's not real. It's an illusion." Cody glances at the crossbow. "There's no such thing as… as… whatever that is."

"I, uhh, think that's a troll," says Ben. "I also think I know why those men we saw are dead."

"Trolls aren't real," says Cody.

"Neither are vampires," I deadpan.

"Or interdimensional travel," whispers Ben.

As if offended by such a large word, the 'troll' snarls and draws back a fist bigger than my entire torso to pound Ben.

"Stop! Go away," I shout, trying to command it, but I don't have any feeling at all of having touched a living brain. I may as well have tried to mentally dominate a pineapple. Oh, great. This thing's the sort of knuckledragger who calls the cops because McDonalds is out of chicken nuggets.

Great. A damn troll. The *last* thing we needed.

19

A GIANT PROBLEM

*B*en stands there paralyzed in fear as the troll's fist comes down.

I fly into him, dragging him aside. The troll punches the dirt with enough force to knock Cody off his feet. Ben grabs on, clinging to me much like Sophia after a nightmare. I stop about twenty feet away, float vertical, and set him on his feet.

"Cody, run!" I yell.

"Make it forget us," whimpers Ben.

"Tried that. That thing is either so dumb it counts as a houseplant, or its brain is on an entirely different, uhh, wavelength."

Cody scrambles to his feet and backs up, firing the crossbow. The bolt plunges into the huge creature's chest in the upper left side, almost disappearing entirely. Despite only the feathers of the bolt remaining visible, the troll doesn't react at all to the hit. "Oh, crap."

"Run!" shouts Ben. He finally lets go of me, grabs my hand, and pulls me up to a sprint.

I run alongside him, glancing back every few seconds at a rapidly closing Cody. The ground shakes under the troll's stride.

"We shouldn't go through that portal," yells Ben.

Cody blows past us, shouting, "Ya think?"

A huge, heavy object whistles overhead, a tombstone shuriken flying at Cody. It smashes into a tree, spraying him with fist-sized chunks. His attempt to dodge throws him into a face-first slide. I swerve toward him, stopping only long enough to grab his arm and pull him upright.

"Ow. Shit!" Cody rubs his arm. Thin trails of blood roll down his face from tiny cuts, the beautiful red color mesmerizes me. He tilts his head in confusion at the way I'm staring at him. He probably thinks I'm about to kiss him, but he's a big Hostess cupcake to me right now.

Ben's scream trailing off into the air snaps me out of my fog. The troll caught up and grabbed him, fist clamped around the boy's legs like a six-year-old about to mash a GI Joe figure into a fine red paste.

"Damn," I sigh.

I fling myself airborne, flying at the troll's forearm, and rake my way around it with as many claws as I can sink in. Eww. His flesh is thick and rubbery, but my weaponized fingernails cut it easily. The troll howls in agony, but doesn't release Ben, so I lunge at its hand and bite down, thinking rageful thoughts. Evidently, Dalton's brief teachings were true. Biting to inflict injury *does* hurt like a son of a bitch.

Even this enormous idiot notices, though it's not a nice reaction—it's the same sort of reaction most people have to mosquitos.

Ben slips from the troll's grip seconds before he smashes the spot I bit with his other hand. I dart down and right. He misses me, though the volume of the *slap* so close is almost as painful as a physical blow. While the giant stands there bewildered at not having crushed anything, I wing up and around behind him and clamp my teeth onto the side of his neck.

Yeah. It's like biting a pair of sweat-soaked underpants that some dude wore for six months straight.

And the blood tastes like toe jam.

I force myself to swallow two mouthfuls before I can't take anymore and disengage. If I throw up, I'll probably lose more blood than I drank. The boys manage to reload the crossbow, though Cody doesn't want to shoot with me so close.

The troll reaches up over his head. I let gravity pull me straight down, ripping my claws over its back on the way. It shivers in pain, letting out a roar so loud it practically knocks leaves off the trees. Maybe if I can piss it off enough, I can lead it away from the boys. It might be able to outrun us on the ground due to the size of its stride, but no way will he catch me flying.

He wheels around, swatting at me. Again and again, I duck his tree-trunk arms and slash at his chest, though I'm not really doing much to him. I feel like an enraged housecat after a drunken tertiary relative stepped on her tail. However, the supernatural pain my claws inflict *is* bothering him more than the crossbow bolt—at least if the increasing red in his face is any indication.

The seventh time I duck and go to pop back up for a claw swipe, he changes pattern and catches me with a wild right-handed slap. One second I'm in the air, the next, I'm on the ground twisted into a pretzel knot. I don't even feel any pain for a few seconds. In fact, I hear myself screaming before the agony reaches my consciousness.

And my legs are numb.

Oh, probably because I'm twisted around a tree, bent over backward with my head between my knees. Yeah, I'm basically sitting on my own skull. Spine's gotta be smashed. Does this count as extreme yoga?

The troll—who's like fifty yards away—turns toward me, squinting like he can't tell where I went. Yay for darkness and thick trees. A streak of yellow flies up from the ground into his face. He clamps both hands over his face and howls. Blood oozes down his chest from the crossbow quarrel stuck sideways through his nose like a bone. Ack. Merely looking at that hurts more than my disintegrated spine.

Okay, not really. But still. Ow.

Once he stops shrieking in rage-agony, he spins to the left and stomps off, chasing Cody. I'm too far away and on the ground, so I can't see a damn thing. Fifty freakin' yards. Holy shit this thing is strong. What's that high-pitched squealing noise? Oh... my skull is knitting where it cracked. Crunching emanates from my neck. Talk about whiplash. A pop comes from my shoulder. The only part of me that wants to move right now other than my eyelids is my left arm. Right one's all tingly plus I'm lying on top of it. Everything below the middle of my chest may as well not exist right now.

I contort my left arm around in front of me, then reach up past my face to grab my butt, pushing it up off my head. At least I'm mostly numb. When I give my ass a shove in hopes of throwing my body out flat in a reasonably normal position, I emit another shriek of unexpected pain. A new fire starts up in my throat. I think I screamed so loud I ripped a vocal cord.

Ugh. Being a vampire *does* have its downsides... like being unable to faint from agony.

Since no one can see me at the moment, I don't fight the urge to cry. I'm in so much goddamned pain I think I'm getting high from endorphins. It's pretty close to the level of debilitating torture experienced by a man having a cold.

My hips crash into the ground, my legs flopping like giant gummy worms.

"Sarah!" shouts Cody. "Where are you?"

Ben screams something incomprehensible. At least the *thud, thud, thud* of the troll running around suggests he hasn't caught them.

"Over here," I yell.

"Little help!" calls Cody.

"Hang on. My spine's not cooperating at the moment."

My right arm decides to stop being a bitch and listen to me again. I drag it out from under me and push myself up a little, but I still can't see anything.

Cody emits a war cry, and the *thwoonk* of the crossbow precedes another roar of anger from the troll. I'd say he's a pretty good shot, but how do you miss something the size of a house? Ben's shouting goes from right to left along with rapid thumping footsteps. Another *thwoonk* comes from that side. Guess they're tossing the crossbow back and forth.

Out of nowhere, a storm of sharp tingles swims over my body from the waist down. Holy crap. I bite my forearm to muffle another scream. Wearing yoga pants made out of needles would be more comfortable. The boys might be screaming. That troll might be thundering around, but I'm completely unaware of everything for a few seconds.

A loud *crack* travels like a hammer impact up my spine into the base of my skull. It didn't hurt, but the sensation is so *weird* it leaves me unable to move for a few seconds. When the disorientation fades, I wiggle my toes.

Okay. Back in the game. Note to self: next time, duck.

I drag myself upright and take off into the air again. As soon as I reach treetop level, the troll is obvious. They've led it even farther away, but it only takes me a couple seconds to fly back in range. Cody's hiding behind a tree right in front of it, dodging side to side as it tries to grab him.

Enraged, the troll grabs the tree in both hands, roars, and yanks the entire thing out of the ground like he's picking a weed. Well, he's doing it wrong. Most of the roots are still there. With a huff, he tosses it aside and glowers down at Cody.

The boy screams and runs. I zoom at the troll and do a high-speed claw rake across its back. He forgets entirely about Cody and spins with a hard backhanded strike, but I'm way out of reach by the time he swings. His chest is a mess of blood and crisscross slashes, but I may as well be attempting to kill a person with a cheese grater.

"Sarah!" shouts Ben.

I swing around in midair and spot him trying (and failing) to climb a tree. "What? Don't climb. He'll just knock the whole tree over."

"C'mere." He waves me down. "It's important!"

"Fine." I zip in and land right next to him. "What?"

He hands me the crossbow. "First, please pull the string. Second. I just realized, that thing's basically a Fey creature. We need iron. It's the only thing that'll kill it."

I crank the string back and hand the crossbow back to him. "Okay. Not like we're going to outrun this thing."

"You can... but you're trying to protect us." He stares into my eyes. "Sorry for being freaked out at seeing you sleep... and wanting to stake you."

"No worries. Iron? Where am I—the fence! Be right back."

Ben nods and leans around the tree, aiming at the troll.

I start to rocket off toward the ruins, but the troll's got Cody by one leg. The crossbow bolt slamming into the back of its head doesn't appear to do much. Hey... head shots are only fatal when something has a brain. And wow, it only penetrated an inch or so. Damn this thing has a thick skull. I swing around in an arc, hold my breath, and claw the hell out of his armpit.

The troll drops Cody, who lands with a heavy *whud*, and throws his head back, howling. I can't even tell if he's in pain or angry.

Before he can slap me again, I zoom off toward the ruins—thankfully easy to see from the air. The troll emits a disinterested/annoyed huff and resumes chasing the brothers. Upon reaching the ruins, I swoop in and land by the remnants of the wrought iron fence. Most of the bars are rusty, but it's not like I have to worry about tetanus.

After a little rooting around, I find a long spar that had to be one of the ornamental main poles. It's easily ten feet long and looks like an all-metal spear, complete with not-quite-sharp point.

Perfect.

Once again, I catapult myself into the air and climb to about sixty feet before racing at the troll. The thing's so angry it's swatting down any tree it gets close to that isn't thick enough to withstand it. Apparently, that thing's strength *does* have limits. Three trees later, it rushes off to the left and lopes up to a run, chasing down Cody who's made the mistake of trying to outsprint it. Or not. He swerves back and forth, using the thicker trunks to force the troll around them in much wider turns than what he needs.

It's really tempting to let out a Valkyrie war cry, but I don't want to give away my surprise.

Silent as a suburban Starbucks ninja can be, I dive out of the air doing my best to line up the point of this rod with the troll's heart. The big idiot spots a hint of motion and looks up at me, leaving his chest wide open. Seeing me flying must short-circuit his three brain cells, since he doesn't even try to swat me out of the air.

A near 140-MPH dive plunges my improvised spear about four feet deep in the troll's chest.

He emits a deep, hollow gasp and starts to swoon backward. Before he goes over, I let go of the spear, flying down and away. He hits the ground with a tremendous *whump* that makes me cringe and knocks dozens of head-sized apples from branches.

The troll struggles to lift his arm and grab the spear, but falls limp. Seconds later, he gasps his last breath.

I drift down and land in a slouch, too exhausted to even fall over.

Cody and Ben drag themselves out of the forest, both covered in hundreds of little scratches. They stand on either side of me, staring at the dead troll.

"Sweet! It worked," said Ben.

"You didn't know that for sure?" I ask.

Ben shrugs with an innocent smile. "I had a strong suspicion."

"You okay?" asks Cody.

"No." I slump to my knees and grab my stomach. Electric shock pains spread outward from my gut. I can't remember ever being this hungry before. "Not really."

20

PORTAL ROULETTE

I kneel on the ground between the brothers, shivering with sporadic twitches.

My fangs are out and won't go back in. I can't look at either one of them for fear of what'll happen. Both boys smell so damn good, my ability to control myself has a lifespan somewhere between snowball in the sun and a politician's campaign promise after winning an election.

"Look, guys," I rasp. "That thing broke me around a tree. And the sun earlier... I need to take the edge off or I think I'm gonna snap. I really hate to ask, but would you mind if I fed from you?"

Cody slaps Ben on the shoulder. "You go first, dude. You've been dying to have her lips on you from day one."

"What about the troll?" asks Ben. "He's got a shitload of blood."

"Umm, that won't work." Cody coughs. "It disintegrated."

"What?" I ask, so hungry I don't think I'd care anymore how nasty it tasted.

"Turned into ashes or something black. Only the bones are left," says Cody.

"Whoa..." Ben whistles. "Good point. Okay. Go ahead. Am I gonna turn?"

I try to shake my head, but I wind up thrashing it back and forth like a patient from a mental hospital. "N-no. Feeding d-doesn't do that or there'd be m-millions of vampires."

"So, umm. How does this work?" asks Ben.

"Easy," I whisper. "Just sit still."

He barely manages a startled squeak when I spring up and bite him. Pizza-flavored blood bursts into my mouth like liquid awesome. I don't allow myself to enjoy it though, instead focusing on the idea of 'do not kill Ben.' Some part of me deep down inside wants to drain him like a Capri Sun packet, but I manage to stop myself after taking a little over a pint. Not wanting to waste a single drop, I drag my tongue over the puncture wound for the gesture of sealing.

Ben shudders.

I pounce Cody next, too hungry to bother speaking to confirm he's okay with it. He better be okay with it. I just had my damn spine snapped in three pieces to save his skinny ass. A blast of French fries hits me in the taste buds. Wow. Pizza and French fries. Of course. What else would teenage boys taste like? A pint-ish from him eases me back from 'eat the entire world' to 'kinda hungry.' I lick his wound closed, then collapse to my knees again, savoring the warmth radiating outward from my stomach.

Both brothers fall over flat on their backs, grinning like fools.

It occurs to me after a moment that feeding from a willing donor has *other* effects on people. Michelle had been secretly wanting sex for a long time, and when she let me feed from her, whatever magic is in my teeth hit her like the climax to end all orgasms. When Dalton fed from Mom, her greatest desire—an escape from the stress of her job and all responsibility—left her loopy for hours. It's not automatically sexual in nature, though these *are* teenage boys. Their brains have three settings: sex, food, and spaceships/explosions. Worse, Ben had a crush on me.

And... yeah. They're both about to break out of their jeans. Damn. I feel all kinds of awkward and dirty like I just did something super wrong with underage boys. Maybe I should make them forget that little part of this 'vacation.' Yeah. I can't let them even remotely associate me with getting off, even if *was* purely a supernatural side effect of feeding.

I should've mind fogged them before biting, but I wasn't exactly thinking straight.

A moment later, they both remember letting me feed from them since I was critically low, but instead of having the mother of all X-rated dreams, they both simply became lightheaded from blood loss.

By the time they come out of the mental haze, my blood meal has settled and I feel normal. Well, as normal as I can feel while terrified that I'm going to get back to the RV and find my family massacred.

"Come on." I grab Ben's hand and drag him upright. "We need to go."

"Where?" asks Ben in a sleepy murmur.

I pause, reaching for Cody. "Umm. Shit. Hell with it. Dealing with a Beast is *not* going to be as messed up as that… that… *thing* that didn't really exist."

"I think it was a troll," says Ben. "But it didn't regenerate at all, so maybe not."

"Regenerate?" I ask.

"He's thinking of the game. This is real." Cody stands. "Okay. Let's head back to the other portal."

We debate the direction to go in for a few minutes before deciding to trust Ben's intuition again and walk the way he wants to go. The boys are a little unsteady on their feet, so I encourage them to eat one of the huge apples each.

Ben's a little more than halfway done with his when he emits a "Mmm!" past a full mouth. He rushes chewing, swallows, then holds up his left hand. "It's glowing again."

Cody and I both hurry over to look.

A purple glow shimmers over about a quarter of the ring, a compass pointer exactly like the teal one.

"We should go this way," says Ben.

"Dude. The last time we followed that thing we almost got eaten by a giant. If we keep playing"—he waves around for a second, trying to come up with a word—"portal roulette, something's going to kill us."

"It wasn't a giant. That was a troll," says Ben.

"I was eye-level to its balls. That was a giant," shouts Cody.

"A giant would've been about double that height."

The brothers explode into an argument about whether that obvious hallucination that kicked my ass should be called a giant or a troll.

I give them thirty seconds before shouting, "Guys!"

They stop, glare at each other for a moment, then turn their heads toward me at the same time.

"We don't have time for semantic bullshit. That Beast could be doing anything right now. I have to get back to my family before he hurts them—and your parents are also losing their minds. We've been missing for a day." I pace around in a little circle, pulling at my hair. "Argh. My dad picked this place for our yearly road trip because he figured I'd be okay in a cave as a vampire. All three of my siblings wanted to stay home, even Mom did... but they all agreed to the trip to make *me* feel better. Like we're still a normal family. And now I'm going to ruin the whole thing by making them freak out and worry."

Cody squeezes my shoulder. "They'll be so happy when you get back to them that they'll forget we were missing."

I take a few breaths to calm down. "Okay. You're right. Positive thinking. We're not going to be missing forever."

"Or die." Ben pats my other shoulder. He holds up the glowing ring. "We gotta follow this when it's on, before it shuts off. And hey, it might be pointing at the portal."

"It's *obviously* pointing at the portal," says Cody. "What's going to come out of this one? A damn dragon?"

"No." Ben shakes his head. "I mean *the* portal. It's the same shade of purple as what we saw back in the campground. Maybe this ring doesn't detect ghosts or vampires at all, but magic. The portal back there at the ruin went to wherever that monster came from. The purple portal goes between here and our world. The color could match up with, I dunno, the frequency or whatever."

"I still think following the ring is dangerous." Cody picks at the crossbow. "I've only got one shot left."

"Do either of you have a better idea than following the ring?" I ask. Silence.

"Okay. Let's go." I point at Ben. "Lead on."

He trots off. Other than a small group of rabbits, no other creatures show themselves for the next hour and forty minutes or so of walking. Shimmering blue light emerges from the trees up ahead: a ring of energy with a dark interior, similar to the portal we came in from.

I dash over to it and bite my lip, debating flinging myself right in. "Guys. I think this is it. I can smell the caverns."

"Umm," says Cody. "Are you sure?"

"We don't have time." Ben swats me on the arm to get my attention and points up. "The sky's starting to brighten again."

"Crap. Oh… screw it. I trust my nose." I jump into the ring and float for a few seconds in total blackness before crashing into a wooden door that bounces open under my weight. Momentum carries me into a graceless stumble, but I don't fall over.

Cody and Ben spill in behind me.

I'm back in that cave chamber… four feet away from a familiar over-muscled man with one eyebrow raised in an expression of bewildered surprise.

The Beast.

"Crap," I mutter, then force a cheesy smile. "Hi. Can I interest you in some Thin Mints?"

21

THE BEAST OF CLARK CAVERNS

I'm lucky I don't need to breathe, because I can't, standing eye-to-pectoral with a mountain of humanity. Or unhumanity as the case may be.

The man studies me, his irises dark chocolate brown with a hint of red. Wild, shaggy dark brown hair drapes over his shoulders, and his beard hangs to the middle of his stomach. A pale grey blazer and nice slacks make him look like a homeless Viking stuffed into new clothes. The room reeks of wood smoke, though after that troll, it's far from unpleasant.

Okay. Dalton said these guys have hair-trigger tempers, kinda like Furies but worse. Maybe I should handle him like I've been cornered by a mountain lion? Wait... how am I supposed to handle being cornered by a mountain lion?

The boys hide behind me.

"Most curious," says the Beast.

I'm not sure why I'm startled to hear him speaking in such a clear tone. Did I really expect him to grunt and growl like a man-bear? "Umm. Hi?"

"Greetings, Sarah." He takes my hand and kisses the back. "Welcome to my home. I am Garrett Alder."

Ben twists back and forth, searching around.

"What?" whispers Cody.

"Looking for the talking candlestick," whispers Ben.

I start to giggle, but clamp a hand over my mouth.

Garrett chuckles. "Clever, but I am not that kind of beast."

"You know my name?" I ask.

"Indeed. I observed you the other night in the woods. I find it curious you still associate with your mortal family."

"Y-you knew I was a vampire?"

He nods once.

Grr.

"You seem frustrated." He strokes a few fingers down his beard.

"Thought I managed to make you think I was a human."

He tilts his head. "Why would you wish to deceive me like that?"

"Umm. 'Cause I'm a dumbass I guess. I'm still kinda new at this and haven't exactly heard the nicest things about your, umm, bloodline. Thought you'd try to rip my head off."

"Ahh." He nods. "I do not take it personally, for I know my kind have certain idiosyncrasies. 'Tis why I have made my home in such a remote place."

"Wait, this guy would've talked to you the whole time?" asks Ben.

I glance back at him, then turn to Garrett. "Why did you put Ben in a cage?"

"Why do mortals put food in refrigerators?" Garrett chuckles.

Ben clings to me from behind, shivering.

"The boy wandered in here on his own," says Garrett. "I would not have killed him, though it seems you have already made a meal of him. He would likely not survive another feeding without injury for a while."

"Wouldn't have killed him? What about those Scraps—or that room full of corpses? We were shitting bricks." I cringe at my hostile tone. "Umm. Sorry. Had a bad day."

"Well…" Garrett looks down, fidgeting. "I do not *intend* to kill, but sometimes I lose control of myself."

There isn't much room to get around this guy with the shelves on both sides of the chamber near the door. Backpacks, flashlights, a few tents, basically camping gear. What the heck?

"Umm. So, what now?" I ask.

"Well, I suppose I *could* drink these two dry and twist your head off."

I gasp, leaning back.

"That *is* what you were expecting, is it not?" ask Garrett.

"Umm." I grind the toe of my sneaker into the ground. "Yeah. Kind of."

He emits a deep, reverberating chuckle that vibrates my bones, then steps back like a butler opening a door for us. "By all means. Please return to where you belong. I am not a monster... most of the time anyway."

I'm a little too scared and suspicious to trust turning my back on him. But I'm also worried that offending him might trigger a beastly rage. Fists clenched, I force myself to smile and walk by.

"But..." says Garrett.

"Gah." I jump and whirl around.

He smiles.

"But?" I ask in a small voice.

"Would you be inclined to do me a small favor?"

"What kind of favor? Does it involve pain? Sharp things? Cattle mutilation? Long periods of tedium punctuated by moments of existential crisis?"

He blinks, stares at me for a moment, then erupts in raucous laughter. "No, child." Garrett gestures up the ramp into the nicer bedroom. "Please, let me invite you in properly. Spare a moment for me to explain?"

"Umm. Okay." I glance back at the brothers and send, *Just go with it* into their heads.

They nod.

Sure... we can talk with him for a minute. Don't wanna piss him off. Not like we've got much to lose.

Other than our lives.

22

FEY AMARANTH

The three of us wind up seated on the edge of the gargantuan bed, which is surprisingly soft and comfortable given that it's deep underground in a cave. I find myself unable to resist running my hand back and forth over the plush burgundy comforter. Garrett pulls a chair away from the writing desk so he can sit close enough to us to have a conversation.

"Forgive me for not offering you refreshments. I do not maintain a stock of blood, or of mortal food. I'm sure you are eager to return to your families, so I will not waste time on pointless formalities. The favor I would ask of you is to go back into the portal and find a particular type of flower. A week ago, I sent in a group of ghouls, but they have not returned."

"Ghouls?" asks Ben.

"Living people given a bit of his power," I say.

Cody holds up the crossbow. "Umm, They won't be returning. I think we found them."

"Damn." Garrett bows his head. "What happened to them?"

"Not sure exactly. Something big smashed them. Maybe a troll."

He blinks. "A troll? That region is supposed to be uninhabited… at least by anything that large."

"Where exactly *is* that?" I ask.

"Another world reasonably proximal to our own. It's close enough that natural bridges have formed and collapsed over the centuries. Most people refer to it as the Realm of the Faerie."

I stare. There is no way in hell I can tell my family about this or Sophia will be insufferable, demanding to see it. There's also not a damn chance I'm bringing her anywhere near that place. She's highly allergic to trolls. And yes, I made that up.

"So, faeries exist?" asks Cody.

"Almost everything that folklore describes exists in one form or another. They arrive in our world via doorways that exist for moments in time then go away. Interactions are so rare that it is easy for most people to regard them all as myths."

"You made that portal?" I ask.

"Not alone. While I have done some research, my nature makes pursuits of an abstract, intellectual nature somewhat cumbersome. A small frustration can enrage me to an unfortunate mental state. An Academic associate of mine assisted in the construction of the gateway. Unfortunately, we committed a mild error in calculation and the other end appeared some distance from where we needed it to be."

"Can't you shut it down and re-make it?" asks Cody.

"The effort necessary to do that is quite great. Oswald, my Academic friend, explained the details, though they mostly went over my head. Something about an infinite number of potential realities existing in parallel with our own. He is certain we connected to the right one, merely an error in the specific location inside the realm. Attempting to make a new portal could lead to many frustrating near-misses where we establish a connection to the wrong reality."

"Oh," I deadpan. "Yeah, that makes total sense."

Garrett smiles at my sarcasm. "We did not miss by *that* much, however, it did create enough distance between the entry point and what I need that I am unable to reach it during one span of darkness. The sun presents a problem I cannot overcome." Garrett smiles at me. "You do not suffer the same flaw, or at least not to the degree the rest of us do."

I pick at the seam down the side of my jeans. "Umm. What's so important about this flower?"

"My associate claims it is a critical ingredient in a concoction that can alter my nature from Beast to Fury. I am so weary of having to dwell here so far removed from civilization... the bouts of going out of my mind with uncontained primalistic urges."

"Umm. Wow. They can do that? Change a bloodline?" I ask.

"It is not without risk. The separation between Fury and Beast is not so large. The chances of my destruction are within acceptable limits."

"Umm, usually most people think the only acceptable risk of destruction is zero," says Cody.

"It would grant me a release from this isolation in either case," says Garrett with a far-off stare.

I let out a heavy sigh. "Have you been stuck here long?"

"My Transference occurred around 1910. I've spent most of my time here."

Wow, this dude's old. I really shouldn't piss him off. "I'm okay with the idea of helping you out, but my family has got to be freaking out about me by now."

Garrett shakes his head. "Time passes differently on the other side of that door. To me, you were gone only a moment. In the time it took me to walk the last several paces to the door after you ran in, you must've experienced hours. You were well out of sight when I opened it. A journey to the grove where the fey amaranth grows would perhaps take ten to fifteen minutes here."

"Hey, my watch is back on," says Cody.

I pull my phone out. It, too, has come back to life, and shows the time at 1:04 a.m., the same day we went into the door. Holy crap. "Wow, he's right."

"If you agree to go, I shall ensure the door stays open, but I do not mean to imply you have little choice in the matter. If you wish to simply return to your families, you are all free to go. The Scraps will not plague you on your way out."

"I'm curious why you don't, umm, you know."

"Put them down?" asks Garrett.

I nod. "I'm told that's what's supposed to happen."

"It is true that the majority of our kind look upon Scraps as beings too tortured or too dangerous to exist. Their condition is not something they asked for, nor my intention. I have already taken their mortal lives during a lapse of control, and do not feel justified in ending their unlife as well."

"Umm. Wow." I stare at this giant of a man, trying to rationalize the monster I thought he'd be with his reality. The man is massive, but he's a gentle soul with the mind of a scholar trapped in a prison of irresistible compulsion and raw bestiality.

Wait. No. that's not at *all* what I mean. Holy crap did I just think 'bestiality?'

I blush so hard Garrett tilts his head at me. I mean, he's stuck suffering the whims of his animalistic side, the raw, umm, vampiric monster part of us. Even I have a hint of it—she comes out whenever someone hits me in the face with the sun. Only, Garrett must freak out like that randomly. Wow. How horrible. Helping him might destroy him (which is what the brothers were trying to do anyway) or help him escape the curse of his existence. Granted, Furies are pretty damn scary too, but getting wicked pissed off at the drop of a hat is a lot more tolerable than going full irrational monster.

Either result will protect tons of people he might accidentally kill in the future.

I can't say no. Especially if it'll only take like fifteen minutes.

"Okay." I stand. "I'll help."

23

THE EXPEDITION

*G*arrett leans back, both eyebrows up. I don't think he could've been more surprised if I erupted vomiting gold coins.

"I do have one question though. Do you have any way to know what the weather is going to be like in there? I can't take bright sunlight, only rainy days."

"We'll help." Cody stands.

"Yeah." Ben slides off the bed and pats me on the back. "We're already down here. Might as well."

"Guys. It's too dangerous for you."

Cody points at me. "You might not make it in the sun without help. We managed last time, right?"

Maybe their bravery comes from not wanting me to leave them in the company of a vampire nest. And, honestly, the forest didn't become dangerous until we opened the wrong portal. "All right."

We head back down the sloped floor into the secondary chamber.

Garrett gestures at the shelves. "Take whatever you need."

"How long is this trip, and where are we going?" I ask.

"Oh." Garrett biffs himself in the forehead. "Forgive me. Sometimes the simplest of things escapes my thoughts as they spend too much time high up in the clouds." He jogs back up the ramp to the bedroom.

Cody grabs more crossbow bolts. Ben straps on a belt with two canteens. I snag a backpack and stuff a bedroll in it along with a tent. Figure if we'd been gone a full twenty-four hours and only a few minutes passed in here, his estimate of fifteen minutes means we'll be camping a few times.

Garrett returns and hands me a map as well as an ordinary magnetic compass. "Nothing technological works in there."

"We kinda noticed that," says Cody.

I look the map over and take note of that giant waterfall I saw in the distance. Being able to fly should let me navigate by this map, assuming the positions of rivers and ridges are accurate.

"Oswald said the flower would be here." Garrett points at a small X drawn on the map near the top of the page. "The door opens to here." He points near the middle, bottom.

"Figures the target and entry point are as far away as possible on the map," says Cody.

Garrett laughs. "I have no reason to map beyond them in either direction. I could include a map for thousands of miles so the two points would appear to be right on top of each other, though such a map would not help you."

"Oh." Cody glances at the shelf. "Right."

Once we've stocked up, Garrett pulls the door open and we step inside again. This time, the portal doesn't close behind us.

"You're really going to stand there for days holding the door?" asks Ben.

"For me, it will be ten to fifteen minutes."

"So weird," mutters Cody.

I shoot up into the sky, take a quick survey of the area, and compare to the map. According to the old compass, we need to travel kinda southwest but more west than south. It shouldn't be *too* difficult to find.

"Oh." I drop back to the ground and approach the door. "Forgot a big question. What's this plant look like?"

Garrett hangs his head and sighs. "You see why I am so determined to free myself of this. It is a long-petaled flower that glows cyan blue. The interior is dark, and the shrub surrounding it has glistening red vines that appear bloody."

"I'm not sure if that's pretty or horrifying."

He shrugs. "Subjective based on the observer's experience."

I again feel awkward for assuming a man this big would be dumb. "Right. Okay. We'll be back as soon as we can."

This time, I lead the way, glancing at the compass every so often.

No one says a word for a while. Damn. I wish I had a way to tell time in here. In the short while we spent talking to Garrett, several days probably passed here. The sun was minutes from rising when we stepped out, and now it's dark again. But how long do we have before daybreak?

"Dude. I can't believe we're helping the vampire who wanted to eat me," mutters Ben.

"Well, he could've done a lot worse," I say. "I didn't want to make him angry. If something set him off, we would've had a real big problem. Even sitting around in his presence is potentially dangerous."

"Huh?" asks Cody.

"My mom once barged into my bedroom and let the sun in. I blacked out for a few seconds. One second, she's opening the door. The next, the door's shut and I'm surrounded in a haze of smoke. Mom said I growled at her like a cougar and my eyes glowed. I totally have no memory of it other than what I saw inside her head. If she'd come too close to me, I might have..." I choke up.

Cody rubs my back.

"It's like a panic attack or something, right?" asks Ben.

"Yeah." I sniffle. "Only with more blood. I think Beasts can do that randomly without warning, not only when they're roasting in surprise sunlight. For me, primal fear of destruction let it out. He could flip at any time and turn into a raging monster who can throw a car over a house."

"Are you guys really that strong?" Cody gawks.

"I'm not. Did you see the size of that guy? He's almost 150 years old. He probably could've knocked that damn troll out with one punch."

The boys laugh.

"Besides... if this only takes a few minutes, how could I say no?" I check the compass again. "That potion—wow did I really just say 'potion' and not mean something from a video game?"

"You did." Cody scratches at his head and yawns. "But we also killed a troll. Vampires are real, and evidently magic works."

I bite my lip, missing my normal life for the first sincere moment since, oh, a few days after I woke up as an undead. Being a vampire has grown on me. It's pretty damn cool. But ugh. This new reality of weird crap is going to take a *lot* of effort to get used to. Better yet, I'll try to ignore it's real as much as I can get away with... once we're out of here.

"Anyway, the thing he wants the flower for is either going to kill him or change his nature. Either way, he won't be a danger to people visiting this park. So, yeah. I had to help."

The brothers get into a debate about whether I'm 'lawful good' or 'chaotic good.' Both seem to think it's hilarious that a vampire would be either one of those. I vaguely remember that terminology from the character games Dad and Sierra like. Cody mentions me sneaking into the cave with him past a ranger, so that means I can't be 'lawful.' Ben doesn't think I'm chaotic or random enough.

I sigh. Great. I'm stuck with nerds. "Says the nerd," I mutter.

"Huh?" asks Ben. "Did you say something?

"No, just wondering how much time we have before sunrise."

"Watch is dead." Cody holds up his arm.

"Yeah. We kind of expected that." I poke him in the side.

We walk for a few hours without seeing anything alive other than plants. I'll take it.

"Cave," says Ben, pointing. "It's been a couple hours. The sun should be up kinda soon, right?"

Not too far off course to the right, a vast rock ridge at the top of a moderate incline spans for miles. A big crack near the bottom appears to be a cave entrance that should provide cover from the sun. I don't feel dawn approaching yet, but we *have* been walking long enough that taking advantage of a good hiding place is a much better idea than risking a fiery death on the off chance we could find another shelter an hour from now.

"Okay." I fly to grab a few apples, then follow the boys up the hill.

It's about a quarter mile out of our way, but the cave is wide and deep enough to keep me well away from any encroaching daylight. Best part? No bears.

The boys unroll their sleeping bags, wolf down an apple each, and sack out. While they probably got some sleep in that hut once they dragged me in out of the sun, they've still been up for a long time. Heck, I'm so worn out I'm almost ready to sleep and the sun's still down.

Also, this cave is severely lacking in amenities. Not even a single-pot serving of complimentary coffee. I roll out my sleeping bag, take my shoes and socks off, then stretch out. Even if I can't sleep until the sun's up, not having to deal with weird shit is a nice, relaxing break.

I WAKE TO AIR SMELLING OF RAIN MIXED WITH TEENAGE BOY AND A HINT of dirt.

The usual sluggishness that accompanies waking up doesn't sink its claws into me. No, that's not a vampire thing. That's a Sarah Wright thing. Sometimes when I was in grade school, my mom had to physically drag me out of bed in the morning. Not that I had a problem with school—other then them starting it at stupid o'clock in the morning. When I grew too big for her to carry, she threw cold water on my face. Around that time, she finally let me have coffee.

Sierra and I share that trait. Sophia though? She's one of those people who's so chipper in the morning you want to hold them face down in a plate of scrambled eggs so you can enjoy the silence.

The brothers both look like they could sleep for the next six hours.

I sit up and pull out the map Garrett gave me, taking an

approximate guess where we are along the rock cliff. Compared to the distance from the opening, I figure we're going to have to stop and shelter for the day one more time before we reach the grove. It's really tempting to fly there. No doubt I could make it there and back in the air. But it would be just my luck that something would happen to the brothers while I'm gone. Going alone would've been better. Maybe. The boys didn't seem too thrilled with the idea of staying at Garrett's without me there. Hell, as nice and educated as he is, *I* didn't really want to be there either. No fault of his, but he could go Tasmanian devil at any minute without warning.

The sad thought hits me that Beasts are likely responsible for the folkloric representation of vampires as hideous monsters and dangerous fiends, when it's quite possible they were also like Garrett. Geez. Talk about a total Jekyll and Hyde situation. No wonder he's willing to risk drinking something that could destroy him. Never did ask what he considered an 'acceptable risk.' It would say a lot about his mental state if that risk is fifty-fifty or worse.

Ugh. Poor guy.

Also, I might need another pair of hands at some point, but there isn't much a pair of normal boys are going to help me with. Well, other than staying out of the sun in an emergency. And we're already a day away from the portal. Without me and the map, they'd get lost. Wait, no they wouldn't. Ben's ring could lead the way back to the portal… not like they'd go anywhere near Garrett without me to protect them.

And if the time thing is right, what feels like three days out and three days back is only like fifteen minutes in reality. Okay fine. I walk.

I creep to the end of the cave and peer out at a gloomy, overcast day that could be eleven in the morning or six in the evening. My tendency to sleep later after an ass kicking makes me think it's closer to six, but there's enough light that I'm offline for now. Grumbling, I head back into the cave to put on my socks and sneakers before repacking my sleeping back.

The boys wake in about twenty minutes and do the whole

stretching, scratching, and walking outside to water the bushes thing. I pull the borrowed backpack on and wait for them to gather their sleeping bags, then head out.

We walk for a little over an hour until the burbling of a creek pulls the boys off course. Oh, yeah… right. Water. Normal people have to drink that stuff. I'm still kinda hungry, but it's mild. Two pints was a big meal. Plus I can't really feed again off these two for a couple months without hurting them.

Cody protests drinking right from the stream, not trusting the water to be free of microorganisms. Ben points out that we A) don't have anything to boil it with and B) are in an alternate dimension. I'm not entirely sure how he finds B comforting. This other world might have entirely new awful creepy-crawlies in the water. He adds a C, I drank their blood so they need to replenish liquids. Before they can make up their minds about drinking from the stream, the skies open up with a downpour.

That solves one problem and creates another.

Cody grabs a broad leaf from a nearby plant and makes a funnel out of it to drink rainwater. Ben follows suit. The rain soaks us to the skin pretty fast, but at least the boys aren't thirsty anymore. Ignoring the downpour, I march onward with the compass directing me. For now, the map stays safe out of the rain in the waterproof backpack.

I'm guessing Garrett didn't expect there to be much danger here or he wouldn't have bought 'deer hunter orange' backpacks. These things are visible from outer space. Granted, he also has a crossbow. Which makes me wonder how his, umm, 'Ghoul Team Six' died. Did they touch that archway and let the troll in? Can the troll open it from his side? Is there something else around here strong enough to smash people like that?

Fortunately, the forest is mostly the same. Flattish ground, trees, bushes. We don't encounter any real obstacles like cliffs or thorn walls or big rivers for several hours. The light doesn't change much, which pushes my initial guess at the time back from six to maybe three. I *really* hate not having a clock. How the hell did people cope with not knowing the time back in like medieval days? Though, I guess they didn't care as much since surprise sun-up wouldn't have killed them.

At least the rain stops.

We keep going, following the compass. Unless my sense of time is completely thrown off, it should be dark sometime soon.

A sudden, loud ripple of crackling erupts off to the left, somewhere between a Leprechaun army firing off a twenty-one gun salute and a giant breaking a bundle of small trees in half. The boys both drop down, crouched, as still as spooked deer. We all look toward the noise.

Motion draws my attention to a not-quite-humanoid figure made of leaves, vines, and brambles sliding from left to right maybe forty feet away. It somewhat resembles a man in a hooded cloak, only it's creeping forward like a snail without any obvious signs of a walking stride. Spots of dim green light hover near the 'head' end, suggesting eyes. It briefly angles its 'face' toward us, revealing six or seven of the glowing spots peeking out from a lattice of thorny tendrils. The 'head' is beyond mannequin simple, lacking any attempt to suggest a human nose or mouth.

"What the hell is that?" whispers Cody.

"A literal forest ranger," I mutter.

They glance at me.

"What? It's made out of forest and its… umm… ranging around."

"Is it dangerous?" whispers Ben.

I tilt my head at him. "Seriously? How would I know? I'm still not sure any of this is really happening. We're probably still all sitting in that cage having a dream together. We should avoid it. Run."

"No. Don't run," says Cody. "If it's predatory, running will make it come after us."

"You're not going to rip it apart?" asks Ben.

Shaking my head, I back away. "No. For one thing, the sun's still up. I'm basically a normal girl right now, and I don't want to die."

"We're not dreaming by the way." Cody also backs up. "People wake up from dreams when they pinch themselves. I think you got hurt worse than a pinch."

I shudder. If there's anything I never want to *ever* do again, it's wearing my own ass as a hat. "Yeah, just a little."

The plant creature stops sliding and turns toward us. Its green orb eyes brighten.

"Crap!" yells Ben. "It sees us."

'Backing away calmly' lasts only another four seconds. When the mound of vegetation glides straight at us, the boys scream and take off at a sprint. Fear gets the better of me. I scream as well and run.

Vines whip in the air behind us. Sharp *cracks* echo whenever it wraps one of its tendrils around a tree to pull itself forward even faster. A deep *whoosh* passes over my head and something brushes my hair. I shriek and pour on more speed, flailing my arms to keep balance in the mud. I may not have my 'powers' at the moment, but at least I don't have to worry about exhaustion. Day or not, I don't get tired.

This thing is pretty damn fast for a pile of weeds.

The afternoon's heavy rain has turned the forest floor into a slippery mess. Cody slips into a sitting slide for a few seconds before somehow managing to get back to his feet and keep running.

Ben goes down head first and tumbles, spinning. I swoop in and grab him by the backpack, hauling him upright and giving him a shove. Vines whip around me, mostly snagging my pack, pulling me toward the creature.

I shrug out of the straps, abandoning the backpack. A wooden tendril wraps around my right ankle two steps later. The creature yanks my leg out from under me, sending me over forward onto my chest—and a face full of mud. More vines grab my other leg and wrap around my body, pinning my arms to my chest. Another coils around my neck, squeezing.

Crap. I really hope this isn't going to turn into one of those creepy Japanese cartoons Ashley likes.

The creature lifts me off the ground and… holy shit it's huge. The 'head' is like twelve feet off the ground and wider than me. Eerie green light orbs behind the interwoven roots pulse with sentience, staring at me. Slick with rain, the creature's wood-and-leaf body glistens in the dim light. I try to force my arms away from my sides, but mortal strength isn't enough to budge these roots. I scream again, both terrified and furious. It swings me around in the air, adding more vines to hold me still. For a second, I'm nearly upside down and my wet hair flops over my face.

Ben runs over and grabs the vine squeezing my left calf, attacking it with a folding knife from his belt. Cody fires a crossbow bolt into the mass of leaves and vines about where its heart should be, but the bolt passes clear through it and comes out the other side without doing much of anything.

I squirm and struggle, but this thing is *way* too strong for me. My mind races with all sorts of nightmares from being trapped in a digestive sac to having acid sprayed on me while I'm tied up in vines.

Ben's knife severs the root holding my left leg.

A shriek like six inhuman voices screaming all at once radiates from the creature's 'head.' A mass of vines lash out at Ben, whipping more than grabbing. He guards his face with his shoulders and continues cutting at the root around my right ankle. A low-lying creeper vine slithers up beside him.

The tendril squeezing my neck prevents me from shouting a warning.

It grabs him, pinning his legs together at the shins, then drags him off his feet, hurling him sideways. He hits the ground with a muddy *splat* and rolls out of sight into the thick underbrush.

I reach up, trying to get a grip on the bundle of vines around my middle. Maybe this thing's like a python and it suffocates its prey to death. Sorry pal, you're going to be waiting a while for me to run out of air. Cody assaults it with a barrage of thrown rocks while dodging around trees to avoid reaching vines. The stones don't bother it at all.

Ben bursts out of the underbrush, charging at me. It grabs him again before he can run in close enough to cut anything, but he resists being thrown aside long enough to collapse the knife and toss it to me. I manage a clumsy catch in both hands while kicking my left leg at another vine trying to grab me. The creature hurls Ben into the weeds again.

It raises me up higher, like it's trying to hold food away from an annoying dog nipping at its legs. Cody slashes at it a few times with his knife. He can't reach me, so he slices and chops at random vines. I open the knife and start sawing at the bundle around my chest. It's a really damn good thing I don't need air. A vine whips out and wraps Cody's chest, picking him into the air, swinging him around once, and chucking him like a catapult stone out of sight into the woods.

Again, Ben comes charging out of the shrubs and hurls himself at the creature. He futilely pulls at the vines holding me. This time, the creature grabs him with roots around the chest and throat. His face goes purple-red in seconds. Pure panic radiates from his eyes as he loses the ability to breathe from a root squeezing around his neck.

I slice two vines around my midsection, loosening its hold. The bundle unfurls, allowing me to slip down. Unfortunately, I wind up hanging by the root around my neck and right ankle, while severed vines wave around above me, spewing sap like out of control hoses.

Oh, this is uncomfortable.

I cling to the root crushing my throat and hack at it with the knife. Somewhere above and to my left, Ben gurgles.

Cody runs out into view holding a burning branch up over his head. With a war cry, he charges at the creature and stabs his improvised torch into the mass of vegetation. The creature shrieks and hurls me to the ground. I land on my side and grab my throat, coughing. Cody raises his hands like he's pointing a gun at it, and a sudden burst of flames spreads inside the creature. Tendrils waving, it rushes off into the forest, leaving a trail of smoke.

"Hah!" shouts Cody. "Burn, bitch!"

Ben moans and drags himself out of the bushes.

"Ow," I deadpan, not bothering to get up. I think I'll just sit here and pluck inch-long thorns out of my neck.

"You okay?" asks Ben.

I take a deep breath, let it out, and sigh again. "Yeah. Just scared. I figured woodland survival would be a challenge, but didn't expect the forest would literally try to kill us."

Cody laughs and drags my backpack over to me.

Ben helps me up. "Seriously. You okay?"

"Yeah." I brush leaf bits off my sweatshirt, then pull my backpack on. "We're off course. I can't fly to check the map yet, so let's just keep going in the right direction."

"What if that thing comes back?" asks Ben.

"It won't." Cody smiles. "And if it does, we burn it again."

"How'd you start a fire?" I ask. "Rubbing two sticks together or something? Everything's soaked from the rain."

He pats a side pouch on his backpack. "Matches… and lighter fluid."

24

THE SANGUINE GROVE

*O*nce the sun finally sets, I launch myself up past the tree canopy for an aerial view of our surroundings.

We haven't veered *too* much off course. Nothing a slight adjustment won't fix. After that damn root creature, I'm even more tempted to tell the boys to wait here and just fly to the end. But... it would be easy to lose them in the thick forest. I could spend more time circling around hunting for them than it would take us to simply walk there and back. Not like the boys have flare guns.

Damn.

I snag four apples, two for now, two for the morning, on my way down.

"I'm so damn sick of apples," says Ben.

Cody shrugs. "You never really liked them. And in here, we don't have much choice."

"Yeah. I hate always eating the same thing over and over." Ben bites his apple contemptuously.

They glance at me.

"Never really thought about it like that," said Ben. "Sorry. That's gotta suck."

Cody groans and throws a piece of apple at him. "That was horrible."

"What?" Ben blinks. "Oh. Hah. Yeah."

"It's not *too* bad. I can still eat normal food for the taste, and blood has different flavors to me."

"How's that work?" asks Cody. "Different flavors?"

As we walk, I ramble about how my perception of the person I bite makes me think the blood tastes like different things.

"What did we taste like?" asks Ben.

"French fries and pizza."

"Dude. Mom said you ate so much pizza you were going to turn into one." Cody chuckles.

"So does it count as cannibalism for me to eat pizza now?" Ben scratches his head.

"Guys, he doesn't actually taste like that. It's all in my head."

We walk for hours. The boys ask me random questions about being a vampire, and mostly I'm honest with them. Other than the sun problem, my particular type of vampirism isn't too much different from normal life. I stray into the topic of being eighteen forever and watching my family and friends grow old around me. Cody thinks it's awesome I won't get old, though Ben inherits my somber mood at the idea I'll eventually be alone. I guess I could adopt new people at some point. People who have cats or dogs are often emotionally destroyed when the pet dies, but they almost always get another one knowing what'll happen again.

I'm not sure if I'll reveal myself to any nieces or nephews, assuming any of my siblings have kids. Ugh. That's so bizarre to think about now. Would they tell their spouses that I'm the *younger* sister if we ever met? By the time (if) any of my siblings marry, they'll look older than I do.

Bah. Forget it. I'm eighteen for real. I need to start acting like it. Anything further away than an hour in the future isn't worth thinking about.

The boys change topics and start discussing things from their hometown: weird neighbors, school friends, teachers, and so on. I get the feeling they're not exactly in the 'popular crowd.' Not that I'm one to talk. Since I didn't fit neatly into any predefined social clique, I fell through the cracks and became part of the scenery. Whenever anyone took a picture of the jocks, the goths, or the geeks, I'd be one of the blurry figures walking by in the background no one really noticed. At least until Scott killed me. Then people realized I'd been there for four years. You know I *still* have people occasionally posting memorial stuff on my Facebook wall, like 'sorry you died, person I never even knew existed.'

I'm so focused on navigating and trying not to worry about everything that might happen over the next sixty years that a warning tingle catches me off guard.

"Crap," I say, looking up. "The sun's coming."

"There's nothing here but trees," says Cody.

"Hang on." I fly up over the treetops, cringing at the bluing in the sky to the north. A quick scan of our surroundings reveals nothing even close to shelter. Wait. *North?* The sun's coming up in the *north?* Crap. We really *are* somewhere else. I drop back to the ground and wrap my arms around myself. Dammit. I should've done this myself. Should've flown. "Shit, you guys. There's nowhere to go."

Ben pulls off his jacket. "Worked once."

"What are the odds we'll find another cabin?" asks Cody. A sudden look of inspiration comes over him and he shrugs off his backpack. "Idea."

"I don't think I'm going to fit in the backpack," I mutter. "And the tent material is too thin to block sunlight."

Cody rummages and pulls out a collapsible shovel. "Not what I'm thinking. Sunlight can't penetrate dirt."

My mouth hangs open. "Are you seriously suggesting burying me? That's like total nightmare fuel."

"More than roasting in the sunlight?" asks Cody.

I fidget.

"And you technically *are* dead. Sorry." He scratches his head.

"I dunno, man," says Ben.

"Look... we just dig out a shallow hole. She lies down in it, we cover her with one of the tents and some dirt. Not deep enough that she can't sit up and get out herself. I'm not saying we *bury* her way down."

I chuckle. "You couldn't dig a proper grave in the time we have with that little thing anyway."

"Maybe you should do it?" asks Cody. "You're super strong and don't get tired."

"Dude." Ben stares at him. "You can't ask her to dig her own grave. That's like totally dark."

"It's not a grave. It's a shelter. Graves are one-way trips. This is temporary." I walk over to the trunk of a thick tree, hoping the branches will add some protection from the light. "Right here works."

Between my claws and Cody's shovel, we hollow out a roughly one-foot-deep pit just big enough for me to lay down in. This is *so* messed up. The boys arrange one of the bright orange tents over me like a blanket, then start tossing dirt on top of it.

"Guys, watch for smoke, okay? If I start roasting, please do something."

"Sure. We got'cha covered," says Ben.

"Dude." Cody laughs. "Wrong."

I might've been scared when that plant thing chased me, but that really has nothing on being buried alive. Holy shit this is terrifying. I can't imagine being buried 'for real' like six feet down, or shut inside a coffin. The more dirt that lands on top of me, the closer I get to a panic attack—but paradoxically, the less anxious I am about the sun.

"Dude, what's that for?" asks Cody. "Dead leaves aren't going to help."

"Camouflage," says Ben.

"From what? There are no people here."

"Umm. Whatever."

I imagine the ground is damp and cold. Well, I don't have to imagine the damp part. I'm fully aware of that. One thing I learned from camping as a kid was to avoid sleeping in direct contact with the earth since it sucks heat out of you. What I'm doing now is the exact *opposite* of that wisdom. To distract myself from the sensation of being buried, I picture Ashley's bedroom and all the unicorns.

No, I'm safe at home in bed. Not lying in a shallow grave in some alternate dimension.

A leaden sensation rolls over me—and disappears as fast as it came on.

Okay, weird.

Did I sleep and wake up?

"Guys?" I ask.

No answer.

Damn. Do I risk moving and potentially incinerating myself? This stirs up a very important yet esoteric question in my mind. Would an Innocent vampire's habit of waking up during the day continue whilst said Innocent lay in a shallow grave where a small amount of motion would trigger imminent foomage? I *really* don't like the idea of being stuck awake and buried not-quite-alive with nowhere to go until the sun sets. I even have to keep my head rotated to the side or the tent mashes my nose in.

"Guys?" I yell.

"Yo?" asks a bleary Cody.

"Did I sleep?"

"How should I know? You're underground."

I growl. "No, dork. I mean… is it still only a few minutes after you covered me, or have hours passed?"

"Oh." He coughs and yawns. "Hours passed. Yeah you probably fell asleep and woke up."

"How is it out there?"

"Still gloomy."

"Gonna test a finger. Help me out if I catch fire?"

Footsteps crunch closer to my head. "Yeah. No problem." Cody yawns again.

I work a hand out from under the tent and poke one finger into the air. No pain, so I sit up. Air is awesome even though I don't need it. My stomach grumbles. I need blood from this day-trekking, but I can't risk taking any more from the boys. They're already down a little over a pint each.

"Guys, I'm getting a little hungry again but I can't feed from you. Our trip back might need to take longer. I gotta save energy, so I should avoid daylight as much as possible. It takes a *lot* out of me to tolerate sunlight."

Cody picks up the shovel again. "Okay."

"Not the grave..." I hold up a hand. "I'll risk it now, but if we find a shelter, I'm gonna go for it."

"Okay."

Ben yawns and forces himself up.

I stand and dust myself off before folding the tent up and stuffing it in the backpack.

They choke down apples while walking, and drink from the canteens they brought.

"Why were you about to risk stream water when you have water already?" I ask.

"Rationing," says Cody, like it's the most obvious thing. "It doesn't make sense to use up limited supplies when there's a ready source available."

"Even if it'll make you sick?"

"We're not on earth anymore. This place might not even *have* microbes." Ben tilts the canteen back, gulping down several mouthfuls.

"It's got trees, rabbits, plants... it has to have microbes," I say.

"Well, it definitely does now." Cody wags his eyebrows.

Ugh. Boys and poop humor. I don't want to know what they used for TP. Another check mark in the 'it's awesome to be a vampire' column for me. I never have to worry about an embarrassing bathroom situation cropping up while stranded in a parallel dimension again.

Less than an hour after we resume walking, we find a huge burrow big enough to walk into that appears to be the work of a large animal. A short tunnel leads into a subterranean chamber with a scattering of leaves and twigs on the ground. It's fortunately empty, and provides a welcome break from resisting the sun.

The boys take the opportunity to sleep some more, spending a few minutes insincerely complaining about their day-night cycle going to hell. I hate wasting time like this, but nothing burns my energy faster than resisting sunlight. With zero sun exposure and no supernatural ass kickings, I can go about a month on a single feeding. Even a short period of tolerating sunlight makes me hungry every day.

To avoid boredom, I doze off as well. I *can* sleep during the day if I want to, and manage to catch a few hours' worth.

Once the sun sets, we resume our trip after a quick flight to compare surroundings to the map. I think we're going to find this grove pretty soon based on where I think we are. Again with the compass out, I take the lead and we walk onward. This part of the forest has slightly different trees, not as tall, with twisty trunks and no apples. The boys' stomachs protest in earnest, though they don't say anything.

A few hours after we leave the burrow, a patch of glowing pale blue light becomes visible in the distance. Hoping that's what we're here for, I alter course slightly to the left. We soon approach a ring of dark blue leaves and blood-red vines with four-inch thorns woven together into a giant wreath. The top is as tall as the troll, and it's way too thick to even consider trying to climb through it.

I pop up off the ground to check it out from the air. It's not a ring, more of a C. A gap about a third the way around to the right opens to the clearing in the center. The same shiny bright-red thorny vines connect the outer wreath to a big flowering shrub in the middle, like spokes to a wheel, only they're as thick as pipes. An interconnected 'cage' of vines forms a dome over the center. I could probably force my way in, but I'd tear myself to bits on the thorns.

Strong cyan light glows from multiple flowers on the central plant. They kinda resemble lilies. Two long petals stretch downward and to either side while a shorter one extends upward. The petals appear to be made out of pure energy, glowing an iridescent moon-blue at the edges with a strip of dark non-glowing violet down the middle. The inner bits are also deep purple.

"That's it!" I land between the brothers. "We're almost done. Just gotta pick one and head back."

They follow me around to the opening. The overhead dome forms a ceiling over the gap in the outer wreath—which is at least twelve feet thick—making it feel like a corridor. Smaller pink and white flowers nest here and there in the indigo leaves, like babies hiding behind the thorns lest something evil grab them. Dark crimson grass covers the clearing inside between the giant red vine 'spokes.' Thorns as big as daggers jut out along the length, progressively longer toward the main plant in the middle. Something tells me this entire thing is one gigantic plant.

As soon as I pass the inner edge of the wreath, I become aware of a pleasant floral smell that, in defiance of all logic, isn't noticeable outside the middle area. A sense of eeriness pervades the place, heightening my already strong urge to go the hell home.

I approach the central bush, eyeing one of the glowing flowers.

"Umm," says Cody.

Two soft *thumps* come from behind me.

I pause and look back.

The boys lay flat on their faces, out cold.

"What the heck?" I hurry over and shake them. "Guys... What happened?"

Neither of them move.

Damn. What now? I check them over for stingers, unable to explain why they both lost consciousness at the same time.

Cracking and snapping comes from the main bush. I spin toward the noise, leaning back in surprise as a thin, genderless figure made of wood emerges from the dark blue leaves. The creature has a generally humanoid shape with branches for arms and legs, though it's as thin as a telephone pole, and a few inches shorter than me. Well, there's a first. For once, I'm taller than the monster.

Two almond-shaped spots of red light on its bulb-shaped head approximate eyes. After a few seconds of blank staring, the eye-spots narrow at me. Though it lacks any sort of mouth, a male voice fills the air. "How is it that you remain awake? How have the aromatic nectars not lulled you to sleep?"

"I have a really high metabolism. And my sister is like crazy into scented candles. I've built up a tolerance."

The wood-thing takes a step toward me, reaching his three-fingered branch hand out to point. "You have come to steal a fey amaranth."

"Actually, I was hoping you had some perennials. My mom really likes Hibiscus."

He stands there silent. Not like the round blob of wood he's got for a face can convey any emotional expression.

"Yes, I'm here for a fey amaranth. Let me guess, you're going to tell me to go kill 300 wild boars for you before I can take one?"

"I do not understand, human."

"Forget it. You're like some guardian of the bush or something, right?"

"I am a forest spirit. This is my home. I offer an exchange. You may take one of my flowers in exchange for them." He points at the boys.

"Umm. No. One, they're not mine to give away, two, they're people."

The wood creature's arm falls to his side with a faint crackle of trampled twigs. "Foolish human. What do you think those flowers are?"

"Umm. Fey amaranths?"

He tilts backward, body faintly shaking as deep male laughter surrounds me from no apparent source. "Those flowers are grown from former fools."

I gasp. The more I look at my surroundings, the more I have the sense those vines are *blood* red for a good reason. Here and there in the grass, I make out the shapes of human bones peeking up. "Whoa. The flowers are made from dead people?"

"You would use the term souls." He spreads his arms out to the sides. "You may take one amaranth in exchange for a soul to replace it, plus one."

"So… you steal souls?"

"It is not stealing to claim what fools forfeit. By entering this grove, you have surrendered. Be appreciative you are able to leave. Most cannot. Most never wake."

I cringe inwardly at the thought of harvesting someone's soul to power a potion. That certainly explains why not every vampire tries to change their bloodline. Still, who or whatever became those flowers is already dead, and bringing one to Garrett will potentially save hundreds of lives.

"I can't give you the boys."

He bows his bulb head. "Alas. My fascination with your lack of sleep wanes. As you refuse to be reasonable, I shall have to claim all three of you." He lunges at me, grabbing for my arm with long, twig like fingers. I lean to the right, avoiding his grip, and pound him square in the face. My punch knocks him flat and sliding—and breaks every bone in my hand.

The wood man sails headfirst into one of the spoke roots with a dull *thud*, flipping up and over it.

"Ow. Son of a bitch." I shake my hand out as the bones re-knit.

Incoherent babbling in the wood creature's voice emanates from everywhere. He waves his arms around like he can't quite figure out how to stand back up. Having little interest in fighting this thing, I dash forward and flick a claw at the stem of the nearest fey amaranth, slicing it off as close to the base as possible.

"Stop!" shouts the wood man, sitting up.

I clamp the stem in my teeth and run, grabbing the brothers by their backpacks and dashing out of the grove, dragging them, their arms and legs flopping around.

The wood creature chases, but only to the edge of the wreath. His branchy fingers swipe at me, but I'm way too fast for him. I stop after about twenty yards and look back. Wood Man glares at me from the wreath for a moment, then storms back inside, disappearing into the bush.

Okay, now I have questions.

Does Garrett know what these flowers are?

Did he deliberately send multiple ghouls in here expecting to make a trade?

Would ghouls have been able to resist the sleeping gas in there?

Did Garrett fail to warn us of that and let the boys go expecting I'd have to broker them for a flower? Or did he not know any of this?

I look down at two *very* unconscious teenage boys.

"Shit. This is *not* what Mom meant by boys being baggage!"

25

WILD DREAMS

*W*ell, I suppose it's a simple matter of waiting for the poison fumes to wear off, right?

Still holding the fey amaranth stem in my teeth, I drag the boys along at a jog, hurrying back to the sunken burrow. Once inside, I take their backpacks off and lay them beside each other. I'm no doctor, but as far as I can tell, they're still alive, breathing normally, and their heart rates sound fine.

Considering the two-ish hours it took to go from here to the grove, and back here, I don't have enough night left to get far before sunrise. I'm also quite in need of a snack, so I can't afford sun exposure.

Oh well. May as well make myself comfortable. I remove my sneakers, peel my soaked socks off, and drape them over the backpack. My clothes have mostly dried out by now, but it will be days before my sneakers recover from that downpour.

The fey amaranth glows from where I left it on the ground. It hasn't dimmed at all, nor does it look withered. Then again, no flower really withers within two hours of being picked. It's eerie, but I have the strangest feeling it's looking at me. When I try to 'mind read' it, there's no connection at all, so I disregard the odd feeling as my overactive imagination. It might've consumed 'soul energy' to create that flower, but I don't think it's a 'trapped soul' that still has any sort of awareness.

I take the blanket out of my backpack, wrap the flower as carefully as I can, and ease it back inside. That done, I set up my sleeping bag and sack out.

CONSCIOUSNESS RETURNS THE NEXT AFTERNOON.

Worry about my family comes out of nowhere, but I hold it back by chanting 'fifteen minutes' to myself over and over for a while. The least I can do for them is to handle this weird shit myself and leave them out of it. If they remain clueless that anything bizarre happened during our vacation, I'll consider it a win. And I swear, this is the last time I complain about a vacation being boring. How could I have known the universe listens to me now?

I force myself up and stretch. Socks are dry but sneakers are still damp inside. Ugh. If I didn't have a three-day hike, I'd say screw it and go barefoot. Despite knowing my feet would heal in seconds from stepping on anything sharp, it still hurts. So, gritting my teeth, I suffer the spine-wiggling sensation of putting on cold, wet sneakers. The only feeling worse than that is putting a cold, wet swimsuit bottom back on. No point re-soaking the socks, so I stuff them in my pocket.

The boys are still out cold. Prodding and shaking doesn't do any good.

I peel open Cody's eyes with my thumbs and dive into his mind, but it's blank. I've only seen a head that empty once before. No, I'm not going to say Bree Swanson. I'm thinking more of Scott whenever one of his sportsball teams was on TV.

"Okay, that's really messed up. There's nothing going on in there at all." I check Ben, and he's the same. "Whatever they breathed in like turned them *off*. They're not even dreaming."

They're still both breathing, heartbeat seems okay.

I edge up to the tunnel and peer out. It's kinda bright, but not instant-death sun.

A few minutes pass as I stand there looking back and forth between the way out and the brothers. *Are* they going to wake up or is that permanent? Could they get worse? Dammit. Grr. I can't sit around.

"Sorry guys," I say to my dry socks, before putting them on. "Gotta cover my ankles."

I take the blanket from Cody's pack and set it aside before borrowing his socks for mittens. I pull Ben's coat off to take his shirt, which I wrap around my head, covering everything except for a narrow eye-slit. I put his coat back on him, drag the brothers onto the floor, and strap them into their backpacks. After donning my pack, I wrap myself in the blanket so I'm basically a Pac Man ghost, and grab their packs.

About halfway up the exit tunnel, the sun hits me... and the boys' weight drags me over backward, sliding back into the room. Grr. As a mortal, I'm nowhere near strong enough to drag them both at once. I could probably carry either one of them without a backpack, though it wouldn't be fun. And there's no way I can carry both without my vampiric strength. I can't even drag them both in 'normal mode.'

"Dammit! We're stuck here." I slouch. "Well... I tried."

I put all clothing back where it belongs and hang my socks up again to dry. Since I'm going to be here until dark, I might as well leave my sneakers off so they air out, too. At least I'm saving energy and won't make myself famished. Hours of mind-numbing boredom drag by.

"Whoa," says Cody in a drawn-out, sleepy voice. Seconds later, he erupts in laughter.

"You're awake!" I yell, leaping to my feet.

"Pickles," says Ben.

"What?" I ask.

"The stars are on fire," mutters Cody.

"No, the marshmallows are rebelling." Ben points at the ceiling. "King Peep is going down."

I lean over and grasp his cheeks, making him look at me. Junior year, Ashley got some weed and *totally* overdid it. She couldn't even stand. Cody looks twice as high as she'd been that night. One of Scott's friends once had something he called Khadafy Weed, basically pot mixed with LSD. No, I didn't try it, but these two look like they stole the entire stash.

"Girl," says Cody. He tries to point at me, but sticks his finger up my nose.

"Gah!" I jump back.

Ben starts laughing.

"Ugh." I sit back down on the floor. "At least you guys are awake… sorta."

They proceed to babble random nonsense and make strange noises for the next few hours. Ben tries swimming in place. Cody makes popping noises like a fish trying to breathe air before discovering he has fingers and staring at them in total awe, mystified at how he can move them by mental command.

By the time it's become dim enough outside that I can tolerate it without mummifying myself, they've tamed down to random giggles and a thick mental fog. Whenever I try talking to them, they react a few seconds late. That beats unconscious dead weight. DMV sloths I can work with.

I pull my sneakers back on without socks since they're still a bit squishy inside, then put the backpacks on the boys like I'm dressing toddlers. Ben complains that the walls are melting after I pull him upright. Cody screams, staring at his feet.

"What's wrong?" I ask.

He keeps screaming.

I dive into his head. He sees himself sinking into the floor, the stone melting and tentacles coming up to grab him. Ugh. To save time, I give them both a mental command to follow me and ignore anything weird. They stumble along as I herd them out the tunnel into the woods. Even the almost-twilight gloom makes me hungry as hell, but I am so *done* with this place it's not even funny. Sheer determination to go home keeps my growling stomach quiet.

The boys stop laughing randomly after a while, and we walk in silence through the night. By the time sunrise feels imminent, they've returned to their relatively normal—though foggy and sluggish—selves. Ben raises his arm and points while emitting a zombie-like moan.

"What?" I ask, for a second almost hoping it's another troll. Disgusting as it tasted, I'd still force myself to drink that blood.

"Hut."

"Oh." Yeah, the sky's bluing again. I veer to the right and climb a bit of a hill to the same decrepit shack the boys took me to the first time the sun snuck up on me in here. Good enough.

After collecting six giant apples, we hurry inside before the sun peeks over the forest canopy. Each boy takes an apple and savages it like they haven't eaten in days.

"What happened?" asks Cody past a full mouth. "I think I blacked out."

"Me too," says Ben. "I remember going into that place with the glowing flowers, then we're walking in the woods and everything is hazy and weird."

"That plant gives off some kinda sleeping gas. Both of you fainted in seconds of walking into the middle part. Some creature came out of it and wanted to take your souls. I think people who go in there usually, umm, don't get back up."

They stare at me.

I start explaining everything in greater detail, but the sun sneaks up on me.

When I regain consciousness, I'm on the cot with a blanket over me. Like *all* the way over me, covering my face, too. Lead in my bones tells me the sun's in a pissy mood. I lay there with no desire to move for some time. The door clatters open, blasting me with hellfire. Fortunately, the blanket keeps the flames to a minimum.

"Ow," I deadpan.

"Don't sit up!" says Ben.

"Yeah, kinda got that feeling from the smoke. It's bright."

Cody laughs. "Nah. Ben's only wearing his briefs. We just cleaned up in the stream."

"You're in your underwear, too."

"Yeah, but I'm not worried my girlfriend's going to see how skinny I am."

"She's not my girlfriend."

"Then why are you glowing red?"

"Stuff it, Cody."

I chuckle under my breath. Rustling and rummaging accompanies them getting dressed. Since the sun is brutal today, I throw myself back into not-dreaming. A hand jostles me awake in what feels like seconds.

"Sun's going down," says Cody.

"Cool." I pull the blanket off my face and sit up. It's dark enough inside the hut with the door closed to qualify as night... and my sneakers are missing. "Shoes?"

"Oh. Put 'em out in the sun for you so they dry." Cody stands. "I'll get 'em." He goes outside and returns a moment later with my sneakers, which feel mostly dry.

"Cool. Thanks." I dust my soles off, then slip the sneakers on. "You guys ready to get the hell out of here?"

"You know it," says Ben, holding up his left hand to show off his glowing ring. "We're close enough to detect the portal."

A six-ish hour walk brings us to the small clearing where Garrett stands in the portal waiting for us. Seeing that doorway kills all my worries and makes the most pressing matter on my mind a long, hot shower. I don't care if I have to share the tiny bathroom with all three of my siblings at once, a shower is happening the instant I'm back at the RV. I've had enough 'roughing it' for a century.

Garrett watches us from inside the door, his expression one of astonished bewilderment... like he saw a guy dressed as Darth Vader playing the bagpipes while riding a unicycle.

I step through the portal and bask in the stale fragrance of the caverns. Ahh... reality. Normality. Sanity... or some pretend combination thereof. At least the trolls here only exist on the Internet. "Hey. Why the face?"

"It was most bizarre watching the three of you walk out of the forest as if on fast-forwarded video. You appeared to cover several miles in seconds."

"Oh. Yeah. I can see why that would be weird."

Garrett grasps me by the shoulders, making me feel super tiny. "Did you find it?"

"Yeah. Relax. I have it." I shrug off the backpack as the boys step in. "How much do you know about the fey amaranth?"

He scratches his head. "Only that it exists and there's a grove." I can't see into his head, but his demeanor seems genuine. "Why?"

"Ghouls wouldn't have worked." I unpack the flower and explain about my encounter with the wood man.

"Oh." He turns toward the brothers. "I am truly sorry that you faced such a risk."

They unload their backpacks and stick everything on the shelves.

"No problem," says Ben, not looking at him.

"Here." I hold up the glowing flower.

Garrett takes it in both hands, as awestruck as a small boy meeting Santa Claus. "It's magnificent. Far more beautiful than I ever imagined." He sighs. "But, this is a soul?"

"I don't know if it *is* a soul or only made from one. Either way, the person is dead. You might as well use it. Not making that potion won't change what happened. And I picked it, so the thing might wither and fade anyway."

"Knowing the true cost of this fills me with regret, but you raise a valid point." He clutches the stem. "I shall not waste this opportunity you have provided. You have my deepest thanks."

"No problem. We can find our way out."

Garrett nods.

The three of us walk gingerly behind him as he returns to his bedroom. The instant he's no longer between us and the way out, I scurry up to a brisk trot. I'm sure he's painfully aware that we all want to be away from him as fast as possible in case has an 'episode,' but he shows no reaction. Being back in the real world gives the boys a second wind.

It's still the middle of the night here, so the cavern lights are off. As much as I want to race to the top, I force myself to stay with them as they're navigating by one flashlight. According to my—yay!—once again working iPhone, it's 2:53 a.m. by the time we climb all the way back to the cave entrance.

I take the flashlight from Cody and return it to the bewildered park ranger who's still standing near the entrance. He's kind enough to donate a pint and a half or so of blood that tastes like trail mix.

The brothers stand there watching me feed with raised eyebrows.

Hmm. Should I make them forget everything? Honestly, the amount of time they've spent knowing I'm a vampire—seven days or so—would be really hard for me to eradicate. Aurélie could do it, but I'm not about to drag these two to Washington. Screw it. I'm quite sure they're well beyond wanting to 'destroy me.' Besides, people already consider them 'the weird brothers,' and if they told anyone they went with a vampire girl into an alternate dimension at the bottom of a cavern where we fought a troll-like thing, who would believe them?

They'd wind up in a mental hospital.

Once I finish feeding, I nod for the boys to follow and hurry down the trail away from the caverns. "Okay. So… things."

"Umm, is this where you make us forget everything?" asks Ben.

"Well, I was thinking about that. We spent like a week in there. I'm still new at this and I don't know if I can erase so much time, saving each other's lives more than once, and everything. Besides. I trust you guys. You're both smart enough to not want to spend the bulk of your adulthood in a mental facility."

They laugh.

"No, shit," mutters Cody. "No one, not even Mom, would believe that happened."

"I'm still not entirely sure we didn't just spend an hour on the floor of Garrett's cave while he messed with our heads to make us *think* we experienced another world." I sigh.

"Why would he do that?" asks Cody.

"I dunno. Why do 'eccentric' old people do anything bizarre."

"Yeah." Ben nods. "Your secret's safe. Thanks for saving my ass."

I smile. "Thanks for saving mine."

We share a brief group hug before splitting off to our respective RVs. I'm so worn out and grateful to be back here in one piece—without my family knowing anything happened—that I stroll right into the main bedroom and peel off my disgusting clothes in front of my sleeping parents. Besides, if they sit up and see me standing there naked, they will forget it happened.

I grab a towel, wrap myself in it, snag a long T-shirt, and duck into the bathroom.

The shower is fawesome. For the first few minutes, the water rolling off me is so black I feel like a melting licorice popsicle. Sierra's first shower in this thing took about twenty minutes, so I figure that's my time limit. I enjoy the first five just standing there basking in the water before reaching for the soap and lathering up.

Rattling comes from the door.

"Occupied," I say.

More rattling.

"I'm in the shower," I call, a little louder.

Silence. I resume soaping up.

Click.

Sam barges in, tosses a screwdriver in the sink, and proceeds to drop his PJ pants and sit on the toilet. I about shriek and face the corner of the shower, my back to him with both hands over my rear end. Argh! Little brothers. I can't even enjoy a shower at four in the morning! I'm not sure if I should be embarrassed or furious at the imminent stench he's going to trap me with.

Well, I don't have to breathe, so maybe that's not *too* much of a problem.

I bonk my head into the corner of the shower stall repetitively, grumbling at wasting water time. He better not still do this to me when he's older. I peek over my shoulder. Through the foggy sliding glass, I can sorta make out his blurry shape on the bowl, slumped forward like he's asleep. Wow, I've heard of sleepwalking before but sleep-pooping?

"Sam, you okay?" I ask.

"Pooping," he mutters.

"Are you awake?"

"Yeah, but tired. Sorry. Couldn't hold it. I'm not looking. Eyes are closed."

I resume washing myself but still keep my back to the room. It won't be long before he's grown up. He'll eventually be an old man... and then be gone. As awkward and irritating as nine-year-old Sam can be, maybe I should treasure these moments while they last. If this happened to Ashley or Michelle (not that either of them have a little brother with a weak concept of personal space) I'd find it hilarious.

Really, all I can do is laugh at the situation.

At least until I can't breathe.

"Good grief Sam, what did you eat?"

He chuckles, proud of himself.

Ugh. Boys.

CATCHING UP

The next afternoon, I awake in bed, safe within my sanctuary at the back end of the RV.

General lethargy is a good indication that the sun's in hell mode again today, but after six full days of walking, I'm *totally* fine with being trapped in bed. My iPhone says it's 4:02 p.m. Hmm. Slept in a little. Not surprising given the week I had. What is surprising, however, is the lack of pain. Still, I don't recommend Troll Chiropractic.

I wonder how my friends and Hunter are doing back home. Adding an extra seven days to this vacation that didn't change the calendar date is a bizarre sensation and it makes me want to hop in the driver's seat and take us home right now. Except for that whole dying a fiery death issue.

A movie while lounging in bed is more like it for vacation. No more supernatural weirdness please. I'm off duty.

"Sarah?" asks Mom, with a knock at the door, around 5:30. "Are you awake?"

"Yeah." I pause the movie. "What's up?"

"If you're hungry, there's a really annoying woman two spaces over who keeps trying to sell me a subscription to this health shake powder stuff."

I laugh.

"Would you mind asking her to forget we exist?"

"Sure thing, Mom. Let me know when the sun's in a better mood."

"Okay, hon. It is a bit hot today. We went to the caverns again. The kids are worn out."

I wince, thinking of my sisters and brothers near a Beast. Then again, he can't wake during the day, cave or not. "Cool."

"Okay. Gonna get started on dinner. I'd ask if you want to help, but it's too damn bright."

"Thanks for the warning," I say.

A movie and a half carries me to evening, when it's safe for me to leave the bedroom. After a week stuck in the same T-shirt and jeans, I pull a Sophia and put on a sundress before heading out barefoot. Mom and Dad recline in the shade under the awning, watching the littles run around with the Frisbee. The remains of dinner litter the small folding table, looks like grilled chicken with something green.

"That's cute," says Mom. "I didn't think you still had dresses."

"Did you smuggle a surgeon into the bedroom to remove those jeans?" asks Dad.

"Ha. Ha."

"Careful flying in that, dear," says Dad. "Anyone could look right up and see your underwear."

I shrug. "No they can't. I'm not wearing any."

Dad sputters his tea all over his chest. Mom blinks at me.

"Gotcha. I'm teasing by the way. And trust me, I don't fly in dresses... or overly loose sweat pants. Already made that mistake once. So where's the health nut I need to erase?"

Mom points at a smaller RV two spaces over where a late-twenties woman with dark hair tends to three sub-five-year-olds in a kiddie pool.

"Oh, seriously? You want me to bite a soccer mom? Ugh. She's going to taste like peach green tea."

The parents laugh.

"At least get her to stop trying to give me sign up forms," mutters Mom.

"You okay, hon?" Dad brushes tea off his shirt and looks up at me. "Kinda making me think you're either exhausted or in a weird mood."

"Just had a really crazy dream of walking in the woods. Feels like I spent a whole week marching cross country. Trying to convince my brain it happened in a dream, not for real." Hopefully that's close enough to the truth not to trip Mom's lie detector. I never have been a good liar. Too guilty too fast. Though, this half-truth is for *their* benefit, not mine, so I'm not guilty at all. And, maybe if I keep telling myself that magical portals into other realms didn't really happen, I'll eventually forget it.

"Sare!" shouts Sierra, after winging the Frisbee at me.

I catch it. "Looks like I'm being paged." I hurry out to the field and toss the thing back to Sierra, making her run a bit to catch it.

We play Frisbee until it gets too dark to see it flying. I take the opportunity to go say hello to the young mother. She's super excited about these 'healthy' nutrient shakes. While I don't bite her, I do implant a notion that she doesn't need to talk to my parents about buying stuff again.

That done, I take the littles for a walk around the campground to spend some outdoor time with them.

An hour or so later, we're all done with walking around.

We return to the RV and hang out, talking about their third trip to the caves. Once the kids are asleep and the parents retreat to the bedroom for some movie time, I head outside (having added yoga pants under my dress) and fly a couple miles west to a small town. From the air, it kinda looks like someone's game of *Civilization*. The downtown area is almost entirely made up of neat square blocks arranged in long rows from east to west. A few signs tell me the town's called Whitehall, and it doesn't take me long to find a snack—a lone figure wandering around a football field at the northern edge of the built-up area. Houses and other buildings continue for some miles, though much more spread out.

Turns out, it's Whitehall High School, and I just ate the groundskeeper.

He'll be fine. Though I should probably send him to the hospital to get checked out. His blood tasted like cheap frozen pizza. Must be my association with high school cafeteria food.

Anyway, being in town offers a certain particular advantage I was hoping for: cellular signal. I stroll around the field beside the school, enjoying the feel of grass between my toes, and start off a barrage of texts to Ashley, Michelle, and Hunter.

Basically, I tell them I'm fine, all is normal, and we'll be back in a few days. Sibs are good, though Sierra is clearly ready to go home. Camping is kinda lame, but I guess it's family time and all. Hunter misses me. Ash and Michelle are both overwhelmed by their jobs. Ash sums up this summer with: 'I hate adulting!'

<How R U coping w road trip?> sends Ashley.

I laugh. <Oh, it's fine except for the trolls.>

Hunter replies with <LOL.>

<Yeah, they're freakin' everywhere,> sends Michelle.

<Don't feed the trolls,> bleeps in from Ashley.

I did feed the troll. Four feet of iron straight to the heart. <Right. I won't.>

We chat for a while more, which consists mostly of:

Ashley talking about these adorable, but sickly, kittens she's taking care of.

Michelle complaining about one of the lawyers at her practice.

Hunter glad to hear from me after a few days of no contact.

Oh, and he misses me.

I tease him a little about having to step up his game due to competition from Ben. His replies come short and confused, so I end the joke early saying Ben's only a fourteen-year-old with crush issues. Oh, and he fancies himself a vampire hunter.

All three of them send back variations of 'lmao.'

<U gotta tell us the full story,> sends Ashley.

‹I will. In person.›

‹When are you coming back?› asks Hunter.

‹One more day before we hit the road.› I glance down and sweep my foot back and forth across the grass. I'm *still* tired from walking. Or tired *of* walking. Montana's nice, but I crave familiar surroundings. Dad's gotta move the RV again anyway to refill the water tank. Stupid campground doesn't have hookups at the parking spots. I might try to gently convince him to just go home tomorrow.

I think maybe even Dad's had his fill of this road trip. We trade texts until they all want to go to sleep.

When I return to the RV, I find my father outside alone, gazing up at the clouds.

"Hey," he says, trying to be quiet and not wake the kids. "There you are."

"Yep." I flap my arms. "Here I am. Flew to Whitehall for cell signal and a snack. Wow, you're up late."

"How are your friends?"

"Doing okay. Are you?"

He looks up at me for a long moment. "I guess. Still trying to figure out how you grew up so damn fast."

I chuckle and sit on his lap. "Yeah, well. Stuff happens. Not quite the same, is it?"

"What's that?"

"The road trips."

He sighs. "Yeah. Bit different after fifteen years."

"Fifteen?"

"We started when you were three. One little random idea became a 'family tradition.'"

"Aww, Dad. It's not a bad tradition. Honestly, the caverns are pretty cool, but I think the kids might like something a little more exciting. Sam would love Gettysburg."

"We did that already."

"Yeah, but Sam wasn't around then."

Dad brushes a hand over my hair. "You're all growing up so fast. There's too many places to go and not enough years."

"Well..." I fake an innocent face. "I could ask a few questions of Aurélie on how to do certain things and add three more vampires to the family so they stay little."

"And I could kick your ass," says Sierra from the window above us.

I crack up.

Dad's expression is too worried. Oops. He didn't realize I was kidding.

"Joke, Dad. I could never do that to them. It involves death first, remember?"

He exhales in relief. "Right. Joke. Guess that means I'm tired if I missed it." He leans his head back to peer up at the window. "And what are you doing out of bed at this hour?"

"Eavesdropping," says Sierra.

That gets a laugh from Dad. "Go back to bed, Sierra." He pats me lightly on the back twice, a 'please get up' gesture. "And I think I'm going to take my own advice. Don't stay up too late, okay?"

I hug him. "I won't, Dad. Night."

He pauses on his way inside and turns back to hug me. "I love you, Sarah. Thanks for putting up with this trip, even if it was boring as hell for you."

"Oh, I wouldn't say that. It was nice." I squeeze him. "Love you too, Dad."

LOVE BITES

*M*y family dives eagerly back into normal life when we return home.

Sierra's committed to making up for a week's lost video gaming. Sam goes straight to Daryl's house. Sophia throws on tights and spends the day going over stuff from her dance class. It's Mom's turn to spend hours soaking in the bathtub. Dad disappears into his office, but he's unwinding with a video game on the computer, not working.

I'm still 'jeaned out,' so I spend the whole day in an oversized T-shirt, then throw on a dress when it gets dark. I'm sure there's a trick to flying in a dress that I haven't figured out. Maybe if I fly headfirst at the ground, then swing around to put my feet down, I'll be good. Flip flops will fall off in midair and I'd feel like a dork wearing sneakers and socks with a dress, so I go for ballet flats. Hmm. Those might still fly off me in midair. Boots? Bleh. Screw it. I'll skip shoes. Not like I'll be walking much.

A little after nine, I fly to the mall and practice coming in for a landing without giving the world a view of my underpants. The headfirst dive, quick flip, and slow glide straight down works like a charm. I still catch a bit of billow, but it's not too bad.

I find what I'm looking for—a plush Snoopy—in one of the shops on the upper level. Hunter used to have one of those until his asshole father ripped it up because 'boys don't need stuffed animals' or some macho bullshit like that. Since that man is probably never coming back, I think it's time Hunter had a replacement Snoopy. I doubt he's going to sleep with it, but even sitting on a shelf, if it makes him think of me, it's a win.

He should be getting off work at Mi Tierra soon. I hug the Snoopy plush on the flight across town to Woodinville. Again, I use the trees in the small cemetery where Dalton locked me in a mausoleum overnight to land in the shadows.

Hunter's giant Buick is easy enough to spot in the parking lot. I perch on the hood with the plush concealed behind me. Ooh. I want to see him so bad, it's hard to make myself wait out here. I can't believe he still wants me despite my being a vampire. In the span of six minutes, I go from adoring everything to crying in guilt to all revved up and back again. There's a reasonable chance I'm going to drag him into the back seat. Or I might just hold him for an hour.

Okay, Sarah. Get a grip. You've only been away a week. No, check that, two weeks.

He emerges from the back door a few minutes after ten and trudges over. Once he spots me, he hurries up to a jog and scoops me into a spinning hug.

"Hey you." He grins. "Welcome home."

I lose myself in his kiss for a few minutes, but it's not long enough.

"It's good to see you again," says Hunter.

"Got you something."

"From the caverns?"

"Naw. Their gift shop was kinda basic." I hold up the Snoopy.

He blinks at it. Part of him wants to laugh, a bit of him cringes at the memory it triggers of his father. His emotions settle in a few seconds, and he takes it with a guilty smile and a little blush. "Thanks."

"I remember you said you had one." I wink. "And no, I don't expect you to take it to bed."

Hunter laughs.

I pull him down by a finger in his shirt collar. "I expect you to take *me* to bed."

His eyebrows go up.

HUNTER WINDS UP SPENDING THE NIGHT IN MY ROOM.

I hung a sock on the knob, which hopefully prevented any sibling invasions before I woke up. The sun is in a good mood today, or maybe it's more accurate to say the *clouds* are feeling helpful. I enjoy lying there with him for a while, both of us wearing only the sheets. Eventually, he wakes up.

We kiss and fool around a little, then drag ourselves out of bed, get dressed, and go upstairs.

The sibs are all off doing their things. Sam's up in his room with Daryl and Jordan, Sophia's in her room with Megan and at least two other girls, and Sierra's attempting to perform some manner of Borg-type meld with the PlayStation in the living room. I think she's going on sixteen straight hours.

Mom's out in the yard 'gloom-bathing' with an iced tea in hand. We find Dad in the garage cleaning up, so Hunter and I wind up helping him out for a while. He hangs out with me all day at home, having dinner with us, then surprises me with concert tickets to an Imagine Dragons show in Seattle.

"Umm. Wow. You shouldn't have. You need money for school."

He cringes. "It's okay. They didn't cost that much. You don't need to feel sorry for me."

"All right. We better get ready then."

"Back in a half hour." He winks.

While he heads home to clean up and change, I do the same here. After a pleasantly uninterrupted shower, I run downstairs and change into black jeans with a black lacy babydoll top that's a little heavy on the goth... and my Doc Martens. I'm not about to dye my hair, but I've at least got the paleness down.

I fill the parents in on the plans while waiting for my knight-in-tarnished-Buick to show up. A gloomy morning and early afternoon has become a nice overcast evening with a slight chance of rain and a constant, fresh breeze laced with sea air. Damn, it's nice to be home again.

When Hunter pulls up, I run outside, hop in, and we suffer a tedious drive into the city. I'm a little annoyed that Ash and Chelle are so busy with work, but they're all for me having fun tonight with Hunter. I stop texting them as we pull into the parking area for the concert.

It makes sense why the tickets weren't a big deal to Hunter's budget—we're out on the grass again, but that doesn't bother me at all. We lounge there together listening to the opening act for a while. Eventually, Imagine Dragons comes out on stage and the real show starts.

Of course, that gets me wondering, if vampires and trolls are real...

Nah.

"Oh, hey," says a familiar voice.

I glance up at Amy, Luke, and Dante walking up to us.

"Hey yourself," I say.

"Cute outfit." Amy winks. "You need to dye your hair black though."

"Pass."

The Seattle Outcasts flop on the grass next to us. Luke is totally doing some James Dean thing with a white T-shirt and that bad boy pose. The guy can even make reclining on the lawn look bad ass. Dante, despite his being a fury, looks chill as hell. Amy's cross-legged right next to me in a dress that can't figure out what color it wants to be and barefoot. She's totally ready for Woodstock 2.0.

We appear to be hanging out and listening to the show, though the four of us have a telepathic conversation catching up on the whole issue with Petra, that crazy Sybarite who tried to kill me. When I tell them that one of my friends is a Shadow who basically threatened to destroy her if she messed with me again, Amy cackles in glee.

I lean to my left and kiss the side of Hunter's neck for no particular reason than being happy I'm home and able to spend time with him.

"So," asks Amy, "have you bitten him during sex yet?"

My face burns with blush as a few people nearby glance back at me. They don't know what she really means, but it's still embarrassing.

"Umm, no," I say barely over the music in hopes of keeping our conversation to us. "I don't feed on people I know."

"Not feeding." She nudges my shoulder. "Just little 'love bites.'"

"Any requests?" asks Luke.

Amy glances at him. "They're a band, not a jukebox."

"You thinkin' what I'm thinkin'?" Dante grins. "Little Leppard?"

"I'm on it." Luke stands, straining to stare at the lead singer.

I chuckle into the crook of Hunter's neck. He wraps me in both arms, rocking me side to side. The current song ends, and the singer murmurs something about a sudden urge to play a cover.

The Outcasts all start snickering as soon as the first few notes play. I glance at them, clueless, then look at Hunter. At the first line of vocals, Hunter blushes.

"Okay, what joke am I missing?" I ask.

"The song." Amy play-punches my shoulder, then snaps her teeth at me. "*Love Bites.*"

I pretend to nibble on Hunter's neck. "Like this? I dunno. Not really into weird stuff."

"It's intense," says Amy. "Really intense. But maybe you shouldn't. Once you do that with him, you'll ruin the poor boy for any other woman he'll ever be with."

Hunter brushes his fingers over my hair. "It wouldn't matter, since you're the only girl I'll ever want."

"Wow." Amy rolls her eyes. "Ease back on the cheese, man."

I tilt my head to look him in the eyes. His sincerity is like a warm blanket. If anything ever happened to me, I have no doubt he'd be alone for the rest of his life. It's an overwhelming feeling to have someone care *that* much about me.

A little choked up, I rest my head on his shoulder. "It's not cheesy when he really means it."

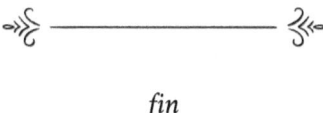

fin

ACKNOWLEDGMENTS

Thank you for reading Vampire Innocent #4!

Special thanks to my beta readers:
   Dianne Webb, Brandy Yassa, David Lee Cox, Leslie Whitaker, Louise Feagans, Lee Hargrove, & Katie McMahan.

Additional thanks to Alex Thompson for the beautiful cover and interior art!

ABOUT THE AUTHOR

Originally from South Amboy NJ, Matthew has been creating science fiction and fantasy worlds for most of his reasoning life. Since 1996, he has developed the "Divergent Fates" world, in which *Division Zero, Virtual Immortality, The Awakened Series, The Harmony Paradox, and the Daughter of Mars series* take place. Along with being an editor at Curiosity Quills press, he has worked in IT and technical support.

Matthew is an avid gamer, a recovered WoW addict, Gamemaster for two custom RPG systems, and a fan of anime, British humour, and intellectual science fiction that questions the nature of reality, life, and what happens after it.

He is also fond of cats.

Visit me online at:
    Facebook: https://www.facebook.com/MatthewSCoxAuthor
    Amazon: https://www.amazon.com/author/mscox
    Pinterest: https://www.pinterest.com/matthewcox10420/
    Goodreads: https://www.goodreads.com/author/show/7712730.Matthew_S_Cox
    Email: mcox2112@gmail.com

OTHER BOOKS BY MATTHEW S. COX

Divergent Fates Universe Novels

Division Zero series

- Division Zero
- Lex De Mortuis
- Thrall
- Guardian
- Harbinger
- The Shadow Fixer
- Neuroshock

The Awakened series

- Prophet of the Badlands
- Archon's Queen
- Grey Ronin
- Daughter of Ash
- Zero Rogue
- Angel Descended

Daughter of Mars series

- The Hand of Raziel
- Araphel
- Ghost Black

Virtual Immortality series

- Virtual Immortality
- The Harmony Paradox

Prophet of the Badlands Series

- Prophet's Journey
- Prophet's Mercy

Divergent Fates Anthology

(Fiction Novels - Adult)

The Roadhouse Chronicles Series

- One More Run
- The Redeemed
- Dead Man's Number

Faded Skies series

- Heir Ascendant
- Ascendant Unrest
- Ascendant Revolution

Temporal Armistice Series

- Nascent Shadow
- The Shadow Collector
- The Gate to Oblivion
- The Queen of Discord
- The Burning Alchemist

Vampire Innocent series

- A Nighttime of Forever
- A Beginner's Guide to Fangs
- The Artist of Ruin

- The Last Family Road Trip
- The Phantom Oracle
- How Not to Summon Demons
- Ordinary Problems of a College Vampire
- A Vampire's Guide to Surviving Holidays
- An Introduction to Paranormal Diplomacy
- A Vampire's Guide to Adulting
- How to Stop a Vampire War in Six Easy Steps
- Ancient Vampire Death Cults and Other Annoyances
- Hunting Vampires for Fun and Profit
- A String of Seriously Unlucky Events
- The Summer of Completely Usual Strangeness
- Demonic Crisis Management for the Modern Vampire

Standalones

- Wayfarer: AV494
- Axillon99
- Chiaroscuro: The Mouse and the Candle
- The Spirits of Six Minstrel Run
- Sophie's Light
- The Far Side of Promise anthology
- Operation: Chimera (with Tony Healey)
- The Dysfunctional Conspiracy (with Christopher Veltmann)
- Of Myth and Shadow
- The Girl Who Found the Sun

Winter Solstice series (with J.R. Rain)

- Convergence
- Containment
- Catalyst
- Catacombs

Alexis Silver series (with J.R. Rain)

- Silver Light
- Deep Silver
- Silver Quarrel
- Silver Crucible
- Silver Heart

Samantha Moon Origins series (with J.R. Rain)

- New Moon Rising
- Moon Mourning
- Haunted Moon

Vampire For Hire series (with J.R. Rain)

- Moon Master
- Dead Moon
- Lost Moon
- Vampire Destiny
- Infinite Moon
- Vampire Empress
- Moon Elder
- Wicked Moon
- Moon Blade

Maddy Wimsey series (with J.R. Rain)

- The Devil's Eye
- The Drifting Gloom
- Dark Mercy
- Primal Wrath

Samantha Moon Case Files series (with J.R. Rain)

- Blood Moon

Immortal Operative (with J.R. Rain)

- Broken Ice
- Broken Wing

Four Elements series (with J.R. Rain)

- The Elementalist
- The Black Rose
- The Wakefield Curse

Witches series (with J.R. Rain)

- The Witch and the Hangman

Zeb Clemens series (with J.R. Rain)

- The Beast of Devil's Creek
- Wanted: Undead or Alive

Young Adult Novels

The Eldritch Heart Series

- The Eldritch Heart
- The Cursed Crown
- The Sapphire Soul

Evergreen Series

- Evergreen
- The World That Remains

- The Lucky Ones
- Nuclear Summer
- The Nuclear Frontier
- The World We Make
- The Threat Unseen

Progenitor Series

- Out of Sight
- Out of Mind

Diary of a Teenage Fey

(Short story series)

- Elder Horror
- The Hag of Barrow Falls
- Babysitter's Nightmare
- Lharakki
- Bauble for a Soul
- Simulacrum
- Amorphous
- Manticore

Standalones

- Caller 107
- The Summer the World Ended
- Nine Candles of Deepest Black
- The Forest Beyond the Earth

Middle Grade Novels

The Adventures of Ubergirl series

- My Dad is a Mad Scientist
- Aliens Ate My Homework
- The End of all Halloweens
- Dr. Infinity and the Soul Smasher

Tales of Widowswood series

- Emma and the Banderwigh
- Emma and the Silk Thieves
- Emma and the Silverbell Faeries
- Emma and the Elixir of Madness
- Emma and the Weeping Spirit

Standalones

- Citadel: The Concordant Sequence
- The Cursed Codex
- The Menagerie of Jenkins Bailey